D1529011

THROUGH THE TRIANGLE

C.P. STEWART

Outskirts Press, Inc.
Denver, Colorado

Outskirts Press, Inc.
http://www.outskirtspress.com

ISBN: 978-1-4327-4036-8

Library of Congress Control Number: 2009928926

Outskirts Press and the "OP" logo are trademarks belonging to Outskirts Press, Inc.

PRINTED IN THE UNITED STATES OF AMERICA

"There is a time for departure even when there's no certain place to go."
.... *Tennessee Williams (1911-1983)*

Chapter 1

A red shouldered hawk circled lazily over the evening landscape, searching for something, anything, to satisfy her growing hunger. She hadn't eaten but two insects since last night and was searching for anything that moved. She had almost captured a field mouse earlier, but it had seen her in enough time to make cover. A hundred twenty feet below, a wide double ribbon of asphalt stretched to both horizons, separated by a strip of tall pine trees. This held little interest for the hawk, other than using the warm updrafts from the hot surface to give her lift, because small animals were usually more plentiful in the grasslands and swampy areas away from it. Objects moved on the ribbon, but they didn't interest her either because they were too large to capture and moved far too fast. Her sharp eyes flicked back and forth until sudden movement in the grasses lining the ribbon caused her to cock her head, her keen eyes focusing on the small animal as it moved quickly. It headed for the ribbon and then stopped, obviously thinking better of running further, intimidated by the large objects that moved quickly by. The hawk began a spiraling descent, trying not to alert the animal to her presence until she could dive from a lower height.

She was low enough now and began to dive by pulling in her wings; the wind rushing silently by as she focused on her prey. The animal, a rabbit, sensing danger, took off on a dead run across the asphalt ribbon, narrowly avoiding certain death as the tires of a large silver-colored car squealed while quickly changing direction as it sped past. The hawk pulled out of her dive and glided over the ribbon, trying to relocate the rabbit, to no avail.

The I-95 traffic was light as the southbound driver alertly swerved to avoid a rabbit that darted in front of him. He swore under his breath while checking the mirrors to verify he had missed it, and then resumed attempting to keep pace with a black SUV about 200 yards ahead. He reasoned that as long as he wasn't driving erratically or passing everything in sight the police wouldn't pull him over and delay his trip. A sign flashed by declaring a speed limit of seventy miles per hour, which amused him because he and the SUV were doing close to ninety.

Allen Cranston had driven this way for most of the trip, cruising about five miles per hour over the limit until a car or group of cars passed him, and then let them get a sizeable distance ahead before trying to match their speed. Any speed traps ahead would get the lead cars, allowing him to back down to the posted limit before being caught. He had checked out radar detectors, almost bought one last year, but he preferred this method of avoiding detection. He just wasn't sold on how reliable they were, and if they were totally undetectable by police.

Continuing in this fashion, he wandered blissfully about his upcoming vacation and the fun he was anticipating. It had been at least two years since his last vacation and this one couldn't have come at a better time. It had been many years since Allen had gone deep-sea fishing, and he looked forward to being able to relax and unwind on that fishing boat. He also planned to finish the rest of the week in the Keys before heading home. Rest and relaxation. He could almost feel the tension evaporating as he glanced at the orange sun tickling the tops of the Carolina pines to the right.

He was jarred back to the present as a Jaguar swung out to pass a semi, moving into the path of his Mercedes. Hitting the brakes and horn about the same time caused the Jag to swerve back into its own lane. "I'd better keep my mind on the traffic," he said out loud.

The radio station he had been listening to was fading due to driving out of the station's range. He took his eyes off the road long enough to locate the scan button. Only two stations paused the radio to give a sample of their offerings, neither of which interested him. He reached into the packet attached to the sun visor and retrieved a CD, which he inserted into the player.

"Now, that's much better!" he murmured as Jimmy Buffet's "Cheeseburger in Paradise" resonated through the premium sound system. The song conjured an image of a large juicy cheeseburger with a side of fries, reminding him that he hadn't eaten since 11:30. His hunger, though, wasn't too bad yet, so he figured on driving a little farther before stopping.

After another half hour, he looked for an exit to get some gas. Just then a Lodging sign spelled out the motels available at the next exit, Food and Gas signs followed. "Looks good for a stop," he thought aloud as he veered his Mercedes onto the exit ramp and to the stop sign at its end. He spied an Exxon station to the right and decided it would do.

He pulled to the pump and extricated himself from the seat that had housed him for several hours. His legs and back were stiff, so he stretched and twisted back and forth a few times at the waist to help alleviate the soreness. After punching in his debit card PIN and starting the flow of gas, he checked out his surroundings. Fast food restaurants littered both sides of the road intensifying his growing hunger. *Might as well eat here rather than stopping later.*

After retrieving a printed receipt from the pump, he started the Mercedes and waited for five cars to pass before pulling across the road. Wheeling into the parking lot, he found a space across the lot behind the restaurant. Getting out, he checked the money in his pocket; satisfied there was more than enough to cover a quick dinner, he remotely locked the car and walked to the entrance.

Once inside, he headed for the restroom. Locked. *Crap,* he thought. *I don't want to spend more time here than I have to.*

He leaned against the wall and waited. After a couple of minutes, the door opened and a clean-cut man who looked to be about Allen's height stepped out, briefly met his eyes and walked around him. Recognition welled inside but stopped short of completion; Allen thought the man looked familiar but couldn't place him. He decided to study him in more detail when he returned to the dining area. Entering, he locked the door and stepped up to the only urinal in the small restroom.

"Not the cleanest place," he said under his breath, surveying the room with several discarded strips of toilet paper decorating the floor and the beginnings of some rust stains on the wall. The odor of urine and disinfectant were noticeable but not as strong as he had expected from the appearance of the room. After finishing, he washed his hands while looking at his reflection in the mirror above the sink. His hair was beginning to gray along the temples, but other than that he figured he could pass for several years younger than his 46 years. The navy blue windbreaker he wore was emblazoned with the neat gold and white logo of the pharmaceutical company that he served as Chief Sales Representative for a three-state region. The logo held his attention a little longer than the rest of his cursory self ex-amination; it represented his lifestyle and possessions, but it also symbolized the reason he had missed solid relationships in his life. He spent so much time on the road that it didn't permit him the luxury of serious monogamous dating. Well, that would change when he returned from this vacation because he was going to try to cut back his traveling and concentrate on using the wealth he had accumulated to start living. He might start with Kaitlyn, the receptionist for a medical facility in Charleston, because she openly flirted with him every time he visited. Yes, Kaitlyn was young and pretty, and seemed to be interested. He would call her when he returned and see where it leads.

The paper towel dispenser was empty and the hot-air dryer wouldn't work, so he shook the loose water from his hands and finished drying them on his khakis. "It figures!" he muttered, so disgusted he thought of going somewhere else to eat, but that would mean another stop and additional time.

Studying the menu board suspended above the counter, one of the value choices caught his attention, so he stepped to the counter and ordered. He watched two overweight workers in the kitchen area prepare his food and then a girl, who looked to still be in high school, brought the food forward and placed it on his tray.

"That will be eight forty-six," she announced, her face and voice expressionless. After pocketing the change, he gathered some ketchup and salt from the condiment table, and vainly surveyed the dining area in search of the man he had seen earlier; not seeing him, he chose a table close to a window where he could keep an eye on his car.

The silver Mercedes was one of the possessions that his

career had afforded him and represented what he had made of his life. Although planning to scale back on his work time, it still brought him pleasure to not only drive it, but also to stare at it.

He shifted his attention to a fussy child that looked to be around four. She was whining about not wanting to eat her fries while a boy, probably her slightly older brother, ate with a constant smirk as he watched their harried mother try to calm the unruly child.

As Allen ate, he thought back to his grandfather and his first deep-sea fishing experience. Allen's parents had been killed in an auto accident, and his aunt, uncle, and grandfather raised him. He felt "Pap", as he had always called his grandfather, had greatly influenced his life by instilling a love of hunting and fishing. Even now, in those rare free weekends, Allen had indulged his outdoor hobbies, further lessening the chance for a serious relationship.

He recalled the vacation spent with his family along the Outer Banks of North Carolina when he was about fourteen or fifteen. Pap had rented a fishing boat for just the two of them. They got up early and arrived at the dock before sunrise. The owner of the boat had a tanned muscular young kid around Allen's age working with him. They caught some tuna that day and Pap landed a swordfish that he fought for nearly an hour. Pap was so proud of that swordfish that he had it mounted and displayed above the fireplace. It was one of the first things his aunt and uncle got rid of when Pap died two years later; Allen never forgave them.

Having finished his meal, Allen deposited his wrappers in the trashcan and placed the tray in its receptacle on top, keeping his unfinished drink for the ride ahead.

Stepping outside, he was aware of how cool and dark it had become and mentally chastised himself for parking close to the end of the lot. Carrying his drink in his left hand, he pulled the keys out of his right pocket and remotely unlocked the driver's door as he approached the car. Still holding the drink in his left hand, he opened the door with his right. Suddenly his head was moving involuntarily forward, and before realization set in, the roof edge of the car wiped away any thought ... forever. The cup fell, its contents escaping in a splash pattern on the asphalt, interspersed with glistening pieces of ice.

Later that night after closing, a young boy cleaning up around the restaurant threw the empty cup from the lot into a trash bag slung over his shoulder – an act done with hundreds of discarded cups in the ten months since he had been lucky enough to get this job.

Chapter 2

Thursday, August 11, 2005
9:18 PM

M anny Contraldo forced the unconscious body across into the passenger seat, wrestling legs over the console, quickly surveyed his surroundings to satisfy himself that nobody had been watching, and then slid behind the wheel and started the Mercedes. He backed out of the parking space and quickly exited the parking lot, turning left instead of toward the interstate. He wasn't sure just what his next move was going to be, but he would know it when he saw it.

He glanced at the slumped figure in the seat next to him, noticing the gash across his forehead and the blood that was beginning to soak the front of his shirt.

"I gotta dump this guy before he stains the interior," Manny growled under his breath.

He peered through the windshield, trying to find a suitable place to pull off and check the comatose figure beside him. Ahead to the right was a large business sign with panels missing; all that could be read was " –wood" and underneath, *FAMILY DINING*. The letters that remained were terribly faded, indicating to any observer that this establishment had been vacant for a long time.

He slowed before a plywood-windowed building sitting at the far end of an asphalt parking lot littered with grasses and weeds growing through several cracks. Cautiously steering the Mercedes into the lot, he pulled close to the abandoned restaurant before dousing the lights and turning off the engine. He stepped out of the car and quickly shut the door to extinguish the interior light, while furtively glancing around. Satisfied that his movements were not being observed, he opened the passenger door and pulled the bleeding man out onto the parking lot. He checked for a pulse, and finding none removed the windbreaker, cleaning out his pockets and throwing everything through the open window onto the passenger seat. He dragged the body to the rear of the vacant building and found the back door standing askew; obviously, he wasn't the first to break in.

Manny forced the door open enough to pull the body inside and leaned it against a wooden cabinet in the kitchen. He started flapping at his head, trying to dislodge a cobweb he accidentally contacted, sputtering, "Agh! I hate spiders!"

Still rubbing his hair, he returned to the car with the man's blood-soaked shirt, where he removed the gas cap and slid one of the sleeves down inside. The newly filled gasoline soaked the sleeve and moved upward into the rest of the shirt through capillary action. He replaced the cap and took the dripping shirt back into the kitchen where he dripped some gasoline on the body and then swung it in circles, spraying gasoline onto the kitchen surfaces. He then wadded the garment and placed it beneath a receptacle mounted in a wooden panel. He knew that firemen could tell arson from the pattern of a fire and hoped this might make them think the fire had started in the outlet. His lighter ignited the shirt, which blazed readily and spread in waves with a *whoompf, whoompf, whoompf.*

He pushed the broken door as close to shut as possible and hurried to the Mercedes, started the engine and drove to the road; luckily, there was no traffic. As he pulled out in the direction of the interstate, he glanced back at the derelict restaurant, and with a grunt of satisfaction saw a bright glow already emanating from the rear of the building.

Manny turned onto I-95 southbound and drove to the next exit, where he pulled into a service station and parked at the far end of the lot away from the pumps. He could now take his time to find out how to profit from the confiscated material on the seat beside him. He already had the car, which was his main objective, and anything else was gravy.

In the wallet were several credit cards, identification, and $236 in cash, which he stuffed into his pocket. He studied the identification and whispered, "Allen G. Cranston, Morgantown, West Virginia." Manny was somewhat familiar with Morgantown having grown up in Pittsburgh, less than a hundred miles north. "We were almost neighbors buddy," he said out loud. "Sorry 'bout that."

Manny reflected how different his life had been compared to the life he imagined Allen Cranston enjoyed. Allen was probably raised with loving parents, and undoubtedly had nearly everything he wanted. Manny's mother had vanished when he was three and his father spent more time with a bottle than with his son, and when the old man *did* spend time with him, Manny usually first felt his disgust, and then his belt. He still had nightmares about the night he awoke screaming when he found a large spider in his bed and his father beat him for disturbing his sleep. On top of everything else, he had been named Manford, a cruel trick played out on a child. His name, in addition to his home life, forced him to become self sufficient, leading to many other activities while trying to prove his worth to peers. There were the gangs, car-jackings, rapes, and fights. He accepted, and even embraced the lifestyle until his final arrest. Twelve of his twenty-eight years had been spent in various correctional facilities, reform schools, local jails, and prison, but his last arrest on felony armed robbery had him looking at ten to twenty years of hard time … until his escape. Unfortunately, a cop was killed during that escape, which immediately placed him on a *Most Wanted* list. That was the reason for his southward trek, heading to a perpetually warmer climate, and hopefully out of the country.

In his favor were his demeanor and looks. He had been told many times how good-looking he was, and he could feign sincerity with strangers. He sounded well educated when he wanted to, and had charmed his way out of many jams in the past.

He lit a cigarette and took a deep drag, then searched and found nothing of interest in the glove box. "Where were you headed?" he whispered.

Twisting to put the wallet in his back pocket, Manny's foot bumped against something under the seat. He reached down and pulled out a clipboard holding several pieces of paper. He examined the papers in order without removing them from the clipboard and murmured softly, "My, my, what an organized person you are ... were." Included were receipts for gasoline and meals, confirmations for hotels, an AAA Trip-Tik to Ft. Lauderdale, maps of Southeastern States and Florida, and a confirmation for a deep-sea fishing trip set for the day after tomorrow. The trip was to originate at Cape Arthur, which appeared on the map to be a little north of Ft. Lauderdale. This last document held Manny's attention, "What a great way to skip the country," he said louder than he meant to, and glanced around to make sure nobody had heard. *I got this guy's car to make the trip to Florida and I can get a boat there to make the trip to Cuba or Mexico. Thank you Allen Cranston for my ticket outta here!* He gunned the engine, and wheeled the Mercedes back toward the interstate.

A passing motorist had summoned the local fire department, but by the time they arrived the building was fully engulfed; all they could do was attempt to save enough of the structure to determine the cause. As his crew battled the flames, Chief Hal Stanford contacted the owners and was assured that all utilities had been disconnected when the establishment closed more than three years ago. This information spurred him to notify the fire marshal, who said he was ten minutes away and would be right over.

The fire marshal sat in Chief Stanford's Explorer while he gathered needed background information, and watched as the fire was reduced to a final few hot spots. He exited the vehicle and slowly walked toward the remains of what had once been *The Briarwood*, a marginally successful family restaurant until most of its interstate clientele was lured to the growing number of fast food establishments closer to the exit. The ruins were still smoldering under the steady streams emanating from two separate two and a half inch lines, but the heat even now prevented a closer approach. He surveyed the scene while moving laterally, the air heavy with smoke and burnt wood. Stopping beside Pumper 302, he watched as one of the firemen turned his position at the nozzle to another and walked toward him.

"You the new fire marshal?" the fireman asked, removing his helmet and smearing sweat from his face.

"You got 'im. Lou Dawson at your service," he said offering his hand. "What's up?"

"Lieutenant Montenegro. You got your gear with you?" the fireman replied while shaking hands.

"Always, why?"

"I suggest you gear up; there's somethin' in there you need to see." Dawson nodded and strode to his pick up, where he donned his fire gear and grabbed his helmet.

The lieutenant was talking to Chief Stanford as Dawson returned, and asked while adjusting his helmet, "What'd you find?"

"A body."

His attention quickly shifted back to the fireman, "You know who it is?"

"No idea … could be a homeless person crawled in for the night and got caught by the fire or it could be the arsonist; regardless, there's not much left. I think identification's going to be a problem."

"Show me." As he followed the fireman, Dawson yelled over his shoulder, "Chief, you better call in forensics and the sheriff!"

"Done!" He headed for the Explorer.

Chapter 3

Saturday, August 13, 2005
5:45 AM

Mason Bankowski carried his cup of steaming coffee through the sliding patio doors and leaned against the deck railing. He was six-one and his 220 pounds had shifted over the years from the imposing athletic body he once had to battling a paunch around his waist such that his trousers now buckled somewhat below his belly instead of around it. He was dressed in jeans, a white uniform shirt with "Bankowski Tours" embroidered in blue above the left pocket, and a white baseball cap to keep afternoon sun out of his eyes and off his receding hairline. Since the sun hadn't yet come up, the hat was pushed back slightly on his head and a pair of sunglasses perched atop the bill. A light jacket completed the ensemble.

Mason spent many hours on this deck since he built it two years ago, especially with a coffee early in the morning, like now, or during the evening hours covered in shade from the house. Usually he was gone before sunrise, but on those rare occasions he wasn't, sunrise was a sight to behold.

The morning was cooler than usual for the east coast of Florida, but it showed promise of turning into an exquisite day. Because of the cooler temperatures, fog had settled in overnight and it was all he could do to see *Oblique View* twenty yards away, even with the dusk to dawn lights situated along the walk. Those lights progressed from being clearly visible to merely faded halos closest to the dock.

Oblique View was his refuge, his return to sanity, and also a source of supplemental income. Mason was a licensed welder and performed union work up to five days a week, but weekends were his, and he spent them deep-sea fishing. He purchased the 1976 forty-eight foot Pacemaker sports fisher with twin Detroit 600 horsepower diesels twelve years ago, and had never had a moment's regret about that decision. Now through a special permit, he was allowed to operate from his own personal mooring located on the Intracoastal Waterway behind his house.

Soon, two paying fares were to arrive for a day of deep-sea fishing: a man and his son from Maryland and a sales rep from West Virginia. Both had sent checks in advance, so if one or the other didn't show, the non-refundable deposit was Mason's to keep. Last night, he added 200 gallons to the fuel tank at the local marina and had stowed other needed supplies, such as bait, food, and beverages. He also checked over the poles and other equipment; everything seemed ready.

A woman slipped up from behind and wrapped her arms around his waist as he leaned on the railing.

"Ready for the day?" She asked.

"Everthin's in order, now all we need're th' guests." he answered in the deep voice she had loved since they first met.

"Who's on for today?"

"Some northerners. One's a first-timer, so it should be fun. Ya know I usually take only one party, but this time there'll be two 'cause they're both small and neither objected to sharin' th' trip."

"Ooh," she teased, "Twice the money for the same trip. Nice. Where you taking me to celebrate?"

"Hey, take 'em as ya get 'em. I'll make sure they catch some nice'uns and they'll get excited, go home with some great stories 'bout how they fought and fought 'til they landed 'em. They'll get their money's worth, Maggie. And to answer yar question, how 'bout ya think 'bout it and let me know when I get home tonight?"

"I'll do just that, and I know they'll have a great time, after all, they have the best in the business working for them."

Maggie shivered against the morning chill. "I'm going in now, make sure you tell me goodbye before y'all leave."

"Ya bet," he called after her and watched her glide into the kitchen, marveling at her grace. Even after twenty-two years of marriage, she was still his inspiration, his shining star and proverbial soul mate. Without her encouragement, he probably would have passed on buying the boat because of certain debt. She was the one who knew his innermost feelings, and convinced him to finalize the purchase because of the extra income possibilities; to his core, he knew she did it mostly to make him happy.

"Hello," a voice sounded. Mason turned to see two figures approaching him on the walk that leads from the street around to the rear deck. "Are you Mr. Bankowski?"

Mason regarded the man as he ascended four steps to the deck, estimating him to be in his mid thirties to early forties, about five-ten, of medium build and solid. He was wearing jeans, a printed shirt over a white crew t-shirt, running shoes, and a windbreaker. His hair appeared dark in the dim porch light, but neatly trimmed, long enough to cover the top of his ears. This was longer than Mason would have liked his own hair, but on this guy it looked good.

"Ya got 'im. Ya must be Mr. Myers and this must be yar son," Mason answered while holding out his hand and looking toward the youth, who appeared to be in his mid-teens and a couple of inches shorter than his father. His black jeans and hooded sweatshirt covered a body that seemed somewhat softer than a boy his age should have. He wasn't heavy, but certainly appeared to be out of shape.

"Jake, please, and this is my son Nathan," the man replied. "It's nice to finally meet you in person."

"Same here. Did ya have a good trip from Maryland?"

"Not bad. We ran into lots of traffic around Richmond where 295 meets 95. We must have spent twenty minutes going two miles. We spent the night just up the road so we would be on time this morning."

"Well, ya're here now and I'm still waitin' on th' other guy."

"Yes, you mentioned him in our phone conversation. Where is he from?"

"West Virginia, Morgantown, I think."

"That's not too far from us. Maybe we'll have some common ground to talk about on the trip."

While the two men were conversing, Nathan moved to the edge of the deck, climbed up onto the railing and pulled headphones out of his sweatshirt pocket. As he was putting them on, Jake called his name with a tone imparting disappointment in his actions. The youth scowled at his father before slipping off the railing, but continued with the headphones and CD player as he leaned against the rail.

"Sorry about that," Jake apologized to Mason without taking his eyes off his son. "We've been having some problems lately."

"That's okay," assured Mason. "Th' railin's plenty strong enough. No harm done. What d'ya say we move down to th' boat and make ready to shove off as soon as our other fisherman gets here." This was more statement than question as he started down the steps toward the boardwalk leading to the boat.

Mason reached *Oblique View* first and stood aside as Jake stepped over the side and into the boat. Nathan was about ten yards behind and seemed in no hurry, forcing Mason to wait until his arrival at the end of the dock. He finally reached the boat, but stood on the dock instead of stepping over the side.

"I don't want to go," he said and turned to walk back up the boardwalk. Jake scrambled back onto the dock and caught up with Nathan after a few long strides.

Stepping in front to face him, Jake implored in a voice slightly above a whisper, "What do you think you're doing? We're here to spend some time together!"

"Look, this is *your* idea of fun, not mine, so why don't you go and have your fun! Mom wouldn't have gone either!"

"Nathan," Jake still whispered, "I can't help what happened between your mother and me, and I can't help it that she ... " his voice trailed off. "God knows I wish I could have helped ... been there for you and her! Now it's just the two of us." His voice softened, "Please give this ... us a chance."

Nathan's eyes lowered toward the boards on which he was standing, and he slowly turned back toward the boat. "All right, but I'm not going to have fun, just remember that," he muttered under his breath while walking.

As they reached the side of the boat and prepared to step in, a figure materialized out of the fog from the direction of the house.

"Mr. Bankowski?" the man inquired.

"Yeah, that's me, ya Mr. Cranston?"

"Allen Cranston at your service," the man answered with a broad smile as he extended his hand.

"Mason Bankowski, and these are th' other passengers, Jake Myers an' his son Nathan."

Faced with the presence of two other people, Manny's smile faded and he fixed a questioning look at Mason.

"They're the ones I told' ya 'bout when we talked on th' phone last time. Remember?"

"Oh, yeah. I forgot. Well when do we leave?"

"Soon as ya're all on board," replied Mason. "It's 6:15 and time to leave. Make yarselves comfortable while I run up to th' house for a minute."

As Mason walked briskly toward the house, Manny climbed aboard, mind reeling. He thought he would be alone with the boat's owner, which would make getting rid of him and taking the boat child's play. Now that there were three of them, it might be a little trickier. *No matter,* he concluded, *they're expendable ... two more won't matter.* He used his lighter to light a cigarette and took a deep draw, holding the smoke before letting it escape through his nose.

Mason entered through the patio door and was met by Maggie. "Are you ready to go, Spanky." He smiled inwardly at the pet name his wife had called him since their second date.

"Couldn't leave without sayin' 'bye to th' best wife in th' world," he answered as they kissed. "By th' way, did Juan call to say he'd be late?"

"No, I didn't hear from him. Do you want me to call his cell?" Just then they heard someone running alongside the house. Mason quickly retreated to the deck and saw a figure run past on his way toward the boat.

"Juan!" Mason yelled.

The boy stopped so quickly he almost lost his balance. Mason chuckled over how comical Juan had looked at that instant.

"Hey Boss, I was afraid I was too late!" the boy cried between gasps of breath while slightly bent over, resting his hands on his knees.

"I was wonderin' if ya were comin' today."

"I stopped to help a lady change a flat about a mile from here and she wouldn't stop talking after I finished. Thought I would never get away from her."

"No problem. Let's shove off."

"'Bye y'all!" Maggie shouted in her native Georgia drawl. "Have a good day and catch lots of fish!" Mason waved back to indicate she had been heard as he and Juan walked toward the boat.

"This here is Juan Morales, my first mate," Mason said as they climbed onto the boat, "and this is Allen Cranston, Jake Myers, and Nathan Myers. "

"Pleased to meet all of you," Juan grinned and then moved to cast off while Mason climbed to the flybridge.

The twin inboard diesel engines rumbled to life as Juan cast the mooring lines onto the dock. Oblique View moved away from its berth and progressed south through the channel as an occasional dock or tree would become visible and then evaporate in the gray netherworld of the miasma.

Jake sat on one of the two elevated fishing chairs watching what he could make out of the shoreline slide by, while

Nathan reclined on a coil of rope and listened to music with closed eyes.

Manny stood leaning against the ladder to the bridge, fingering the knife in his jacket pocket and thinking about how things had gotten out of hand. Instead of dispensing with the captain and then immediately heading the boat toward Cuba, this was going to take some planning, and it was going to delay leaving until later in the day. He had planned on being past the Keys by the time anyone missed this boat and sent out search parties.

Damn! he thought. There were too many people on board to get rid of, and by then the search parties would be out. *Damn!*

Manny studied each of the individuals on board, trying to figure the best way to dispose of each. The captain was a few inches taller than Manny's five-ten frame and looked to be about forty to fifty pounds heavier, so he figured he would have to use surprise and kill him quickly. The first mate was a couple inches shorter than Manny and lighter, although he seemed to be all muscle, which meant he could probably hold his own in a fight; surprise would also be needed on him. The other two, although roughly about his size, didn't seem to pose much of a threat; they should be easy. He flicked what remained of his cigarette into the water, and then moved to the empty elevated chair.

Chapter 4

*O*bliques *View* passed from the Intracoastal Waterway into the Atlantic Ocean between two narrow strips of land. Through the fog a ghostly apparition materialized on the leftmost strip of land, a huge rock promontory that stood about ten feet tall. It looked natural but resembled a light-house. Jake thought how appropriate that rock was, located at the mouth of the inlet as they set out to sea. The fog swallowed it as quickly as it had appeared. The boat lurched a few times as it encountered the ocean's waves in line with the surf crashing on the shore to either side of the inlet.

Jake felt exhilarated by the moist early morning air, the smell of the sea, and the vibration of the inboard engines under the aft deck. He looked over his shoulder and saw Nathan reclined on the coil of rope, hood up, eyes closed and arms crossed. At first he thought Nathan was sleeping until he noticed one of his feet moving nearly imperceptibly, obviously to the music in his headphones. He had hoped his son would take an interest in healthy activities, but now wasn't sure this trip was as good an idea as he had originally thought. So far it had only alienated him further.

As the shoreline faded into the lingering mist, Jake's mind reflected two months to … no, he would think pleasant thoughts instead.

Lisa. Sweet Lisa. They met in Qualitative Analysis lab his sophomore year at Towson State University. Jake remembered the beautiful brunette whose lab station was across the room. He had trouble concentrating on his lab work while straining to see her through the labyrinth of pipes and lab apparatus that seemed to exist only to frustrate his efforts, and on more than one occasion he had discarded the portion he was supposed to continue running tests on. Then one day she was standing alongside him as he washed out some test tubes. He looked up at her, she smiled, and he dropped four test tubes into the sink, breaking three of them. She laughed and helped him pick up the pieces. After that, she came to him often to ask questions or get clarifications on what she was supposed to do. Study sessions followed, and then occasional dates. They both needed to complete their studies at a larger university, and as luck would have it, both were accepted to Penn State University. Locals refer to the State College area as Happy Valley, an appropriate name in their case. He hinted at marriage one evening on the steps of Old Main and formally asked her in front of the Nittany Lion statue a week later. They were married a month after graduation and moved into an apartment just outside Baltimore. Good times, good years; oh how he wished for those things again.

Three good years followed with both following their respective careers, she as a pharmacist and he as a chemical engineer. Their combined incomes permitted the purchase of a house with a large, but manageable mortgage in an upscale neighborhood. A year later Nathan was born, and Lisa cut back her hours to take care of him. That decision forced Jake to step up his time at work to enable them to meet the unrelenting bills. Overtime led to accepting consulting jobs in distant places, finally helping with plant design and development, which meant weeks away from home.

He enjoyed his time at home watching Nathan grow and helping around the house, but his time away was damaging the marriage more than he realized. Gradually, disagreements became frequent and then incessant, making road trips a relief. Calm days at home became rare as the nagging and fighting took more of their time together. Finally, he was served divorce papers.

That was it. He couldn't bear to think about Lisa any more today; he was going to try to force some enjoyment into his life. This trip was about healing and he was going to try to force some enjoyment into Nathan's life also... whether he liked it or not.

Searching the internet Jake had found *Bankowski Tours*, which promised an unforgettable ocean adventure - fishing, lunch, a knowledgeable and experienced guide, a well-equipped fishing boat, and plenty of large game fish. He phoned Captain Bankowski, an affable man, who told him that he already had a fare for August 13th. When informed that the trip had to be taken before school began, he said he would call back. About an hour later, Captain Bankowski called back saying he had contacted the other fare and was assured he was fine with having two others along; even thought it would be fun.

Observing that the fog had lifted and the sun was sitting on the eastern horizon, Jake removed his windbreaker and began smearing sunscreen on his neck, face, and arms while continuing to ponder where his relationship with Nathan was heading. This trip was becoming anything *but* fun, nevertheless Jake hoped it could help Nathan and him to get their minds off things for a few days. The drive and motel stay had been unpleasant; with Nathan's sullenness and his own emptiness, communication was beyond difficult. He felt that he was walking through a minefield by sidestepping Nathan's mood swings while trying to keep things pleasant and on an even keel. Tomorrow was sightseeing and travel to the Disney World and Universal theme parks, where they would spend four days, and then two days at the beach before returning home. Hopefully, things would improve by the time they got back.

Lost in thought, Jake didn't notice the passenger beside him slip out of the other fishing chair and move toward the cabin.

Manny took a deep draw on a new cigarette, still concerned about how to dispatch the others so he could take over the boat. Time was of the essence, but so far the placement of everyone didn't lend itself to quietly eliminating them one by one. The helper, what was his name again, something Latino, regardless, a short time ago had taken off his shirt to reveal someone built similarly to himself. Had he looked less formidable, there would be little problem; he would do the captain first with confidence that he could handle the other three, even take them all on at the same time. The problem was that he only had two knives, one in his jacket pocket and a back-up hidden in his right sock, held in place by a narrow strip of Velcro wrapped around his ankle. A gun would have made the process so much easier, but he assumed nothing beyond a knife would be necessary to kill the captain and take his boat. Knives were his weapon of choice; they were quiet and very effective if you knew how to use them. Now with three others on board, the situation had totally changed. His first priority now was to find the opportunity to get the helper in a way that nobody else would notice, and then do the captain. The other two would soon follow.

Just then, Juan came up from below deck and paused for a brief moment as he came face to face with Manny.

"Excuse me Mr. Cranston," he said with a smile and smoothly moved past as Manny stepped aside.

The boat slowed and pitched as its wake caught up with it. Mason climbed down from the bridge and announced, "Time to do some fishin'!" At this, all but Nathan turned their attention toward the captain.

Juan moved to the aft storage compartments where he pulled out some fish that would have been what they called *keepers* back where Jake was raised. Removing two long poles from storage containers in the rails alongside the deck, Juan set one in the cylindrical holder located directly in front of each of the two fishing chairs, and played out some line from each pole in turn. He placed a large piece of fish on each hook, and then threw them over the back of the boat. This done, Mason restarted the forward motion of the craft, markedly slower than before.

"Okay, man the seats!" Mason shouted over his shoulder from the bridge.

Jake offered his chair to Nathan, who looked up, shook his head and closed his eyes again. Jake figured he might change his mind when he saw some fish being caught, so he remained in the chair on the right and fastened his seat belt.

Manny panicked. He couldn't even consider his plans if he was captive in a fishing chair with a pole in his hands. He had to think quickly because he was supposed to be here to do some fishing and the captain and helper were looking for him to take his place. A plan formed as he began moving toward the chair. Watching the deck floor, he found what he was looking for, a duffle bag lying on the deck. Quickly memorizing its location, he raised his eyes toward the chair, and as he reached the bag he made sure to trip on it and fall to the deck. Juan hurried over to help him.

"Ohh, my shoulder," Manny complained. "I think I

pulled something." He was holding his right shoulder as Mason came back down the ladder, concern on his face. No accident had ever happened on *Oblique View* since he started running his charter fishing business, and he was aware of what a lawsuit could do to his future.

"How bad is it?" Mason asked, trying to keep panic out of his voice.

"I think it'll be okay, but I better rest it awhile," answered Manny. "I better not try to fish right now ... maybe later."

Mason, masking his profound relief, patted Manny on the left shoulder and told him that he was probably right; to sit down and rest. He then climbed back up and regained the controls.

After Manny was seated in a deck chair, Juan squatted beside Nathan, startling him by his presence. He spoke quietly to Nathan as Jake watched over his shoulder, trying to hear what was being said. Nathan removed his headphones and sweatshirt before walking to the other fishing chair. As he climbed in and Juan tightened the seat belt around him, Jake looked over and smiled.

"Welcome sport, glad to have you beside me. Now let's have at those fish!"

"Okay. I'll try," replied Nathan in a monotone, as he looked out over the boat's wake toward where the lines seemed to converge where they entered the water.

Manny sat, rubbing his right shoulder, grimacing in pain but smiling inwardly.

Chapter 5

10:00 AM

Richmond Aiken Walters strode through the door into the welcome coolness of the municipal building and headed directly for his office. He immediately closed the door behind him, tossed his hat onto a vacant chair, lifted the phone handset and punched in some numbers before sitting.

"Dr. Simmons please," he spoke absently while searching through a wealth of papers scattered on the desk, and after a few seconds, "Just tell her the sheriff wants to speak with her."

After a short pause, a familiar voice resonated into the earpiece, "Hello, this is Dr. Simmons. How are you R.A.?"

"Could be doin' better Gina … and you?"

"Not bad but the workload's a bear. I take it this is a business call?"

"Yeah, this time. I was wonderin' what you came up with on the body from the fire."

"Hold on until I check the file," she continued while walking across the lab to her desk, "but I can tell you the body was male, and he didn't die of natural causes."

"Kinda what I figured. What was the cause of death?"

"Here it is," she said while opening the file. "C.O.D. was head trauma, had a nice crack across the forehead. Somebody hit him hard with some type of narrow weapon. From what was left of the skeletal structure, I estimate him to be older than thirty, maybe up to fifty. No other distinguishing features ... oh wait, there was a healed broken arm, left one, both radius and ulna about 6.5 centimeters from the base of the hand, looks like an old one. Teeth are pretty much intact so dental records should help identify him. Is that all you wanted?"

"Thanks, hon. Are we still on for tonight?"

"That depends on whether you can tear yourself away from that office of yours. I don't particularly relish being stood up."

"Yeah, sorry 'bout that; couldn't help it with the fire and all. I'll make sure nothing keeps me here past seven and I'll pick you up at eight. Okay?"

"Okay, you're on. See you at eight." As an afterthought she added, "Sharp."

"Deal, see you then."

"Bye."

He hung up and leaned back causing the familiar chair creak he had heard everyday since becoming Sheriff three years ago. He stared at the calendar on the far wall, fingers interlocked behind his head. He enjoyed this job, with lots of prestige as he swaggered around town or drove his cruiser through the county. Thankfully, Jackson was usually a nice quiet county. Prestige was nothing new to R.A, after all he was a legend in this part of the state. Twelve years ago the press had nicknamed him *Rifle Arm,* insisting that's what R.A. stood for the year he led the Glennville Warriors to the state football title game. What a disappointment that game was; torn knee ligaments in the first quarter relegated him to Spartanburg Hospital's Emergency Room where he listened to the radio as his team's 14-0 lead disintegrated into a devastating 42-17 loss. After the injury, scholarship offers dried up forcing enlistment in the Army. Two tours of duty had jaded R.A.'s opinion of military life so much that he passed on reenlisting for a third. Late one night, while eating a sandwich and searching through want ads, Mayor Flagstan and Councilman Johnson showed up on his porch. They told him Sheriff Kendall Finnegan was resigning due to health problems, and R.A.'s name had come up as an appointed replacement for the thirty-year veteran lawman. General consensus was that his eight years in the Military Police should be ample experience to allow him to fill out the remainder of Finnegan's term and then run for the office in the next election.

Refocusing on the present, he wondered why somebody would leave a murder victim in this county ... instead of some other county. He always had a lingering fear that un-solved cases would reflect poorly on his record. *Oh well, I guess I better see what I can find out about Johnnie Doe,* he thought as he rose and grabbed his hat on the way out.

As he reached the front door a nasally voice said, "Sheriff, Lieutenant Evers just called in and wants you to meet him at the fire scene. He says he found something that might help."

"Thanks Doris," he responded to the dispatcher. "Tell him I'm on my way."

"Yes sir," she replied while watching R.A. leave the building; she had always been good at watching, especially when it came to R.A. Walters. She remembered him from high school, but then again *everyone* remembered him from high school. He was the *yummiest* as one of her girlfriends had put it back then, and Doris didn't disagree, even though they felt he was in a class of his own and ran with a totally different crowd. He never glanced her way back then, but now here she was, working in the Jackson County Sheriff's Office ... and he was the sheriff! It didn't matter that he was seeing the deputy coroner; he was here, she could see him everyday, and who knows, maybe one day he would actually see her.

The ruins of the old restaurant were still smoldering two days after the fire, and the smell of burnt wood permeated the air as R.A. left his cruiser and surveyed the scene. Seeing Larry Evers headed his way, he walked to meet him.

"Doris said you found something."

"Yeah, over there in the weeds," the detective said while

pointing toward some brush located to the right of the ruins. "Follow me. I didn't move it." R.A. followed the detective, one of eight supported by the county. Although only two years younger than R.A. and appearing somewhat nerdish, Evers had demonstrated a penchant for police work, becoming the youngest detective in Jackson County history and earning the rank of Lieutenant quicker than anyone in the state. Several times over the past couple of years R.A. thought that Evers might soon challenge him for the office of sheriff, but that was something that would have to be dealt with when it happened.

"I was poking around the perimeter of the fire scene and found a shoe in the weeds over here," Evers explained as they reached the edge of the pavement.

"What does that have to do with anything?"

Evers moved the weeds aside with a stick to expose a cordovan loafer and explained, as he patiently had on numerous occasions, "I am fairly certain this shoe belongs to our John Doe, and since it looks to be an upscale brand, I would surmise he wasn't a transient or somebody seeking shelter for the night."

"Well, how do you know somebody else didn't drop it?"

"I guarantee someone would search for a lost shoe like this until he found it. Also, the last rain we had was Thursday morning, and this shoe's drier than if it had been in that rainstorm; if you remember, it was a gully buster. It has some water damage but I think it inadvertently got kicked in the weeds by one of the firemen."

R.A. started to reach for the shoe but stopped when Evers grabbed his arm. "What did you do *that* for?"

"With all due respect, I suggest the vic's fingerprints are probably on the shoe so we should do all we can to not contaminate it."

"Oh, yeah… right. Take care of it." Evers watched the sheriff retreat to his cruiser. Why that incompetent bastard was ever appointed was as much a mystery as the apparent murder case they were presently working. Shaking his head, he turned his attention to the task at hand. Retrieving a digital camera from his car, he returned to where the shoe was lying, clicked several photos and then bagged it.

Driving back to headquarters, Evers wondered if R.A. had even bothered to check the missing persons reports. Crimes of this nature didn't happen around here very often and he wanted to get it solved as soon as possible.

R.A. sat in his office eating a fast-food burger while poring over every missing person notice he had. So far nothing seemed to match the victim. He wondered why this guy, who apparently wasn't close to being destitute, hadn't been reported missing; maybe he wasn't gone long enough to be missed. More information was needed on the victim in order to request dental records. He realized his aptitude for this job might not be the greatest, but even *he* knew you couldn't just request dental records from every dentist in the country. He hoped Evers could get a lead through the fingerprints.

"Sheriff." R. A.'s attention shifted to the thin woman with far too much makeup standing just inside his door.

"What is it Doris?"

"This fax just came in and I thought you'd want to see it," she said, handing him two sheets. She remained standing close to his desk as if awaiting further orders.

He glanced up from the papers and said, "That will be all Doris. Let me know if anything else comes in."

"Thank you sir," she said, and added as she turned, "Anything you say."

The fax was an FBI fugitive notice on a Manford Pierce Contraldo, wanted for murdering a police officer and flight from justice. It said the murder occurred in Pittsburgh, Pennsylvania minutes after his armed robbery conviction. It further stated that the fugitive is considered armed and dangerous. The last part caught R. A.'s interest: witnesses had reported seeing a person who strongly resembled Contraldo at a truck stop on I-95, approximately twenty miles north. R.A. studied the mug shot on the fax and recognized the photo that had been flashed on the news the past day or so.

R. A. was wondering if the burned body was Contraldo when the ringing phone startled him.

"Sheriff Walters."

"Sheriff, this is Evers. I'm at the crime lab and they lifted two decent prints off the shoe. So far they haven't got a match, but AFIS is still running them."

"Okay, let me know if you get something."

"Will do, but keep something in mind. If this guy doesn't have a record or doesn't have his prints on file in the system, we won't get a match."

"Duly noted. Let me know either way." R. A. returned his attention to the fax.

Two hours later Lieutenant Larry Evers reported that no match was made on the fingerprints. That settled it, they would have to wait until somebody bothered to notice John Doe missing and reported it. In the meantime, R.A. figured he had better notify the FBI and request Contraldo's dental records just in case.

Chapter 6

Same day
11:30 AM

Jake's muscles ached from fighting the last two tuna he had caught. Each weighed in excess of ten pounds ... ten pounds of pure fight and determination. The past three hours were rewarding, but exhausting. At least the ocean breeze had helped to moderate the ninety-degree temperatures. About an hour ago, Nathan cried out for help because he had hooked a *big one*. Until then, he had caught only a few small fish and Jake was worried that his son's experience wouldn't be as rewarding as he hoped. To his amazement, Nathan had hooked a medium sized marlin. With Juan's guidance and the captain's expert use of the throttle, he finally brought the big fish alongside, where Juan used two grappling hooks to hoist it onto the deck. While watching the action, the sight of the grappling hooks brought a nearly imperceptible smile to Manny's lips.

"You've got yourself quite a trophy there!" Juan excitedly

told Nathan. "You should get it mounted and hang it above the fireplace!" Jake was pleased to see Nathan grin broadly, but just as quickly as the smile had appeared, it faded.

"No thanks," Nathan said as he walked back to where he had left his Discman. After exchanging glances with Juan, Jake held up his hand in a gesture to not pursue it for now.

"Time for lunch!" Mason announced and headed for the galley with Juan close behind, but just before descending the stairs, he paused to scan the horizon.

"Did you see the sky?" Juan asked Mason after joining him in the galley.

"Yeah, I been keepin' an eye on it; looks like we might have some rough stuff comin' in. If it keeps comin', we might have to cut this day a little short an' head back. I hate to do that to 'em, but it'd be better'n bein' out here in a storm. I judge we got 'bout two hours 'til we gotta start back in."

"You're right. We should have enough time to eat and fish maybe another hour before packing it in."

During the next half-hour, each person was able to create his own sandwich from the ingredients provided, and choose from several picnic-type sides. Soft drinks, beer, and water were also available. While they ate, Mason and Juan cast wary eyes on the horizon and exchanged concerned glances. Clouds in the distance were turning dark faster than they had anticipated and occasional flashes of lightning could be seen, although far enough in the distance no thunder was heard. The boat was rocking more noticeably as they finished eating and the wind had increased.

Mason and Juan quickly gathered the remaining food and containers, then made their way back to the galley. Jake stood, stretched, and moved to the side of the rear deck, where he leaned on the railing with both hands while looking at the waves that were becoming rough. Nathan walked to where he could look at the marlin lying on the deck. Manny was growing more impatient with each passing minute. Time was becoming more enemy than friend; he had to do something soon, but he couldn't chance it as long as the captain and helper were together. He had to separate them, and quietly get rid of each one.

A distant clap of thunder caused everyone to look toward the eastern sky. Dark clouds and lightning were evident and the water was becoming choppier.

"Are we in any danger?" Jake called to Mason as he prepared to climb back to the bridge.

"We're in th' Gulf Stream," explained Mason. "Storms often come up quick; this one seems to be comin' a little faster'n usual. We'll be okay, but if ya're worried, we can try to outrun it to land."

"Aw, we have complete confidence in you and your abilities," responded Manny. "I vote for riding it out." Going back to land before taking over the boat was the last thing he wanted. At least he might get to push someone overboard during the storm, and nobody would be wiser.

"What do ya guys want to do?" Mason directed toward Jake.

"I guess it's alright if you feel it would be safe," answered Jake. "But I don't think we should take any needless chances."

"I agree," replied Mason. "Juan, pack in th' gear!"

While the adults were discussing, Nathan had been watching a distant speck grow larger on the eastern horizon. By the time Juan had secured the fishing equipment in storage containers the approaching speck could be identified as another boat, which seemed to be pulling the storm behind it. The waves were increasing in height and menace.

Oblique View's radio came to life, spurring Mason to climb the ladder to his controls.

"This is David Callahan on pleasure boat *Blue Heron*. Our heading is two eight zero, attempting to outrun squall to the east. Over," came the voice from the radio.

Mason keyed his radio microphone. "This is *Oblique View*, charter fishin' vessel, Mason Bankowski, captain. Are ya in difficulty? Over."

"One of my inboards is overheating, may need assistance. Over."

"I've got a visual. We were headin' in but we'll wait on ya if ya need an escort. Over."

"Affirmative. Thanks for the offer. Storm's catching us. Waves getting worse. Over."

"Coast Guard. This is fishin' charter *Oblique View* callin' Coast Guard. Come in. Over."

"*Oblique View*, You have United States Coast Guard Integrated Support Command, Miami. Is there a problem? Over."

"Coast Guard. This is Oblique View. We're in a squall with pleasure boat Blue Heron. They're havin' engine problems. Please advise on estimated duration of storm. Over."

"*Oblique View,* we have no indication of any storm on radar. Must be ... " The rest of the message was obliterated by static.

"Coast Guard. This is fishin' charter *Oblique View* callin' Coast Guard. Come in. Over."

"*Oblique View,* this is the Coast Guard. We repeat, there is no storm showing on our radar. What is your location? Over."

"Coast Guard. This is *Oblique View.* GPS is fluctuatin' for some reason, but estimate forty nautical miles east o' Cape Arthur Inlet. Over."

"Coast Guard to *Oblique View.* Keep us informed of your situation. We are sending a cutter in your general direction and will notify Key West Naval Air Station and Patrick Air Force Base to stand by if needed. Over."

"Copy that, Coast Guard. Will keep ya informed. *Oblique View* over an' out."

Oblique View was rolling from side to side with increasing amplitude, causing everyone to grab on to integral parts of the vessel to keep from being thrown overboard. Jake led Nathan down to the relative safety of the vessel's interior, while Manny noticed Juan moving to the front of the boat and followed. He knew this was the best opportunity to eliminate him.

The other boat was still about five hundred yards away, so he figured anyone on board wouldn't be close enough to witness what he was about to do. Juan was standing on the fore deck as though *Oblique View* were in still water.

Manny cursed when he realized Juan was too far forward; the captain's elevated position afforded him an unobstructed view. Just then, Juan turned and approached. Manny, holding on to a rail to the right of the bridge and hidden from sight, slowly pulled the knife from his pocket and held it behind his back. His mouth salivated as he waited for his prey to get close enough. Rain started to fall, quickly becoming a torrential downpour when Juan was still about six feet away.

"Mr. Cranston, you should move back to where it's safe," Juan shouted, thinking the passenger had been caught in the wrong place and might be scared by the motion of the boat.

"Okay!" Manny shouted over the wind. "Help me!"

"Glad to!"

Just as Juan came into range, Manny shifted his weight to get a better thrust but slipped on the wet deck. His knife fell behind, bouncing into the ocean, as he had to also use his right hand to grab for a handhold to keep from pitching overboard.

"Easy there!" shouted Juan as he grabbed for him. "Did you drop something?"

Manny thought quickly. Obviously Juan hadn't seen what had dropped. "My lighter!" He shouted back while mentally chastising himself for losing one of his knives. Now he was down to one.

"Well, let me help you to where it's safer!"

As Juan grabbed his arm Manny swiveled hard, attempting to send Juan overboard but the kid seemed to have remarkable balance, and even had to hold on tighter to Manny to keep him from pitching headfirst off the deck.

They returned to the aft deck where Juan helped Manny down the stairs into the cabin, reuniting with the other two passengers.

"It's getting nasty out there," Manny said to nobody in particular, while trying to shake the abundant moisture from his hands.

"It's best if you all stay put until the storm plays itself out," advised Juan before retreating back up the stairs.

The other vessel was fast approaching when the radio crackled with static and then words, "This is *Blue Heron*. Port engine shut down due to overheating. Over."

Mason keyed his mike. "*Oblique View* here. We'll head in together. Stay 'bout fifty yards away so we're not forced together. We'll both make it in. Over."

"Affirmative and thanks. Will keep safe distance. Over."

"How many on board? Over."

"Seven passengers; two male, five female, and three crew, male. You? Over"

"Three passengers an' two crew, all male. Over."

Both vessels started toward land, keeping far enough apart that the rough seas wouldn't throw them together. The storm was growing in intensity and the passengers were being tossed around aggressively. Nathan was thrown against the starboard wall and then the aft wall alongside the stairs before he had time to brace for either collision. He fell on the floor with blood beginning to form on his forehead. Jake recovered his balance and moved to him.

"I'm all right," he said as Jake examined the knot on his head and dabbed the blood with his handkerchief.

Another round of being tossed about followed. Manny felt like he was a ball in one of the pinball machines he had played down at Larry's, just outside the Strip District as he was growing up. More rocking. It was increasingly difficult to keep from being pummeled against fixed objects in their surroundings. Objects fell off shelves and clattered to the floor, only to roll haphazardly under foot, making it harder still to remain upright.

Mason had his hands full trying to keep *Oblique View* positioned perpendicular to the wave fronts and staying a safe distance from *Blue Heron*, while remaining close enough to attempt a rescue if she foundered. Another worry… fog was closing in fast. How was he going to keep *Blue Heron* in sight? He decided to contact … what was the other captain's name? Dave something … Callahan, that was it, Callahan.

"*Blue Heron*, this is *Oblique View*. We have a fog problem. What d'ya advise? Over."

"Copy that, *Oblique View*. It's moving in fast. I'm losing visual on you. Over."

"Suggest we try to ride it out here. Can't maintain safe distance in fog. Over."

"Affirmative. Over."

"Affirmative, *Blue Heron*. We'll move on some an' stay put. Stay on radio and answer back on horn blasts. Over."

"Affirmative, Oblique View. Over and out."

The fog already obliterated *Blue Heron*; it was dense and a funny color, reminding Mason of faded pea soup. He had never seen fog move in as fast as this. While reflecting about the fog, a realization dawned on him: *Oblique View* wasn't rocking; she was sitting as solid as if she were in dry dock and the rain had stopped. He looked over the side but couldn't see the water because of the fog's density. He descended the ladder to the deck and quickly moved to the starboard side. He couldn't believe what he saw - the water was perfectly calm, no ripples. He turned and ascended the ladder back to the controls where he sounded five quick blasts on the horn and waited for *Blue Heron's* obligatory response of five blasts. When he heard none, he keyed his mike.

"*Blue Heron,* this is *Oblique View*. What happened to yar signal reply and what's with this fog? Over."

No response.

"*Blue Heron,* this is *Oblique View*. Come back. Over."

No response.

"Blue Heron, this is *Oblique View*. Come back. Over."

No response.

"Captain Callahan, what's goin' on over there? Come back. Over."

No response.

Mason looked up from his attempts to contact *Blue Heron* and took note that the fog had moved out a short distance, to what he estimated as ten yards. The exposed water surrounding *Oblique View* was like glass.

Jake, Nathan, and Manny emerged from below decks and stood in astonishment at the condition of the water and the dense fog beyond.

"Weird," Nathan mumbled while holding his father's handkerchief to the wound on his forehead. "That's definitely weird."

Chapter 7

Afternoon

Calm. Calm. Calm. As choppy as the ocean had been during the squall with waves topping six feet, it was now totally smooth. The water appeared to consist of something gelatin-like, or at least a substance much more viscous than normal water. Jake's science background made this situation seem even more implausible. He dipped the end of a grappling hook into the water and watched as ripples moved away, but only a few inches before dying out. This wasn't the way water was supposed to be ... the ripples should have moved much farther, even as far as the pale green fog that still surrounded them at a distance Jake estimated to be between twenty-five and thirty feet; beyond that, there seemed to be nothing. He had never experienced being on the Atlantic Ocean, but he knew this was not normal.

The air was hot and stuffy, but not nearly as humid as before the storm when sweat was common to all on board. And the light; even though they were surrounded by dense fog, it was somewhat bright within their cocoon, as if a low wattage fluorescent light was somehow illuminating the fog, but without shadows in spite of the brightness. The fog was different too, no dampness like this morning's fog; it felt as if they were surrounded by a plastic curtain.

Mason was trying to make sense of his instruments. In his twelve years of taking out charters he had never encountered anything remotely as strange as this! The engines ran, but it seemed as if the boat was fastened to some gigantic, invisible pylon. Maybe it was an optical illusion brought on by lack of visibility or the fact that waves wouldn't perpetuate and died out quickly. He tried steering in a circle but all he could feel was the vibration of the engines as they increased and decreased with the throttle. He focused on the compass needle, which was slowly rotating even when the boat was supposedly stationary. In addition, the GPS screen had them constantly changing position, and the last time he checked they were somewhere between Nova Scotia and Greenland. He had tried several times but still couldn't raise either Blue Heron or the Coast Guard, and this unnerved him more than most things had in his forty-eight years.

Glancing at his watch because he wanted to be back before Maggie was forced to worry, Mason knew that the squall had started about quarter past twelve and it had to have been at least a half hour since then, maybe an hour. *12:28? Impossible!* Maybe his watch wasn't running. He checked the control panel where a digital clock in military time was located and it showed *1226*. He stepped to the top of the ladder and called down to the others.

"What time do you have?"

Jake looked at his watch and reported, "Twelve twenty-eight ...wait, that can't be right." He removed and shook his watch, and then looked at it closely. While he was doing this, Manny and Juan communicated other reports of twelve twenty-five and twelve twenty-two. Nathan wasn't wearing a watch.

"These times can't be right," commented Jake, examining his wristwatch. "Mine's stopped. Check yours." All were in agreement that their individual watches had stopped. Mason then relayed the problems he was having with the navigation system and radio. He tried to remain calm while emphasizing his confidence that this situation was merely temporary... and hoping he was right.

Mason recalled that *Blue Heron* was about a hundred yards off the port stern when he had last seen her before the fog descended. He walked to the furthest point on the aft deck and shouted in the direction of his last sighting of *Blue Heron*.

"Hellooo. *Blue Heron!* Can ya hear me?"

Silence.

"*Blue Heron!* Can ya hear me? Come back."

Silence.

"Well, I guess all we can do is wait for this fog to lift. Make yarselves comfortable," suggested Mason in resignation as he returned to the controls.

Time passed. The fog remained. Nathan fell asleep listening to his Discman, Jake was lost in his thoughts, and Manny was cursing his damn luck because it was looking with increasing certainty that he would have to return to land. His only option seemed to be returning to the captain's house during the night, eliminate the captain and his wife, and take the boat. He had to get out of the country before the cops closed in on him. Who knows, the police might be waiting for him when they got back. With nothing to do, Juan settled in a deck chair and dozed off.

Jake's thoughts again drifted to Lisa and the life they could have had. He regretted the wasted years and how everything had affected Nathan. Thoughts of those who had expressed their condolences and love flooded his mind. It was too much; he had to concentrate on clearing his mind before he was forced to remember more.

He was concentrating ... and then he was waking up. He didn't remember falling asleep, only waking. He became aware of something different ... sweat, and the sound of small waves lapping at the boat. He stood and looked around. "Hey, the fog's gone!" he shouted. At this, the others either awoke or emerged from their thoughts.

Mason had been engrossed with entering their experiences of the day in his log and hadn't noticed the change in conditions. He immediately surveyed their surroundings, seeing nothing but gentle swells. He snatched up his mike.

"*Blue Heron*. This is *Oblique View* callin' *Blue Heron*. Come in. Over."

Static.

"*Blue Heron*. This is *Oblique View* callin' *Blue Heron*. Come in please. Over."

Static.

"This is Mason Bankowski on *Oblique View* callin' David Callahan on *Blue Heron*. Come in. Over."

Static.

"This is *Oblique View*. Over an' out."

Mason didn't know what happened to *Blue Heron* or the people on board, and for now he didn't want to speculate. It was sufficient to know that they were no longer anywhere within sight and weren't broadcasting.

"Coast Guard. This is charter fishin' vessel *Oblique View*. Do ya read? Over?

Static.

"*Oblique View* callin' the Coast Guard. Any Coast Guard vessel or station. Do ya read? Over."

Static.

"Damn! Radio must be out." Mason said. At least the compass seemed to be functioning again, so he started the engines and turned on a heading of 270 degrees. He figured they would find the east coast of Florida if they traveled due west, and he wanted to go as far as possible before the compass malfunctioned again, and if it did, he planned on ignoring it and maintaining this direction.

Nobody had any idea of the time, even though all time-pieces on board had strangely resumed at about the same time, which they deduced was approximately twenty minutes ago. How long they had been inoperable was anyone's guess, but Jake figured it had to be a couple of hours; at least it seemed that long.

Mason kept the engines at full throttle while keeping an eye on the compass and other gauges. He was grudgingly optimistic, waiting for integral systems to malfunction while praying they didn't. He kept thinking, *so far, so good*.

Now that the boat was headed toward land, the mood on the aft deck was much lighter than before. There was hope now, in everyone but Manny. He now knew for a fact that he would have to knock off the captain and his wife later tonight, and take the boat. He also realized there was a good possibility that cops could be lying in wait for his return. Cranston's body might have been found and identified by now, and his car traced to where it was parked in front of the captain's house. Going back to prison was not an option; he would choose *suicide-by-cop* rather than be taken alive.

Chapter 8

Afternoon

At the first sight of land Mason began to relax. He finally had a visual target he could focus on and stop worrying about the instruments. He searched the approaching shoreline for any familiar landmark; seeing none, he chose to move in as close as he dared, and head southward along the coastline.

Ten minutes of searching the shoreline turned up nothing that looked familiar, and Mason was having trouble hiding his growing trepidation. Not only did he not recognize any landmarks on the shoreline, the entire shoreline seemed different. There were no condos, homes, boats, sunbathers, tourists, airplanes ... nothing but occasional palm trunks, a few with sparse leaves. It was as if the east coast of Florida was deserted.

"Anything yet?" Juan was beside him on the bridge.

"Look at the shore. Anything strike ya as strange?" Mason asked quietly so nobody else could hear.

"Nothing."

"Yes, there is. Look again."

"I meant there is *nothing*. Where are the people, boats, houses ... anything?" Juan whispered back. "Where *are* we?"

"Since there shouldn't be any land between th' coast an' where we were in the Gulf Stream, this has to be th' Florida coast. It don't make sense. I don't remember this much deserted beach. Maybe we got farther off course than I thought ... or maybe this is an island I didn't know about. Anyway, it has me wonderin'."

Suddenly, Juan pointed to a structure on the other side of the beach dunes.

"Look, over there. What is that, a military base?"

"Dunno. Never seen anythin' like it, but at least we might find someone there who can tell us where we are. Let's anchor an' take th' raft ashore."

Mason descended the ladder after shutting down the engines. Juan followed and moved to drop anchor and prepare the raft.

"We're takin' th' raft ashore to find out where we are. Y'all are invited to go with us," announced Mason.

"Nathan and I'll go," Jake replied while Nathan rolled his eyes.

"I better stay behind and watch the boat," volunteered Manny.

"Okay, Mr. Cranston. If anythin' happens, fire a flare straight up, an' we'll get back as soon as we can. Juan, bring me th' flare gun!"

Juan went below and retrieved the flare gun within one minute. He then returned to preparing the raft while Mason instructed Manny on how to load and fire the flare gun.

"Raft's ready!" Juan shouted when the raft was inflated and lowered over the side.

Juan slid over the side into the raft, and held it in place while the others climbed in. They shoved off, and Juan rowed toward shore. When they reached shallow water, he jumped out and pulled the raft through the surf onto the beach. The others stepped out, and Juan dragged the empty raft well past the high water mark into dry sand.

"This way." Mason indicated a low area between two shallow dunes that were covered sporadically with sea oats along with some other kinds of dried grass, and started off with the others following.

On the boat, Manny watched the raft head toward shore and couldn't believe his luck. All he had to do was wait until they were out of sight, haul up the anchor and leave, not having to waste anyone, not even one! No one murdered. That thought reminded him of one of his counseling sessions in prison. He had been forced to attend mandatory weekly sessions with the prison psychologist, Dr. James Burrows. He recalled how smug the man was, how much he tried to impress people with his so-called intellect. Burrows had once told Manny he couldn't be rehabilitated because he didn't have a conscience. Inside, Manny always knew he had a conscience; it's just that his conscience was expendable under certain circumstances. Now he was about to achieve a desperate goal without killing anyone ... else.

"See, Dr. Burrows," Manny said with a smile. "I do have a conscience. Wish you were here ... but if you *were* here, my conscience would have to take a short vacation."

The landing party disappeared behind the dunes, so it was time to act. Manny had watched Juan lower the anchor, so it was an easy process to reverse the winch and wind it up. He hurried rearward, swung around onto the ladder, and climbed to the bridge. He looked over the instruments and decided he could handle it ... and then his heart dropped.

"Where are the damn keys?" he exclaimed, frantically searching the control panel, all compartments, and even around and under the seat cushion. Nothing. The captain must have taken them with him. He considered hot-wiring the ignition, but the wires seemed to be housed deep within the console, and he couldn't locate an access panel.

"Damn! Damn! Damn!" Manny shouted, and then sat on the captain's chair, resigned to having to stay until the landing party came back. He lit his last cigarette and drew the smoke deep into his lungs, held it, and then blew it out through tight lips. Once finished, he flicked the butt into the water, went back to the deck winch and again lowered the anchor. He then examined the flare gun, figuring, if need be, it could be a damn fine weapon.

Emerging from the dunes, the landing party was confronted with about six or seven strange looking buildings, all resembling plastic igloos, but slightly more pointed. There were no other structures as far as the eye could see, only sand and sparse vegetation. Upon closer approach, the buildings were connected. One large igloo seemed to be in the center with straight structures connecting it to the smaller igloos. Each of these was in turn connected to the igloos bordering it. The entire structure loosely resembled a wheel, with one igloo located at the hub and the others on the rim at the end of the spokes. Jake stepped forward and ran his hand over one of the igloos.

"It seems to be constructed of some type of polymer, something extremely hard and smooth," he said, while examining the surface.

Nathan showed only mild interest as he slowly walked a short distance around the accessible perimeter of the structure his father was investigating. Mason and Juan walked around the entire structure searching for signs of life.

"What do ya make of it?" Mason asked, when he and Juan reunited with Jake and Nathan.

"It's probably some type of military building, possibly Coast Guard. Its design makes sense in this area; I bet it's immune to whatever nature throws its way," answered Jake, stepping back to take in as much of the structure as possible.

"Why do ya say that?"

"First is its shape … parabolic. The parabola is an underlying shape in nature. For instance, a baseball thrown from the outfield to the infield follows a parabolic path;

satellite dishes have a parabolic shape; the reflectors behind light bulbs in flashlights and headlights are parabolic; if a chain is allowed to hang while supported at both ends, it will assume a parabolic shape and that shape will describe an energy curve."

"I couldn't follow much of what ya said, but how's that make it better?"

"Well, if the shape is that of natural energy, then it will be the most stable of structures. It should easily withstand a hurricane, and maybe even a tsunami without damage. In addition, the material it's made from is strong and smooth, eliminating windows and common roofing materials like shingles. This place seems practically indestructible."

"But as ya said, there's no windows … and no doors either. How could anybody get light inside or look outside? And how could ya get inside with no doors?"

"I don't know, but I'd like to find out. Maybe it's lit from inside and you can't look out. If it's military, maybe they don't want to look out … or have anyone looking in," supplied Juan.

Mason pondered this a moment. "Well then, let's see if we can find someone inside an' get some questions answered."

"Let's go."

Mason led the way with Juan bringing up the rear. They circled the entire structure, but found no doors and no tracks in the sand. They pounded on each igloo-shaped pod with no response from inside. There were five pods surrounding the central pod, each connected by what seemed to be a hallway covered in the same material as the pods. Each connecting segment's exterior shape was also parabolic in cross-section and no more than ten feet in length. The entire structure was in the shape of a pentagon with a pod at each vertex and one in the center, all connected.

"Maybe it's solid," Mason speculated. "There's no way in."

"Nobody would build a solid structure out here. What purpose would that serve?" supplied Jake.

"Dunno, but I don't see any way in. Do any of ya see somethin' I missed? There's no footprints other than th' ones we left, so where's th' door?"

Nathan, who was getting bored and hot, sat down and leaned back against a connecting section between two outer pods while his father and Mason discussed the structure. Juan squatted beside him.

"We're not gettin' anywhere here. Let's go," said Mason, frustrated.

"Okay. Let's go."

As Nathan rose to his feet, he placed his right hand on the wall to support himself. As his hand lost contact with the surface so he could follow the others, a section in the outer rim opened. He turned, saw the opening, and called to the others, "Hey! Look here!"

Jake and Mason hurried back and peered into the opening that seemed to exist without a discernable physical door.

"Anyone in there?" shouted Mason into the gaping rectangular cave. Hearing no reply, he repeated the query into the opening.

"Don't seem like anyone's home," Mason concluded. "Let's go in."

"Hold on. I, for one, don't want to get trapped in there. How can we be sure the doorway won't close after we enter? If it does, how can we get out? Nathan or Juan, did either of you find this doorway?"

"I don't know what happened. I just got up and it was there," answered Nathan.

"Did you trip any levers ... or touch anything?"

"I don't know."

"Well, we were already walking away, so odds are that something one of you did caused the door to open. Show me what you did."

Juan squatted where he had been a few minutes earlier. Nathan sat down where he had been, and then stood up, brushing the wall. The doorway disappeared.

"Now ya've done it!" shouted Mason. "Now how're we gonna get inside?"

Jake placed his hand where Nathan's had been. Nothing happened. But when he removed it from the surface, the doorway reappeared. He tried it again, and the doorway disappeared; again, and it reappeared.

"Well, now we know how to open the thing from the outside, but the inside's still a mystery," said Jake.

"So, how do we do this?" asked Mason.

Jake handed Nathan his wristwatch.

"Captain Bankowski and I are going inside. You two watch the time, and if the door closes, reopen it in fifteen minutes. Got that?"

Nathan nodded.

"Before we go in, make sure you can work it."

Nathan placed his hand on the wall and then lifted it. The doorway disappeared, and reappeared when he repeated the process.

Jake turned to Mason. "Let's go."

Juan watched the two men walk through the opening and then turned his attention to Nathan. "Where you from?" he asked.

"Around Baltimore," Nathan answered with obvious reluctance, while staring off into the distance.

"I never been farther north than Georgia; got an aunt, uncle, and two cousins live just east of Atlanta. I'd like to go to New England sometime. You got any brothers or sisters?"

"Nope."

Juan was hoping to get Nathan to open up a little, noticing how withdrawn he had seemed earlier, so he continued trying to make conversation.

"I got a brother, Miguel, and two sisters, Rosa and Maria. Miguel's the oldest, he's twenty two, just graduated from UM in May and got a job with Jericho Corporation in Pensacola. He's supposed to start Monday, so we're going to help him move in tomorrow. Rosa's twenty and works in a dentist's office; she's engaged and plans to get married next year in October. Maria graduated from Cape Arthur High in June and she starts at Seminole U in two weeks."

"Seminole U? What's Seminole U? I never heard of it," queried Nathan, focusing on Juan.

"Florida State University. You know, the 'Noles ... Seminoles."

"Oh yeah, I saw them play on TV. Good team."

"You talking about football or basketball?"

"Football."

"Do you remember who they played? You know, the game you watched."

"I don't know, I think Florida."

"Oohh, the Gators, huh? That was probably a great football game; the Gators and 'Noles are big rivals down here. Gators hate 'Noles and 'Noles hate Gators; been like that for a long time."

"Yeah, I think it was a good game. I don't usually watch football, but I think I watched most of that one. You like football?"

"I played the last two years but canned it this year to get some money built up for college in two years. Wrestling's my sport."

"Wrestling. Why wrestling? I think you could get hurt bad wrestling. I saw those wrestlers on TV slamming each other and picking someone up and throwing him down on the floor. I'd never want to do anything like that."

"No, you've got the wrong idea. Wrestling is a sport;

what you saw on TV is a show, they're more actors than athletes."

"They *have* to be athletes, just look how they're built."

"Most of them are athletes, or had been at one time, and they have muscles, but they act out most of what you see. Sorry to disappoint you, but I've heard those guys sometimes know weeks in advance who is going to do what, and who is going to win. Then they get together and practice, or at least make sure they have an idea of what's going to happen and in what order. My type of wrestling is different."

"How?"

"Well, there are twelve weight classes and we take turns wrestling one member from the other team who weighs about the same. I did well last year … made it to states as a sophomore.

"Wait a minute. How old are you?"

"Sixteen, why?"

"I don't know, I thought you were a lot older than me. I'm only a year younger than you."

"Yeah, I thought we were about the same. So, tell me about you."

"Not much to tell. I'm going to be a sophomore, and do okay in school. There's not much more."

Juan decided to change his focus as he realized Nathan wasn't about to open up, "Tell me about your parents; your dad's kind of cool, what about your mom?"

"I don't want to talk about it … them … whatever,"

Nathan said as he looked straight ahead, then turned his head to gaze into the distance.

Juan, knowing he had somehow crossed a line, kept silent for a few moments.

"Sorry, I didn't mean to pry." They resumed their vigil in silence.

Chapter 9

Afternoon

U pon entering the building, Mason and Jake didn't need to wait for their eyes to adjust to the dark; it wasn't dark. The walls glowed as if totally backlit, and although bright enough to see clearly, the light was dim enough that their eyes felt comfortable, even somewhat soothing.

They moved into the pod to the immediate right of the doorway. This room was approximately twenty feet in diameter and, unlike the exterior, had a horizontal ceiling and vertical walls. The walls, or rather *the* wall because it was circular, seemed to consist of the same material as the building's exterior. The room was devoid of furnishings. Two lighted panels were set in the wall about four feet above the floor and a black triangle was embedded in the wall approximately eight feet from the panels and at the same height. The leftmost panel was glowing pale yellow and the right panel glowed orange. They looked to be the same size, approximately four inches wide and eight inches high.

"What do you make of this?" Jake asked after studying the panels, while Mason had been trying to determine how the walls were lit.

"Make of what?"

"These two panels. They must serve some useful purpose or they wouldn't be here."

"Don't know. If this is military, it might launch a rocket or somethin'. Better not touch'em. That triangle looks like an emblem of some type, maybe has somethin' to do with the builder. Let's check out the rest of th' place."

They moved through one of the hallways, which also had a horizontal ceiling and vertical interior walls. Each of the perimeter pods was identical to the first one they examined, including the same two lighted panels and black triangle. The central pod was identical to the perimeter pods, except for two things. It was larger, about thirty feet in diameter and there were four lighted panels: pale yellow, pale tan, orange, and pale green, but the black triangle was missing. All floors were alike and seemed to be made of the same material as the exterior.

"Well, nobody and nothin's here," said a disappointed Mason. "Whoever was here seems to've moved out. The place is deserted, so we may's well get outta here."

Mason exited through the still-open doorway while Jake hesitated.

"Hold on a minute," Jake said. "I want to see if I can open the door from inside."

He tried various places on the inside wall alongside

the open doorway, until it closed. He tried again where it seemed to work before, and it reopened. He mentally set the triggering spot a foot to the right of the doorway and four feet above the floor. Satisfied he could open this door from inside and outside, he stepped out into the sunshine. Suddenly, a thought struck him, and he began walking counterclockwise around the entire structure.

"What's he doin'?" Mason asked Juan.

"Don't know. I suppose he'll tell us when he gets back."

"Guess ya're prob'ly right. I wish he'd hurry. I gotta get back home b'fore Maggie starts to worry."

Jake came into view from the direction opposite where he had started. "There's a doorway in all five connecting hallways. Now we know how to get into this thing if we need to. Let's go back to the boat."

As they passed between the dunes, a movement caught Nathan's eye. He looked down, relieved to see that it wasn't a snake, just a large ant scurrying along the dune to the left … and then it was gone.

"Find anybody?" Manny asked as the raft reached the starboard side of *Oblique View*.

"Nothin' but a strange lookin' buildin', prob'ly somethin' military. It was deserted. Any problems while we were gone?" Mason responded.

"Nope."

The landing party climbed aboard and Juan tied a rope to the raft so it could remain inflated, then pushed it away from the side of the boat. He raised anchor while Mason assumed the controls and started the engines.

"Where're we going now?" Manny shouted to Mason over the throbbing of the engines.

"Farther south. That's where most of th' cities an' people are!" Mason shouted back and then accelerated *Oblique View* to full throttle.

The wind felt refreshing to Jake, who by now was sweating profusely. Ever since the fog lifted, the sun was bright but seemed filtered as if shining through a translucent layer of sky. Few clouds were evident, so they weren't blocking the sun's rays. Also, he couldn't really put his finger on it, but the air felt different, thicker, and he found he had to reapply sunscreen more often because he was starting to burn. He passed the sunscreen to Nathan who was also becoming red. Now, with the boat moving swiftly, things felt more normal.

Juan climbed the ladder and joined Mason at the controls.

"Did you try to raise the Coast Guard again?"

"Yep. Just static. I forgot about my cell in this compartment," Mason gestured toward one of the storage compartments built into the control panel, "But when I tried to call Maggie, nothin' happened."

"Is the battery charged?"

"Yep. Take a look." Mason handed the phone to Juan, who found a full four bars showing.

"Mind if I call my brother?" Juan asked.

"Go ahead. I hope you have better luck'n me. If you get 'im on th' line, tell 'im to call Maggie an' th' Coast Guard. I hate to admit it, but I'm lost."

Juan punched in the numbers for his brother's cell phone.

"Nothing. Didn't even get his voice mail. I'll try home." Again, Juan punched in the numbers, waited a few seconds and then flipped the cover closed. "Nothing. What happened to our communications?"

"I'm wonderin' if it's th' communications ... or somethin' else," Mason said, scowling.

"What do you mean, 'something else'?"

"Think about it, Juan. You were born an' raised along this coast. Does any of this look familiar to ya? What part of th' coast are we lookin' at? When we looked at that buildin' back there, what did ya see on th' other side of it?"

"You mean beyond the building? All I saw was more sand and some bushes, or at least beach grass. Why?"

"I don't know ... it didn't feel right. From where we ran into that squall, we shoulda come straight in an' been within 'bout twenty miles, give or take, from where we left. Ya agree?"

"I suppose, but remember we sat out there for a long time and could have drifted far off course during that time."

"Yeah, I guess ya're right, but why didn't we see th' Intracoastal Waterway beyond th' buildin'? If we was anywhere between Canaveral an' Stuart, it shoulda been there."

"You're right, but don't forget that we didn't try to go inland; the land might've been too wide to see the Waterway from where we were."

"True, but th' land gets pretty narrow in some places an' I ain't seen nothin' like that th' whole way along here."

"Maybe we're too far south."

"If that's the case, we'da run into Riviera or West Palm by now. They're heavily populated down there."

"I see what you mean. I just want to get home. We're helping my brother move to Pensacola tomorrow. What are you going to do?"

"I'm gonna make this baby fly. Jus' keep an eye out for anybody or anythin' so we can find out where we are."

The sun was getting lower in the sky when Juan grabbed Mason's arm.

"Hey, there's a bunch of buildings over there!" he exclaimed.

"Gotcha!" Mason uttered as he throttled back the engines to idle.

The passengers had been sitting in silence, watching the shoreline pass when suddenly they were pitched forward by the rapid deceleration of the boat.

"What happened?" Jake called to the two men on the bridge.

"We found some houses and we're going ashore!" Juan replied as he descended the ladder and scurried forward to drop anchor.

Mason cut the engines, descended the ladder, and walked

to the aft deck where he reeled in the raft they had been towing.

"Everyone ashore this time!" Mason ordered. "I don't think we have ta worry about anyone stealin' the boat. We haven't seen anybody since we came ashore."

Manny knew that he would arouse suspicion if he protested, which would raise questions about why he wanted to remain on the boat, so he didn't object. All five piled into the raft, and again, Juan rowed them to shore. After jumping into the surf and pulling the raft onto the shore, Juan waited until everyone had vacated and then dragged it far up past the tide line.

The group then set out toward the buildings, approximately three hundred yards away. This time they had to go over a twelve-foot high sand dune since there was no break to walk through. Walking and sliding down the other side, Jake stopped suddenly, causing Nathan to pile into him, knocking both off their feet. Mason and Juan looked around to see what happened.

"Hard to keep yar feet in this sand," commented Mason.

"Look over there," urged Jake, pointing southward along the dunes as he regained his feet. They turned and saw a huge lighthouse-shaped rock, leaning noticeably to one side and half-buried in the sand.

Chapter 10

Late afternoon

W hat the hell..." Mason's comment trailed off as he stared at the object about twenty yards away. Then his frustration, mixed with anxiety took over. "Where the hell are we? What happened? How in the hell'd that get here?"

Everyone else stood dumbfounded except Manny, who hadn't noticed the rock when they first passed it because his mind had been too focused on his goal for the day. He just mimicked the rest, showing surprise. Mason and Juan trudged their way through soft sand to the rock, where Mason brushed some sand away from its southern side. He stopped and slowly stood. By that time, the others had joined them.

"That's it. That's the rock beside the inlet for sure," Mason said with a bewildered expression.

"How can you be so sure?" asked Jake.

"Look where I dug," explained Mason, "and you'll see

two chips out of it 'bout an inch apart. A coupla weeks ago, some dumb-ass kid got himself arrested for shootin' at that rock … hit it twice on that side 'bout an inch apart."

"But those would be fresh chips if it happened only a couple weeks ago, these are old and weathered," Juan replied after examining the wounds carefully.

"Yeah, an' this rock wasn't half covered by a sand dune this mornin' either!" Mason half shouted. "Somethin's definitely screwed up!"

While they were talking, Manny's attention shifted to the buildings in the distance. They were shaped like igloos, or L'egg's Egg pantyhose containers sticking out of the sand. If they were painted pale blue, that's exactly what they resembled. Since something had drastically changed, and there didn't seem to be any people, much less cops, he put his escape plans on hold. He thought he could see how this whole thing played out; there would always be time to escape later if things didn't work to his advantage.

"Hey, it's getting late. Let's get to those buildings before it gets dark," urged Manny, the others indicating their agreement by nodding or simply starting to walk in that direction. Mason glanced back at the rock as he walked away.

The air was warm and the sun, now low in the sky, lengthened the men's shadows rapidly as they trekked across the sand to the closest structure. The going was made more difficult by some dense brush with stiff branches and sharp thorns.

When they reached the structures, Mason suggested they divide into two groups to survey their surroundings and report back in fifteen minutes. He took Manny with him while Juan accompanied Jake and Nathan. When they reunited, the consensus was that all structures resembled the one they had encountered earlier, except for the number of perimeter pods, which varied from three to six. Feeling confident about being able to gain access to these buildings, Jake walked to one and tried the same technique that had worked previously. Nothing happened. He retried with the same result. Nathan and Juan separated and tried the technique on other buildings while Jake circled his building, trying at various locations. All failed.

The sun was setting and they still weren't able to enter any of the buildings. Mason suggested they return to *Oblique View* and return in the morning when they could see. As they were about to leave, Manny had success while using the techniques he copied by watching the others.

"Well, at least it looks like we have a place to stay tonight," reasoned Jake.

"Looks that way," agreed Mason. "Have a look at what's inside. I'll take Juan back to check on th' boat an' secure th' raft."

"Boss, do you think it's wise to leave the boat unattended for the night, especially since we don't have any idea what's happening around here?" asked Juan.

"Yeah, I guess maybe ya're right," responded Mason, then turned to the three passengers. "I think I'd better stay on *Oblique View* for th' night to make sure it's there in th' mornin'."

"How do we know you won't leave us before morning?" asked Manny. "It's your boat and you have the keys and this is your area, you know it like the back of your hand."

"I did know this area like th' back of my hand 'til this afternoon," replied Mason. "I don't know any more than ya'll do now."

"Hey, I have an idea," interjected Juan. "Why don't I boat-sit tonight and everyone else stay here?"

"Okay by me," voted Manny.

Jake and Nathan said it didn't matter to them, so Mason agreed to let Juan stay with the boat. He walked Juan away from the group with his arm around his shoulder.

"Don't take any chances out there, Juan. If anything remotely seems dangerous, take this an' use it." Mason instructed as he pulled a Beretta .38 from beneath his waistband in the back. "I brought it along when we left th' boat. Ya also have th' flare gun; use it if ya need help, but only after ya use th' gun. I'll sleep outside, a gunshot'll wake me up an' I'll get to ya as quick as I can. Take care an' be safe."

"I will. You can count on it." After taking a few steps, he turned and said, "If you can get through to Maggie tonight, please have her call my family and tell them to wait on leaving until I get there." He then continued his trek to the beach.

Mason watched him until he disappeared into the gathering dusk, then pulled his cell phone from his pocket, punched in a speed dial number, waited, and then closed the cover. Dejectedly, he turned and joined the others.

Jake entered the building, and as he had done in the previous building they had explored, moved into the pod to his right. He found the room identical to the ones in the other building, and further examination of the remaining pods verified that, other than having only four perimeter pods, this structure was identical to the one they had explored earlier in the day.

He returned to the doorway and invited the rest in. Juan had already left for the beach and Mason had decided to remain outside when Nathan and Manny joined Jake inside the building. They were in awe, looking around, taking it all in.

"Where's the light coming from?" asked Manny as he looked around.

"I don't know," answered Jake, "but it seems as if the walls and ceiling could be constructed from some type of material that continues to glow once energy has been supplied to it. It might be based on the Photoelectric Effect."

Nathan scrunched his face, "What's a photo ... photo, whatever you called it?"

"Photoelectric Effect. The way I understand it, certain wavelengths, or colors of light falling on certain metals will cause an electric current to flow in the metal. I think it was actually discovered by another scientist, but Einstein's explanation of the phenomenon earned him the Nobel Prize.

I know photocells are based on the principle, but this might extend into fluorescence."

"Fluorescence? What's that?" asked Manny.

"An atom has a nucleus containing protons ..."

"And neutrons," Nathan interrupted and then added in a bored sing-song manner, "with electrons in orbits around the nucleus. The number of electrons is equal to the number of protons in a neutral atom. I remember that stuff from eighth grade science."

"Very good Nathan, you're right. Now do you remember what distinguishes the electrons from each other?

"I don't know, something about energy ... energy levels; that's it, energy levels," Nathan answered, now exhibiting a rare semi-smile.

"That's right, energy levels. The electrons with the lowest energy are located closest to the nucleus and the electrons with the greatest energy are located the farthest from the nucleus. Well, energy absorbed by an atom is actually absorbed by certain electrons, which then jump from their energy level to a higher energy level. They stay at the higher energy level for almost an eternity in atom time, about ten to the negative eighth seconds or a hundred millionth of a second, and then they return to their ground state, or original energy level. When they return to their original energy level, the extra energy is given off as photons, which we see as light. It's possible that the material used to coat the interior walls, floor, and ceiling is a fluorescent substance that continues to glow as long as energy is supplied to it. Neon signs and fluorescent lights use this principle."

"Cool. I never heard of any place like this."

"Neither did I," answered Jake, and then whispering to himself as he turned to walk, "Neither did I."

They moved into the central pod where there was more room. Due to the absence of furniture, they sat on the floor. Manny was trying to make sense of his present situation. He had to keep at least one step ahead of circumstances to survive, and right now he had absolutely no idea what the circumstances were.

"What are these lights?" Nathan questioned as he examined the lighted panels to his right.

"I don't have any idea," answered Jake. "But I don't think we should play with them because the people that own this building aren't home. When we explored the other building this afternoon, it was identical to this one, down to the lighted panels. Captain Bankowski thought we shouldn't touch them, because if it's a military base we might launch missiles or something."

"Yeah, right," groused Manny, and then sneered, "I just *bet* those buttons launch missiles."

"You know, you may be right," said Jake. "Let's get Mr. Bankowski in here and talk over our options."

By the time Juan reached the raft, the sun had dropped below the horizon and it was becoming difficult to see. He was relieved to see the raft and *Oblique View* where they had left them, because so many strange things had happened to-day that something not changing was reassuring. He pulled the raft into the surf, climbed in and rowed to the anchored fishing boat. As he rowed, he studied the western sky with its beautiful colors, but he couldn't recall ever seeing green in a sunset before; for now, a striking green was the most prominent color. After climbing aboard and tying off the raft, he hooked the marlin and dropped it over the side after securing the line, and then performed a cursory inspection of the boat. Satisfied that all was in order, he pondered about whether to spend the night in the sleeping quarters below or on deck, which would permit quicker action if anything should occur. He chose the latter and made himself as com-fortable as possible in one of the deck chairs.

Chapter 11

Evening

Mason turned away and quickly wiped his eyes before entering the building after being summoned by Manny. He had used his isolation to think about how Maggie must be worrying about him. By now, the Coast Guard must have begun a *search and rescue*, trying to find them. He knew they would send out helicopters and cutters, looking for either the boat or debris from the boat. How could *he*, he wondered, let them know *Oblique View* and everyone aboard her were fine and just trying to get home? Regardless of the rescue efforts being initiated, his heart ached for Maggie and he missed her more than he thought possible.

Once inside, everyone gathered in the central pod to discuss the pros and cons of seeing what one of the lighted panels might do. Manny was ready to try all of the panels to see what would happen and Mason thought they should wait until they knew more about them. Jake saw merit to both arguments whereas Nathan showed only mild interest, not caring much either way.

"Alright," conceded Manny. "How about we try just one. That way, we at least have some idea of what they are."

"Well, th' owners seem to've abandoned this place, so I s'pose it might not hurt to try one," Mason said. "Jus' be careful; we don't know what we're dealin' with here."

Since they were in the central pod, they could choose one of four panels and general consensus was to try the first one on the left, the pale yellow panel. Jake and Manny examined the panel but couldn't find evidence of how it was to be used, if at all. There were no raised tabs, which would indicate it was to be pried open through use of a hidden hinge. There was no small button or hole to either push or insert something small and stiff, like the end of a straightened paperclip. There didn't seem to be more room around the perimeter in one direction, as opposed to any other direction, which might indicate that it was to slide. The lighted panel was set flush with the wall and surrounded, as they all were, with a narrow metal molding in a satin finish.

"Maybe you push on it like a button," suggested Manny.

"Maybe. Go ahead and try it," Jake responded. Manny pushed on the panel and nothing happened. "Try the next one." Manny pushed on the orange panel. Again, nothing happened.

"Looks like they don't do nothin'. Maybe they're just for

decoration," offered Mason, watching from the periphery of the room. "Ya may as well try th' other ones while ya're at it."

Manny pressed the pale tan panel with nothing noticeably occurring, but when he pressed the pale green panel, a screen appeared in the wall. All in the room stared at the display.

DIRECTOR SYSTEM J428FB*
SYSTEM AUTHORIZED FOR USE BY:
ANTHONY PATARD JOMBAHK
OWNER LAST ACCESSED:
131 YEARS, 214 DAYS, 34 MINUTES, 16 SECONDS
NON ACCESS TIME EXCEEDS HUMAN LIFE SPAN
SYSTEM MUST BE REPROGRAMMED

While the screen was displayed, the number of seconds steadily increased.

"Just a damned minute!" Mason almost shouted. "What the hell's it mean it was last accessed over a hunnerd years ago? Hell, this place wasn't even here yeste'day! What's goin' on?" He wheeled and stomped out into the night.

"He's right," said Manny. "This thing must be wrong. A hundred years ago would be what ... 1905, and thirty years on top of that would be sometime around 1875. There weren't houses like this back then, I can damn well tell you that!"

"True." Jake replied with a thoughtful expression. "We may be in deeper than we originally thought."

"What do you mean?" Nathan, suddenly aware of his father's statement, chimed in. "Are we in trouble?"

"I don't want to speculate right now. We need more information before we jump to any conclusions."

"But you said ... "

"Not now, Nathan." Jake interrupted him. "Not now."

"Fine!" Nathan exploded and bolted from the room.

"Nathan!" Jake called after him, but he continued running and disappeared through the doorway.

"Damn! I didn't want that to happen; he's got enough on his mind without me yelling at him."

"Don't worry. He'll get over it," soothed Manny. "Now, what did you say about our situation?"

"We need more information," Jake replied distractedly as he turned his attention to the screen and the panel that had brought it into existence. "I'm afraid we are in a unique situation, something I couldn't even imagine before now."

Intrigued, Manny sidled up beside him and watched over his shoulder. Jake was running his hand over the screen, tapping it in various places, but nothing happened. Next, he reached over and tapped the pale green panel, again nothing happened. He then placed his hand on the panel and when he removed it, the screen changed.

SYSTEM J428FB* MUST BE REPROGRAMMED

"Well, *that* tells us something new, doesn't it," Manny said with thick sarcasm. "That's what the damn thing said the first time."

"Yes, but the screen changed. Let's see if I can get it to change again." Jake placed his hand on the pale green panel and when he removed it, the screen changed to:

ARE YOU A VISITOR OR NEW OWNER?
STATE CLEARLY: VISITOR NEW OWNER

"Visitor!" Manny quickly answered.

WELCOME VISITOR
HAVE A NICE DAY!

The screen then disappeared. Manny and Jake looked at each other and then back to where the screen had been.

"We must have to be a new owner to reprogram the system," stated Jake. "Let's try that route and see what happens."

Jake placed his hand on the pale green panel, and when he removed it, the screen reappeared.

DIRECTOR SYSTEM J428FB*
SYSTEM AUTHORIZED FOR USE BY:
ANTHONY PATARD JOMBAHK

C.P. STEWART

OWNER LAST ACCESSED:
131 YEARS, 214 DAYS, 36 MINUTES, 27 SECONDS
NON ACCESS TIME EXCEEDS HUMAN LIFE SPAN
SYSTEM MUST BE REPROGRAMMED

Jake repeated the process.

SYSTEM J428FB* MUST BE REPROGRAMMED

Again, he repeated the process.

ARE YOU A VISITOR OR NEW OWNER?
STATE CLEARLY: VISITOR NEW OWNER

"New owner," Jake enunciated clearly, whereupon a square appeared to the right of the message.

PLEASE PLACE THE PALM OF YOUR RIGHT
HAND ON SQUARE

Jake did as instructed and watched as a light from behind the square moved slowly from top to bottom; when it disappeared, so did the square and the message changed.

CLEARLY STATE YOUR FULL NAME

Jake was taken aback by the question, but gathered his wits and said, "Jacob Richard Myers."

The screen showed:

YOUR FULL NAME IS:
JAKOB RICHARD MEYERS
IS THIS CORRECT? YES NO

Jake thought about the misspellings and was going to say *no*, but thought better of it. He reasoned that it didn't matter if his name was spelled right, as long as the *system* recognized it.

He said, "Yes."

The screen changed again:

CLEARLY STATE YOUR BIRTH MONTH

"October."

YOUR BIRTH MONTH IS OCTOBER
IS THIS CORRECT? YES NO

"Yes."

CLEARLY STATE YOUR BIRTH DAY OF THE
MONTH

"Fifteen"

C.P. STEWART

YOUR BIRTH DATE IS OCTOBER 15
IS THIS CORRECT? YES NO

"Yes."

CLEARLY STATE YOUR BIRTH YEAR

"Nineteen sixty four."

INVALID RESPONSE
CLEARLY STATE YOUR BIRTH YEAR

Jake figured the *system* was programmed to have the year stated in a different format.
"One thousand nine hundred sixty four."

INVALID RESPONSE
CLEARLY STATE YOUR BIRTH YEAR

"Don't you just hate machines," Jake said to Manny in a statement rather than a question. "Let me say it a different way; one nine six four."

INVALID RESPONSE
CLEARLY STATE YOUR BIRTH YEAR

"Okay. Now how else can I say it?"
"You got me. I think you covered all bases," Manny agreed.

"Wait a minute." Jake's mind was racing. "Let's say this thing is from the future and the last time anyone used it was ... what did it say, about 130 years ago. If we add 130 years to today's date, we get 2135 ... and then add, say, another fifty years. That would be around 2185. Let's try that one."

"Two one eight five."

YOUR BIRTH YEAR IS 2185
IS THIS CORRECT? YES NO

"I'll play your silly game," whispered Jake, and then louder, "Yes."

YOUR BIRTH DATE IS:
OCTOBER 15, 2185
YOUR AGE IS:
98 YEARS 7 MONTHS 28 DAYS
HOW MAY I SERVE YOU, JAKOB RICHARD
MEYERS?

Jake thought about figuring today's date. He turned to Manny and said, "Get something to write with and something to write on so we can figure to-day's date."

"What did you say?" Manny was still staring at the screen and hadn't been paying attention to Jake.

"What's today's date?" he repeated. Then in the periphery of his vision, he saw the screen change. He and Manny both turned toward the screen and stared.

TODAY'S DATE IS
JUNE 12, 2283

Chapter 12

Evening

W hat the hell is this?" demanded Mason after being called inside to view the wall screen. "What kinda trick are ya tryin' to pull? That can't be right! That'd mean..."

"Unfortunately, it *has* to be correct," countered Jake. "Just think about what all has happened, the different coastline, these buildings ... and the lighthouse rock that used to be at the mouth of the inlet. What about the technology here?" He indicated the wall screen while posing this last question.

"But," responded Mason with a sweeping motion, "that means *this* is what's left o' Cape Arthur!"

"It would appear so," Jake concurred. "We left this morning from this area ... and returned almost two hundred eighty years later."

As Manny watched the exchange between Mason and Jake, a slight smile crossed his face. He couldn't believe his incredible luck. He was totally free, through the craziest circumstances imaginable he had outlived every lawman and arrest warrant issued for him. Even if the law still had his name on file, it wouldn't matter, because nobody would still be looking for him after two hundred seventy-some years. This was fantastic!

"But, what 'bout Maggie?" asked Mason, continuing to question Jake.

"I'm sorry."

"What d'ya mean ya're sorry'? She's *my* wife, not yars!" Mason's anxiety causing his speech to slur even more than usual. "Dammit, wha's happen'd t'er!"

"Take it easy, Captain Bankowski ... Mason. There's nothing we can do about what's happened. Nothing. Take a few deep breaths and have a seat while we try to figure out what all's occurred and what options we have."

Mason took Jake's advice and forced some deep breaths while leaning against the wall. The exercise had a calming effect and he sank to the floor, sliding his cap back on his head. "Okay," he said quietly after about a minute of silence. "Can ya tell me what's goin' on ... I mean, what happened to us?"

"Hold on a minute," said Jake. "I need to get Nathan in here too." He walked outside into the darkness, and not finding Nathan, called for him.

"Nathan! Nathan, please come here! I need to show you something!"

"Yeah, what do you want?" Nathan answered sullenly

while walking around an adjacent pod toward Jake, hands in pockets. "This'd better be good."

"Follow me," Jake instructed as he re-entered the building and walked to the central pod, joining Mason and Manny.

Jake turned to face Nathan and held him by the shoulders. "Nathan, something happened to all of us today, something ... something that transported us almost two hundred eighty years into the future."

"Yeah, right. Do you take me for an idiot?"

"No Nathan, it's real." Jake stepped back to permit Nathan to see the wall screen and then asked for today's date.

TODAY'S DATE IS
JUNE 12, 2283

"Wha ... what kinda trick is this?"

"Sit down. We all need to talk."

"How'd this happen?" pursued Mason

"Bermuda Triangle," whispered Nathan, and then louder, "I think we might have gone through the Bermuda Triangle."

"What's the Bermuda Triangle?" Manny probed.

"Bermuda Triangle ... Devil's Triangle; an area located off the coast of Florida where hundreds of boats, ships, and planes have disappeared without a trace." Jake explained. "I was very interested in it when I was a kid, read everything I could on it."

"Without a trace?" repeated Manny. "You mean they were never found? What could have caused that?"

"I saw a TV documentary on the Bermuda Triangle a couple of years ago and, if I remember right, they said they had solved the mystery and it was something natural. Methane gas? Yeah, I think it was methane gas. It seems there are huge deposits of methane gas in the deep trenches of the Atlantic in this region and they sometimes release lots of it at a time. They proved it could sink a large tanker and bring down airplanes."

"That's a bunch o' shit!" Mason responded. "I been fishin' th' Atlantic for twenty-five years, takin' charters out for twelve and I ain't never seen no big gas bubbles or heard o' anybody else experiencin' nothin' like that. I heard th' stories, we all have, but believin' 'em is somethin' else. How'n hell can big gas bubbles bring down a ship or plane? Don't make sense to me."

"Well, let's see if I can explain it in a way that you can understand," Jake said. "A ship, or a fishing boat like *Oblique View* floats because water is dense and weighs a lot. The boat sits in the water and displaces water ... think of filling a bathtub completely full of water and then climbing in; the water displaced by you is going to overflow, right?"

"Yeah, that makes sense," Mason answered thoughtfully.

Jake continued, "Well a boat or ship does the same; it displaces the water as it is put into the water. It will sink until the weight of the displaced water equals the weight of the boat, then the boat floats. Methane gas is much less dense than water, so if the boat is in methane, it would need to displace much, much more methane than its own volume to stay afloat ... so it sinks. Methane is also less dense than air and airplanes need air pressure to fly. When methane erupts from the seabed, it quickly bubbles to the surface and then rises through the air. Any plane flying through methane will drop like a rock because methane isn't dense enough to support it."

"Sounds reasonable, but we didn't hit any big bubbles o' methane; hell, we didn't hit bubbles o' any kind," Mason countered. "So ... how'd we get here ... now ... whatever."

"Maybe their explanation doesn't cover *all* occurrences. Maybe it is just a theory. I remember when I watched that documentary, they still hadn't found traces of many of the ships and planes that vanished. Flight 19 for example."

"Was that an airliner?" asked Manny.

"No, it was five Navy planes, Avengers, I think, types of torpedo bombers. They left a Naval air station sometime around World War II and somewhere near where we are now. Anyway, they were on a routine training flight when they were lost without a trace. Another plane flew out to find them, and I think it disappeared without a trace also."

"Didn't they use their radios?"

"Yes. They were in contact with the base, but said their compasses were screwy and the ocean didn't look right. Nothing was ever found of them."

"Th' only thing we had in common with them was my

instruments went screwy in th' storm an' fog," interjected Mason. "I never had that happen b'fore."

"This whole area is supposed to exhibit magnetic anomalies," Jake paused when he saw that neither Manny nor Mason understood what he was saying. He continued, "What I mean is, there are strong electromagnetic fields here, and I've heard this might be one of only a few places on earth where a compass points to true north *and* magnetic north."

"What's so special 'bout that?" asked Mason. "A compass is a compass, an' it points north."

"At any location, other than the few I mentioned, a compass will point to the magnetic north pole, which is a few degrees off from the true, rotational north pole."

"Oh," responded Mason, not wishing to continue.

Manny, on the other hand pressed on, trying to understand more. Beneath his seeming quest for knowledge was the desire to find out if whatever had happened to them could somehow reverse itself. "So, what happened to us?"

"It seems we experienced a time-warp; we jumped into the future," Jake hypothesized.

"How can something like that happen?"

"I don't know. I guess that time exists in layers, much like sheets of paper with a different era on each, and we seem to have moved from one sheet of paper onto another." This oversimplified explanation left Jake unsatisfied, even though he was the one who said it. Wishing to clarify, he continued, "Einstein said that time is relative, it can be made to slow down, depending on your frame of reference."

"Frame of *what?*" Manny asked, not sure he was following any of this, but trying to understand; nothing was more relevant right now.

"Einstein theorized that the faster you go, the more time slows down. Try to follow this. Light reflects from everything and travels out into space at the speed of light. Got me so far?"

"Yeah, I think so. Go on."

Well, let's suppose a light beam falls on a clock that reads 12:02, and that reflected beam travels into space at the speed of light. If you could travel along with it, at the speed of light of course, you would continue to see the time as 12:02, no matter how long you look at it. So, if you travel at the speed of light, time stands still. If you traveled alongside the light beam and your speed was just slightly less than the beam's speed, you would see the time change very slowly. The faster you go, the more time slows down."

"Okay, so how does this apply to us?"

"I don't know. Possibly while we thought we were sitting still in the fog we were moving fast into the future. Or ... or we were still for an incredibly long time while time passed us by. Who knows, we might have just slipped into another layer of time. Maybe this is what happened to other victims; they jumped time into the future."

"Could they jump into the past?" Manny's curiosity was definitely aroused. For him, this was the crux of the matter.

"Not likely. If any of the victims, the people lost in the Triangle had been transported to the past, there would have been a record of them appearing and telling their story about coming from the future. Since I don't recall ever hearing of anything like that, I would say it probably wouldn't happen. Besides, if someone traveled into the past, that person would, or rather, could have an effect on history."

Manny was overjoyed at hearing this. He was here, the cops were in the past, and nothing could bring them together. This turned out much better than he had dared to hope.

"What 'bout th' people on shore? What happened to them?" asked Mason. "What 'bout Maggie?"

Jake tried to answer Mason's concerns as gently as possible. "I would say the Coast Guard came to our last known location and found nothing. I'm sure a search and rescue operation was launched when we didn't return as planned. I'm sorry, but Maggie probably never found out what happened to us, and I imagine she figured we went down in the storm." Mason simply nodded his head, pulled his cap back to its original position and walked back into the night.

"That was hard on him." Jake stated matter-of-factly.

"Yeah, well it wasn't only hard on him!" Nathan fairly shouted. "It's hard on me too! This was all your fault ... you and your 'Let's go fishing so we can get to know each other better!' Well, you screwed things up with Mom and me before, and now you screwed me over again! I had a life! I had school! I had a possible future doin' something I wanted! Now, what do I have? Nothing!"

"Nathan! Come back!" Jake implored after him, but he was gone into the night.

"I better try to get him to come back in here." Jake explained as he started after his son. Not immediately finding him, Jake enlisted Mason's help in looking for Nathan. Jake headed south and Mason headed north, both calling his name. After about fifteen minutes, Jake found him slumped on a sand dune.

"Nathan, I am truly sorry for how things turned out. If I had *any* idea something like this was possible, I certainly wouldn't have brought you here. Please believe me. And also believe that I don't want to be here either; I have a career and ... " Jake's voice trailed off as he realized what he was saying. "I don't care about my career, or my car, or the house, or anything; I only care about you. Please come back to the house. We don't have any idea who, or what, might be out here."

Nathan regarded his father with disdain, but something had softened slightly within him ... or maybe he had become resigned that his former life was gone; regardless, the rage had evaporated. He rose, and without uttering a sound walked with Jake toward the house. When they arrived and Nathan had entered the house, Jake continued north along the dunes in search of Mason. Finding him, they both returned to the house. Jake went in and Mason settled on the ground, facing the ocean with his back resting against the building.

Thinking of the agony Maggie must have endured

believing him to have gone down at sea, tears streamed, accompanied by the distant crashing surf and a chorus of night sounds that seemed much louder than he ever remembered.

Chapter 13

Late evening

After entering the house, Nathan passed through the central pod and continued into one of the smaller pods where he sat on the floor and leaned his back against the wall. Becoming bored, he stood up and walked to the two lighted panels. Studying them, he decided to press one and see what would happen. Tentatively, he placed his right hand on the yellow panel and suddenly a screen appeared in the wall.

DIRECTOR SYSTEM J428FB*
SYSTEM AUTHORIZED FOR USE BY
JAKOB RICHARD MEYERS
OWNER LAST ACCESSED:
42 MINUTES, 35 SECONDS
YOU ARE NOT JAKOB RICHARD MEYERS
ARE YOU A VISITOR?
STATE CLEARLY: YES NO

C.P. STEWART

"Yes."

WELCOME VISITOR
STATE CLEARLY: COMMUNICATION
ENTERTAINMENT

"Cool," whispered Nathan, and then, "Entertainment."

YOU CHOSE ENTERTAINMENT
STATE CLEARLY: YES NO

"Yes."

ENTERTAINMENT
TOUCH CHOICE:

BROADCAST MUSIC
RECORDED MUSIC
BROADCAST VIDEO
RECORDED VIDEO
OPERA
PERFORMING DANCE
MUSICALS
LATINAS
DOCUMENTARIES
NEWS
BIOGRAPHIES

Nathan looked over the list of choices and touched *BROADCAST MUSIC.*

FREQUENCY?
STATE CLEARLY OR STATE: SCAN

Not knowing any local frequencies, Nathan said, "Scan." Numbers flashed on the screen, increasing rapidly until reaching the highest frequency, and then starting over and continuing the process until it had progressed through the entire frequency range five times.

NO BROADCAST FREQUENCIES AVAILABLE AT
THIS TIME

ENTERTAINMENT
TOUCH CHOICE:

BROADCAST MUSIC
RECORDED MUSIC
BROADCAST VIDEO
RECORDED VIDEO
OPERA
PERFORMING DANCE
MUSICALS
LATINAS
DOCUMENTARIES

NEWS

BIOGRAPHIES

Nathan again looked over the list of choices and touched *RECORDED MUSIC*. A list of titles appeared on the screen, none of which looked familiar. He chose one at random and sounds emanated from the walls, but it only remotely resembled any music that he had ever heard. It was not pleasant but he forced himself to wait until the cacophony of sounds ended. The same choices appeared on the screen.

"What's that noise?" asked Jake, walking into the room.

Nathan made another choice without speaking. Another music selection sounded through the walls, and it also didn't resemble the music either one of them was used to. It actually bordered on being painful to their ears. When it concluded, Nathan made yet another choice, and this time the sounds were soothing and pleasant. They waited until it ended before speaking.

"How did you find the music, Nathan?" asked Jake.

"Yellow one." Nathan then moved to the wall and sat down against it.

Sensing that it was useless to attempt communication with his son at this time, Jake reluctantly returned to the central pod.

Manny was sitting against the wall and asked, "What happened?"

"Nathan accessed the system for entertainment and was

checking out the music," Jake answered. "He said he used the yellow panel."

"Were there other things you could do besides music?"

"Dunno. He wasn't in a mood to share information," Jake responded as he picked a spot, not far but not near the other man and sat, leaning against the wall. "I'll check with him later; he might be in a better frame of mind."

What followed was an awkward silence with both individuals staring at nothing in particular, lost in thought. Jake refocused on his immediate environment and a quote came to mind: *"The silence was deafening."* He decided to break the ice.

"Mr. Cranston, what do you do; I mean, what line of work are you in?"

"I work for a pharmaceuticals company, and you?"

"I'm a chemical engineer."

"What does a chemical engineer do?"

"I've done about everything from quality control in a lab to designing and overseeing construction of petroleum refineries. What do you do for the company you work for?"

"Things. Sales. You know."

"I understand you're from West Virginia, Morgantown, right?"

"Yeah, all my life. How'd you know that?"

"Captain Bankowski shared that before you showed up at the boat this morning. How do you like living there?"

"Great."

"I have a cousin that lives in Monongah; that's not too far away from you."

"Yeah, a couple hours."

"No, I mean Monongah, just south of Fairmont."

"Yeah, a couple hours south."

"I've always wanted to go to a Mountaineer football game; how far from the stadium do you live?"

"About two blocks. I've got season tickets." Wanting to impress Jake, he added, "Catch every game I can."

"Really? Wow! That Rich Rodriguez has done a great job there, hasn't he?"

"Sure has ... great quarterback."

"Yeah." Jake's voice trailed off as he regarded the other man, then added quietly, "Yeah. Great quarterback." Silence followed.

Following his father's departure, Nathan sat quietly for about ten minutes before returning to the lighted panels. He again pressed the yellow one.

DIRECTOR SYSTEM J428FB*
SYSTEM AUTHORIZED FOR USE BY
JAKOB RICHARD MEYERS
OWNER LAST ACCESSED:
58 MINUTES, 22 SECONDS
YOU ARE NOT JAKOB RICHARD MEYERS
ARE YOU A VISITOR?
STATE CLEARLY: YES NO

"Yes."

THROUGH THE TRIANGLE

WELCOME VISITOR
STATE CLEARLY: COMMUNICATION
ENTERTAINMENT

"Communication."

YOU CHOSE COMMUNICATION
STATE CLEARLY: YES NO

"Yes."

DO YOU WISH TO CONTACT SOMEONE?
STATE CLEARLY: YES NO

"Yes."

STATE CLEARLY THE PERSON'S NAME
OR
STATE CLEARLY THE PERSON'S VIDEOCOM
NUMBER

Since he obviously didn't know anybody's name, it was clear that he had to say some numbers ... but which ones and how many? He decided to try.

"One, two, three, four, five, six, seven, eight, nine, zero," seemed like a good place to start and as each digit was pronounced, it showed on the screen and an underline space appeared to the right indicating another digit was being requested.

C.P. STEWART

1 2 3 4 5 6 7 8 9 0 _

Now what do I do? I've used all the digits once. I guess I'll start repeating. He spoke up, "One."

1 2 3 4 5 6 7 8 9 0 1 _

"Two."

1 2 3 4 5 6 7 8 9 0 1 2

ATTEMPTING TO COMPLETE LINK

After about ten seconds, the screen changed.

NO LINK AVAILABLE
TRY ANOTHER?
STATE CLEARLY: YES NO

"Yes."

DO YOU WISH TO CONTACT SOMEONE?
STATE CLEARLY: YES NO

"Yes."

STATE CLEARLY THE PERSON'S NAME
OR

STATE CLEARLY THE PERSON'S VIDEOCOM
NUMBER

Knowing now that twelve digits were required, Nathan rambled off a new number and the screen mimicked visually what he said.

3 7 5 2 8 4 1 1 6 7 2 3

ATTEMPTING TO COMPLETE LINK

After about ten seconds, the screen changed.

NO LINK AVAILABLE
TRY ANOTHER?
STATE CLEARLY: YES NO

"Yes."

DO YOU WISH TO CONTACT SOMEONE?
STATE CLEARLY: YES NO

"Yes."

STATE CLEARLY THE PERSON'S NAME
OR
STATE CLEARLY THE PERSON'S VIDEOCOM
NUMBER

A different twelve-digit number was pronounced with the same outcome. Nathan tried six more times with like results, but the seventh attempt bore fruit. A room appeared on the screen and a person was seen passing quickly through the viewing area. Just then a message appeared across the middle of the screen, the room still in evidence behind it.

**DO YOU WISH TO CONTINUE WITH THIS LINK
STATE CLEARLY: YES NO**

"Yes."

**WHEN YOU WISH TO END THIS LINK
STATE CLEARLY: CLOSE**

Nathan peered intently at the screen.

"C'mon," he impatiently whispered, as if he was afraid the person in the room on the screen could hear him. "Come on out and let me look at you." Then it dawned on him that this *was* a communication system and he *could* talk to whomever his system was linked to. "Hello. Hello in the room. Who's there? I want to talk ... I want to communicate with you. Hello? Please talk to me. Hello?"

The room appeared empty. He waited. Nobody appeared; nothing changed. He sat on the floor and waited. He rolled onto his side and stared at the screen. Eventually, his eyes became too heavy to keep open and he drifted off.

After about an hour, the intensity of glowing in the room subsided into near, but not complete, darkness.

Hours later while the communication link remained open, Nathan was sound asleep in the darkened room, unaware of the gaunt-looking hooded figure with light violet eyes, fixedly staring at him from the wall screen.

Chapter 14

Juan opened his eyes to a twilight world, actually pre-dawn he realized when his senses began functioning. He had finally fallen into a deep sleep sometime around two or three o'clock, to the best of his reckoning. He couldn't get comfortable in the deck chair so he had re-trieved some bedding from the living quarters and spread them out on deck, which allowed him the luxury of stretch-ing out and using a blanket as insulation against the damp cold. It wasn't only the uncomfortable positions and hard deck surface, but he thought, or maybe imagined hearing sounds on shore. He wasn't really certain he had heard anything; it was barely audible and might actually have been the sound of waves lapping against the hull or break-ers on shore. Still, he had a gnawing feeling it was more than that.

Still wrapped in a blanket against the cold night air, he lay there looking up into the gradually lightening sky, not quite ready to get up and face the day. This was to be the day he helped Miguel move to Pensacola and here he was, sitting on *Oblique View* waiting for the sun to come up. He was sure his family was worried by now and he had no way to tell them he was safe. It was the most frustrating aspect of this whole ordeal. *Why didn't the radio and cell phones work?* He refused to give credence to the nagging sense assaulting his subconscious that something had changed his life forever.

He had worked for Mason Bankowski for three years and had always enjoyed his work. Mason, even when Juan had started as a thirteen year old, had always treated him as an adult, had appreciated his help. He remembered one time ... his thoughts were interrupted by ... by what? There was something; the sound, the sound he thought he had heard during the night. It was faint, but discernable. What was it? Where was it coming from?

Rolling onto his knees and crawling to the starboard edge of the aft deck, he cautiously peered over the railing toward shore. Through a slight morning fog he saw things, animals of some kind, running along the beach in the pre-dawn darkness. He couldn't make out just what they were ... maybe small dogs; that's what they could be, but there seemed to be many of them, so many that he worried about having to go ashore later to join the others. You never can tell whether stray dogs are vicious or friendly. Maybe they would be gone by the time he went ashore. At least he now knew what was making those noises during the wee hours of the morning.

A concern welled inside, ramming itself into consciousness. If they *had* been dogs running on the beach, then there had to be twenty of them, at least that he could see within the distance the fog encompassed. He thought he had heard them throughout the night, but he heard no barking; dogs barked.

He hurried below deck and searched one cabinet; not finding what he was looking for, he checked another, then another.

"Here you are," he said with relief as he retrieved a pair of binoculars.

Climbing back on deck, he noticed that the darkness had lifted slightly, very gradually being replaced with daylight. He focused the binoculars on the dogs, removed them from his eyes, and then looked again. They weren't dogs ... they were crabs! These crabs were the largest he had ever seen; they *were* the size of dogs; they had to be at least two feet long, on average!

Now things started to make sense. Beach crabs were nocturnal, which explained the sounds through the night, but he was on this fishing boat anchored approximately a hundred yards off shore. He realized he had heard them running across the sand in spite of the sound of the waves against the hull *and* the pounding surf.

Forcing the beach crabs from his mind, Juan started collecting items he planned to take with him when the sun rose.

Mason stirred, opened his eyes and focused his attention on the sand dunes. He stood and stretched, trying to relieve a backache caused by sleeping in a sitting position with his back against the building. The sun was climbing over the ocean's horizon encased within a large glowing halo, but the air was still cold and wet, tasting of salt. He rubbed his arms for warmth and wished he had brought his jacket ashore.

He walked forward and climbed the dune, the rising sun's attempt at warmth a welcome change from the coolness of his resting place in the shadow of the dune. A nighttime fog was beginning to evaporate, and from his vantage point near the top he was relieved to just make out *Oblique View* still at anchor and Juan moving around on deck. After all that happened yesterday, he was ready for normal, anything normal.

Mason's gaze shifted to the ocean, until yesterday his friend, with its glittering sparkles of silver on the dark surface, narrowly converging toward where the sun was rising. It was almost as if nothing had changed, but he knew everything had changed, and the ocean didn't care in the least. His stomach growled and he suddenly realized he hadn't eaten since lunch yesterday. None of them had. They had to find some food. On that thought he turned and descended the dune, but not before staring at the lighthouse rock for a moment, wishing it was right back where it was yesterday morning.

Jake and Manny were still sleeping. The glow had returned to the interior, causing Nathan to open his eyes and look around the room groggily. He hadn't slept well; his dreams had been strange and lying on the floor caused him to wake up several times searching for a more comfortable position. Scanning his surroundings caused dismay that what had happened yesterday wasn't a dream. He remembered the link to some other place and quickly turned his head to look at the wall screen where the room was still displayed, still empty. He wanted to close the link but didn't want to lose this connection to some other site, an actual place where he saw someone last night. Also, he reasoned, once closed, the connection couldn't be re-established because he had said the numbers as they came into his head and he didn't remember them now. He decided to try communicating again.

"Hello, is anybody there? Hello. Please come to the phone. Hello?"

Due to the quietness of the surroundings, Nathan's imploring speech caused Jake to wake up. He listened for whatever sound had wakened him.

"Hello. Please come into the room so I can talk to you. Hello?"

Who is Nathan talking to? Jake wondered. Mr. Cranston was still asleep across the room, so it must be Captain Bankowski ... but it sounded as if he was calling to someone who was not in the room with him. Just then, Mason walked into the central pod from the direction opposite Nathan's location.

Jake scrambled to his feet and crept through the hallway, cautiously approaching the entrance to the pod occupied by Nathan. He reached the entrance, stopped, and peered in. Nathan was talking to the wall, or rather a displayed room in the wall screen.

"Nathan?" Jake called. A startled Nathan whirled around to face his father.

"You scared me! What do you want?"

"I'm sorry, but I heard you talking and wondered who you were talking to."

"Nobody," he clipped with a distinct edge in his voice. Jake tried to ignore his son's surly behavior. Just then Mason sidled up beside him.

"What's goin' on here?" Mason asked in a friendly tone.

"I used the system under *communication* to try to call people," Nathan said matter-of-factly, seeming to respond favorably to Mason's presence. "Nothing happened until this one ... and I swear I saw someone moving through the room. I tried to get the person to come back and talk but he must have left."

Mason and Jake exchanged glances and then both moved forward for a closer look at the screen. They saw a room, much like the room in which they now stood, with the exception of a chair, visible against the far wall. The wall color was also slightly darker than theirs.

"What do you make of it?" Jake asked Mason, without removing his gaze from the wall screen.

"Obviously, th' boy found somethin', jus' what, I dunno. At least we know we're not alone; there's someone else out there somewhere."

"Yes, but the trick is to find him ... or them," Jake replied, still not removing his eyes from the screen. He turned to Nathan and asked, "How did you get this connection?"

"I used the yellow one and chose *communication* instead of *entertainment*. It asked for a person's name or a number. I didn't know any persons, so I gave it a number."

"What number?"

"I made one up. I tried different ones but nothing happened, then I tried this one."

"Do you remember what number you used?"

"I told you I made it up. I don't remember what it was, just twelve numbers. If I had any idea this number would work, I would've tried to remember it."

"I understand. You said you saw someone?"

"When it first connected, I saw someone move past. It was quick, but I know it was a person."

"Why don't we take turns watchin' the screen in case th' person comes back," suggested Mason.

Jake agreed, "I'll take first turn."

"Okay, I'll go out an' meet Juan."

"I'll go with you," volunteered Nathan, and fell into step behind Mason as he left the room.

They walked outside and made their way to the beach in time to see Juan, about forty to fifty yards up the beach, pulling the raft far past the high water mark. Not aware of being watched, he left the raft and walked back toward the surf, studying the sand on his way.

"Good to see ya again!" called Mason, walking toward the lone figure on the beach. "Any problems?"

Juan jumped and turned toward the two approaching figures.

"I didn't see you," he said when they were close enough that he didn't have to shout. "No problems; everything was fine."

"Did you lose something?" inquired Nathan.

Juan returned his gaze toward the sand and walked a few feet. "Come here and look at these tracks." Mason and Nathan joined him and focused on the sand.

"There's a lot of them," volunteered Nathan, "What made them?"

"Beach crabs," answered Juan. Mason looked at Juan and then back at the tracks in the sand.

"Beach crabs didn't make those," he said. "They're too far apart. I've seen beach crabs lots o' times an' their tracks're closer than these ... an' smaller too."

"Believe me, they were beach crabs, *big* ones. I heard them running on the beach most of the night and saw them this morning. At first I thought they were dogs."

"How big were they?" Mason asked.

"Like I said, I thought they were dogs. I figure they averaged about two feet across the claws."

"Impossible!" scoffed Mason.

"Look at them. You said yourself that the marks were

too far apart. Think about the size of crab needed to make those tracks."

"Wait a minute," interjected Nathan. "I saw a big ant back where we stopped before. I figured it was just a grand-daddy ant when I saw it running across the sand."

"Big, huh. How big?" Mason queried.

"About this big." Nathan held up his hand with his thumb and forefinger illustrating the size.

"Looks about three inches," estimated Juan, and then added absently while staring into the distance, "That's a big ant alright."

He walked north on the beach, stopped, and motioned for the others to join him. They approached, and then slowed as Juan held his forefinger to his lips, indicating silence. When they converged on the spot, they saw a hole about ten inches in diameter, surrounded by a crater of sand and many tracks radiating from it. Juan straightened and then motioned for the others to look farther northward. There were more holes in the distance, but they were being obliterated by the incoming tide.

"These are crab holes; I think their size shows how big the crabs are," Juan stated. The other two merely stared.

The three turned as if on cue and walked back to the raft and began collecting everything Juan had loaded. As Nathan gathered jackets and sweatshirts from the front, Juan passed the handgun unobtrusively to Mason, who inserted it under his waistband and covered it with his shirt. Mason then gathered up the flare gun and portable short wave radio, while Juan lifted two coolers. "Is that what I hope it is?" asked Mason, indicating the coolers. Juan winked and gave a slight nod bringing a wide smile to Mason's lips. "Let's go."

Chapter 15

Manny awoke alone in the central pod. He stood, walked outside and then continued around the building, looked back and forth, and when he was sure nobody was looking, urinated.

"How in the hell did people who lived here go to the bathroom?" he questioned aloud. After finishing, he zipped up, and noticed a slight movement as he turned. He searched around trying to locate what had caught his attention. Suddenly he jumped back; on the side of the building was a large spider slowly climbing the wall. It was as large as a tarantula and almost as hairy. Manny danced backward until he stumbled on a branch of driftwood and almost fell. He picked it up and crept forward until within striking distance, and then broke the branch over the spider and wall section. The spider slid to the ground where he jumped on it again and again, mashing it as he would snuff out a cigarette, but more forcefully and with more urgency. He paused to creep closer, jutting his head forward and then retreating slightly until he was sure the wretched thing was dead. He wiped his shoe thoroughly in the sand and then walked back to the entrance.

Manny was sweating profusely from his frightening close encounter and wiped his face with a shirt sleeve. He paused before entering to allow the air to cool him, all the while studying the sky. Discreet rays radiated downward between low-hanging dark clouds.

"Hey there, Mr. Cranston!" Juan called as they came into sight over the dune. Manny turned and raised his hand as a salutation. This was a good day, the beginning of the rest of his carefree life, and he didn't mind this heartfelt gesture at friendliness.

All four entered the building and set their loads on the floor in the central pod. Mason hungrily eyed the coolers as Juan opened one to reveal leftover food from yesterday's lunch and the other contained drinks on ice. Everything was still fresh because Juan had collected all of the perishables from *Oblique View's* refrigerator minutes before heading to shore.

"Let's eat!" commanded Mason, even though Nathan, Juan, and Manny were already helping themselves. Then he called to the other occupied pod, "Mr. Myers, come in here and load up a plate; food's on!"

Jake didn't need to be asked a second time. He walked in, filled a Styrofoam plate with food, grabbed a cold beer, thanked Juan and Mason, then returned to the outer pod to continue his vigil.

"Where's he going?" Manny inquired.

"He's watchin' a phone screen," explained Mason between bites. "Nathan opened a communication link last night an' says he saw someone walk through th' picture. He said th' person didn't come back so we're takin' shifts watchin' for 'im."

"You saw someone?" Manny looked at Nathan. "Who was he? I mean, what did he look like?

Nathan finished chewing his latest mouthful and swallowed.

"I didn't get a good enough look at him ... or her; whoever it was moved through the room too fast for me to see any details, probably on his way out. I was surprised to make a connection, and I wasn't expecting to see anybody."

"I want to see this," Manny said as he stood and walked out of the pod with a half-eaten sandwich in his hand.

"Yeah, me too," Juan rose and followed Manny.

"Well, I guess that leaves the rest o' the food for you an' me," concluded Mason. "C'mon Nathan, eat up b'fore they come back."

Nathan made himself another sandwich, spooned out some macaroni salad, and added a handful of potato chips.

"Don't mind if I do," he responded. "I was hungry."

"Me, too." Mason replied while choosing a cold beer and a soft drink from the cooler. He handed the soda to Nathan.

"Fawnks." Nathan said with a smile and a mouthful of food. After swallowing, he repeated clearly, "Thanks, Captain Bankowski." Then added, "Sir."

"You're welcome."

Jake was eating cross-legged with his plate on his lap when footsteps approached. Manny and Juan entered and stood studying the room displayed in the wall screen. While the other two were watching the screen, Jake took the opportunity to concentrate on his food.

Juan finally turned toward Jake and asked, "Have you seen anything yet?"

Jake swallowed and washed the food down with a long draw on his beer. "Nope. Nothing."

"Nathan made the connection?"

"Yep."

"How'd he do it?"

"Said he used the yellow panel and could choose between 'entertainment and communication,' then was told to say a number; he did, and got this."

"Why don't you close this one down and try another number?"

"I think Nathan said it takes twelve numbers, instead of the ten we used, and he said he tried a number of times before actually getting this connection. He doesn't remember what number he used so we probably couldn't get this one again if we close it."

Juan turned again toward the screen.

"Hmmm," mumbled Manny as he finished his sandwich and then returned to the central pod.

"I'll be back," Juan muttered as he, too, left the room.

Jake continued his vigil while finishing his food and drink.

A little food remained, which was re-stored in the food cooler. The drink cooler still contained a good selection in a mixture of half-melted ice and ice-cold water. Both coolers were moved against the wall and then Mason rose and started from the room.

"Time to relieve Mr. Myers," he said, and then stopped and turned. "Juan, I need to talk to ya." Upon seeing the quizzical expression on Juan's face, he added, "Outside, if ya don't mind."

They walked outside, Mason with his arm around Juan's shoulders. Once outside, Mason suggested they walk along the dune for a ways. As they walked southward, both surveyed the sky, which by now consisted of dark clouds piled upon darker clouds.

"Looks like a storm's brewin'." observed Mason.

"Yeah," agreed Juan, then turning to study the serious expression on his boss's face, added, "This isn't about the weather, is it." This wasn't a question, but rather acceptance that he was about to receive news he wasn't ready to hear.

"Nope," Mason replied, then taking time to gather his thoughts, proceeded, "Juan, I know ya were lookin' forward to helpin' yar brother move today."

"Yeah, and I have to find a way to let my family know I'm safe; I know they're worried. Did you get through to Maggie last night? If not, could you have her call them when you get through?" Juan suggested, trying to ignore the deep feeling that the scenario wasn't possible.

"I'm sorry, that's not gonna happen," Mason explained

in as soothing a voice as he could muster. "After ya left last night, we found evidence that everythin', and everyone we knew'r all long gone. They're gone forever." Tears welled in Mason's eyes as he spoke and a quick swipe of his shirttail was needed to remove them.

"But, how do you know? What happened?

"Mr. Myers tried th' computer system in th' house, an' it said we're now in th' year 2283. From th' time we left yeste'day 'til we came back in, we somehow jumped more than two hunnerd seventy years."

"Impossible! How could that happen?"

"I dunno. They thought the Bermuda Triangle caused it. I dunno what to think. Th' only thing I know's everythin's different; we talked 'bout that."

"But, what about my family? What happened to them?" He knew the answer, but was hoping beyond hope for a different resolution.

"I'm sorry."

Juan started to tear up, and then said, "I need to be alone." As he started to walk away, he stopped, turned to Mason, and said with a quavering voice, "It's not your fault. Th ... thanks for telling me."

Mason watched him walk away and knew Juan was hurting every bit as badly as he was; the only difference was that a captain couldn't be as demonstrative with his emotions. It just wasn't fair. It was as if his and Juan's entire collective families had died suddenly. Actually, they had died over the years while believing the opposite: that he and Juan had died August 13, 2005. It hurt even more with the realization that the families had experienced the same heartache. Respecting Juan's wish and knowing he could do no more for him, he returned to the house and continued through to where Jake was keeping vigil.

"Hey, I'll take th' next shift," he somberly said upon entering the room. "Go take a break."

"Thanks. Nobody showed." Jake stood and stretched. "I'll check back in a little while."

Jake got as far as the doorway, stopped, and looked out through the hall. Feeling satisfied that nobody was within hearing distance, he turned and walked back to Mason.

"What can you tell me about Mr. Cranston?" Jake asked quietly.

"Not much," replied Mason, still staring at the screen. "He's some kinda sales rep for a few states, lives in West Virginia."

"You talked to him on the phone, right? Tell me what all he said."

"Yeah. He said he wanted to go fishin' 'cause he'd gone with his grandfather when he was little. Said he lived in Morgantown, West Virginia, not much else." Then after a thoughtful moment, "I remember he talked a lot about his job, really liked it and was pretty successful. Why do ya ask?"

"I got a bad feeling about him," responded Jake, keeping his eyes on the hallway so he could stop if anyone entered, "I talked to him last night and what he said didn't add up."

"In what way?"

"Well, I'm fairly familiar with that area, Morgantown I mean, and he said Fairmont is a couple hours south of him. Fairmont is no more than twenty miles south; no way it's a couple hours. I also mentioned another town, located within about ten miles of Fairmont and he acted as if he had never heard of it. Yet, he claims to have spent his entire life there."

"Well, maybe he just got confused; maybe thought ya said someplace else."

"That's not all. He said he was a big Mountaineer football fan, that's West Virginia University. He said he's had season tickets for years and went to many games."

"Yeah, so? So he's a football fan."

"The trouble is, he said he lives within a few blocks of the stadium, and I'm pretty sure the stadium sits outside of town. And the clincher is, he called Rich Rodriguez a quarterback."

"So?"

"So, he's the *coach*, has been for about five years. Nobody that follows football as much as he says would make *that* mistake."

Mason turned his attention to Jake.

"I see what ya mean. What do ya think we should do?"

"I don't know for sure. For now, I think we should just keep an eye on him until we figure out what he's up to. I suggest we don't let on we suspect anything."

"Okay," agreed Mason, refocusing on the screen.

As Jake entered the central pod, a heated discussion was taking place between Manny and Nathan. They stopped when they noticed Jake.

"What's going on?"

"He was saying we should move somewhere else that has furniture," related Nathan.

"*And* a bathroom!" added Manny. "These people took everything with them when they left. We got nothing."

"Furniture?" Jake asked incredulously. "You were arguing about furniture? I can't believe it! Here we are, somehow jumped over two hundred years into the future, not knowing anything about what we're faced with and ... "

Jake's tirade was interrupted by Nathan, who had grasped his forearm tightly and was pointing toward the wall screen.

DIRECTOR SYSTEM J428FB*
SYSTEM AUTHORIZED FOR USE BY
JAKOB RICHARD MEYERS
OWNER LAST ACCESSED:
10 HOURS, 51 MINUTES, 7 SECONDS
I SENSE STRESS OVERTONES IN YOUR VOICE.
HOW MAY I SERVE YOU, JAKOB RICHARD
MEYERS?

All three individuals silently stared at the wall screen. Jake finally broke the silence after pondering their situation.

"I need to have instructions on how to use system *jay*

four two eight eff bee star," Jake said, enunciating each letter and number as clearly as he could.

JAKOB RICHARD MEYERS HAS REQUESTED
INSTRUCTIONS FOR
SYSTEM J428FB*
IS THIS CORRECT? STATE CLEARLY: YES NO

"Yes."

IN HOW MANY DIMENSIONS DO YOU WISH
INSTRUCTIONS?
STATE CLEARLY: 2 3

Jake looked to the others for inspiration; Nathan was the only one who responded by holding up three fingers.

"Three." Jake enunciated.

A thin document appeared out of the wall beside the screen and remained, seemingly suspended in thin air. Jake lifted the document from what turned out to be a transparent shelf extending from the wall. Upon removal of the document, the shelf retracted into the wall. Jake held what he realized was possibly the key to total operation of this house, and regarded it almost reverently.

Chapter 16

Juan's worst fear had now been confirmed - that the entire world as he knew it was gone; not only gone, but gone a couple of hundred years ago. How could something like this happen? One lousy fishing trip, like hundreds of others over the last three years, and now his life was turned totally upside down. He felt anger boiling inside. *How could God let this happen?* In a few hours he lost his family, friends, girlfriend, home, chance at being a state champion, and his dream car he was making payments on. It wasn't fair! Not at this time in his life! Not at any time!

He stood, hands on hips, head down, sobbing like a baby in the hot humid air. Tears running down his cheeks were mingled with water dripping from his head as the sky opened and he found himself in a torrential downpour. The rain didn't bother him. The wet clothes didn't bother him. Nothing mattered right now. His world was gone. He missed his family and his life. Falling to his knees, he covered his face with his hands.

Jake sat on the floor, and with Nathan and Manny looking over his shoulder, began examining the documents in front of him. There were few pages, each very thin, yet amazingly strong and stiff. He started reading. After a few minutes, Manny walked away, bored. Nathan, who was caught up in the proceedings suddenly realized his close proximity to his father and also walked away. Both left the room.

Jake was so engrossed in the document he didn't notice that he was now alone. On the first page he scanned the system parameters and requirements, and then moved to the lower portion of the page where information on the manufacturer and designers of this particular system were included. He skipped over what he considered non-essential information and focused on the date of manufacture, 2120.

He found the overall system diagram on the second page, loosely reminding him of a flowchart. After studying the page for about fifteen minutes, he stood, advanced to the lighted panels, and placed the palm of his right hand on the tan panel.

DIRECTOR SYSTEM J428FB*
SYSTEM AUTHORIZED FOR USE BY
JAKOB RICHARD MEYERS
HOW MAY I SERVE YOU, JAKOB RICHARD
MEYERS?

Jake removed his hand from the tan panel and placed it on the orange panel. The screen changed.

C.P. STEWART

WELCOME JAKOB RICHARD MYERS
CHOOSE INTERIOR CONDITIONS FROM THESE
CHOICES.
PLEASE TOUCH SCREEN TO MAKE CHOICE.

LIGHT INTENSITY
TEMPERATURE
ACOUSTICS
FURNISHINGS
PRIVACY
NO CHOICE

Jake touched *FURNISHINGS* and the screen immediately changed.

MAKE FURNISHING CHOICE
PLEASE TOUCH SCREEN TO MAKE CHOICE.

CHAIR
TABLE
FLOOR LAMP
LOUNGER
SUPPORTER
NO CHOICE
REMOVE FURNISHING

He touched *CHAIR*.

AMOUNT REQUESTED?
STATE CLEARLY: 1 2 3 4 5 6 7 8

"Four." A map of the room appeared on the screen, marked off with grid lines.

TOUCH SCREEN AT CHAIR LOCATIONS

Jake studied the map and then touched the diagram at four different locations, each grid becoming lit. When he finished, the grid he had touched first turned red, and below the diagram the top view of a chair appeared. The chair was rotating fairly slowly in a clockwise direction, with a message below it.

TOUCH CHAIR WHEN ORIENTATION MATCHES
DESIRED ORIENTATION

Picturing how he wanted the chair, he waited until its position matched and then touched the chair on the screen. A faint humming sound caused him to look around in time to see a chair moving up through the floor as if lifted by an elevator. The entire process lasted approximately ten seconds and the chair was located where Jake had chosen, facing exactly as he wanted. He walked over to the chair and pushed down on it to see if it was sturdy enough to hold a seated person; satisfied, he sat on it.

"Nice," he murmured, then rose and returned to the

screen where the diagram remained. The grid containing his first location choice had changed from red to yellow and his second location choice now glowed red and the clockwise rotating chair again appeared with the same message.

TOUCH CHAIR WHEN ORIENTATION MATCHES
DESIRED ORIENTATION

He made his choice and watched the second chair appear, just as the first had. He then repeated the process two more times. He now had four chairs in the room. And the screen changed again.

MAKE FURNISHING CHOICE
PLEASE TOUCH SCREEN TO MAKE CHOICE.

CHAIR
TABLE
FLOOR LAMP
LOUNGER
SUPPORTER
NO CHOICE
REMOVE FURNISHING
MAIN MENU

This time, he touched *LOUNGER*.

AMOUNT REQUESTED?
STATE CLEARLY: 1 2 3

"One." The map of the room reappeared on the screen, marked off with grid lines; four of the grids were lit yellow, indicating the chair positions.

TOUCH SCREEN AT LOUNGER LOCATION

Jake studied the diagram and then touched the grid where he wanted the lounger. The grid turned red, and below the diagram the top view of a couch appeared. The couch was rotating fairly slowly in a clockwise direction, with a message below it.

TOUCH LOUNGER WHEN ORIENTATION
MATCHES DESIRED ORIENTATION

Jake repeated the process he had used for the chairs and a couch appeared just where he wanted. When the menu appeared again, he chose *NO CHOICE* whereupon the screen reverted back to a previous menu.

CHOOSE INTERIOR CONDITIONS FROM THESE
CHOICES:
PLEASE TOUCH SCREEN TO MAKE CHOICE.

LIGHT INTENSITY

C.P. STEWART

TEMPERATURE
ACOUSTICS
FURNISHINGS
PRIVACY
NO CHOICE

Satisfied with the accuracy of the instructions, and feeling that the other interior conditions were acceptable for the time being, Jake touched *NO CHOICE*.

THANK YOU, JAKOB RICHARD MYERS

Sitting on the couch, Jake turned sideways, leaned against one soft arm and stretched his legs. He couldn't identify the material of the covering but it was quite comfortable. He returned to his reading just as a thunderclap reverberated in the distance.

Manny and Nathan had ended up in different rooms, both sitting against respective walls while contemplating their pasts and futures. Nathan considered the future to be extremely bleak compared to the past; Manny's view was just the opposite.

Hours later, after the rain had stopped, Juan was jolted awake by hands grabbing at him and pressing on his back as his arms were being forced behind and tied. He couldn't make his groggy mind understand what was happening. All he could think was that he must have fallen asleep, because it was almost totally dark and he didn't remember the transition from daylight to dusk. Something was forced into his mouth before he was jerked to his feet. He looked around at his captors; all four of them wore dark clothing with hoods. Lightning illuminated the world, and in that brief moment he noticed that, even though he couldn't make out any facial features, they all had eyes that seemed to almost glow with color that was a pale shade somewhere between blue and violet.

Chapter 17

Jake was so engrossed in the instruction manual he lost track of time, until Nathan entered the room and headed for the coolers. He stopped, looked around at the furniture that had mysteriously appeared, pulled a soda out of the cold water, opened it and took a long drink. Next he opened the food cooler and began fixing a sandwich of ham, lettuce, and a tomato slice. He was about to add a slice of cheese but thought better of it after finding the slice to be very soft. He put it back, picked up his sandwich and drink, and left the room.

Jake watched his son the entire time but wasn't about to make any comments, fearing Nathan's reaction. No, it was better to observe, rather than attempt any interaction. Maybe later, after Nathan ate. He also felt the stirrings of hunger and stiffness from being in the same position for so long. He rose, placing the instructions aside on the couch, stretched from side-to-side in a twisting motion, then walked toward the room occupied by Mason.

Mason was slumped against the wall, asleep. Jake looked at the wall screen, which still displayed the empty room at the other end of the connection. Suddenly, a black figure moved swiftly across the screen to just out of sight on the left side. A black-clothed arm reached to an area somewhere below the screen and the display disappeared.

Jake couldn't believe what he had just seen; the speed it had taken place had rendered him unable to react. Still staring at the place formerly occupied by the display, he reached down and with one hand shook Mason's shoulder.

"Huh ... wha' ... wha' happened?" Mason slurred as he fought to regain his senses. "Is it time already?"

"I just saw someone on the screen. He moved so fast I couldn't do anything," Jake, still incredulous explained. "Whoever it was shut down the connection."

At this, Mason glanced quickly at the wall where the display had been, then back to Jake. "I'm sorry, must've dosed off," Mason was saying and Jake wasn't sure, but it seemed like he was talking to himself. "Didn't mean to. Sorry." This last part, Jake knew was intended for him.

"Don't worry about it. We'll try again after we eat."

"Yeah, I *am* gettin' a little hungry."

The two men walked back to the central pod where Mason stopped upon entering. "Where'd all this furniture come from?" he asked.

"I've been reading up on the computer system that controls this place. Seems since it thinks of me as its new owner, I can access quite a few things."

"At least we have a place to sit," Mason remarked as he made his way to the coolers with Jake close behind.

As they were fixing sandwiches, Manny entered.

"Whoa! Where did this stuff come from? Rob another house?"

"No," answered Jake. "Just figured out how to do it. The furniture is under the floor; I just used the instructions to get them."

"It's nice anyhow." Manny said approvingly as he headed for the coolers.

As they feasted on the last of the edible food, Jake related how the furniture was acquired, and other pertinent information. Manny asked some questions that Jake answered to the best of his knowledge. Mason mostly just ate without saying much, and then apologized for falling asleep on his watch, saying he was emotionally wrung-out.

Jake told Manny about the mysterious black-clad person that hurriedly closed the connection. While he was relating the incident, Mason seemed agitated, looking around.

"Where's Juan?" Mason asked. "I told 'im 'bout us bein' in th' future an' all, an' he was pretty upset ... but that was earlier ... this afternoon. Did he come back?"

"I didn't see him," answered Manny.

"Maybe he's with Nathan," speculated Jake. "I'll go check." He stood and walked from the room.

Entering the room where Nathan was downing the last of his soda, Jake looked around and quickly ascertained Juan's absence. "Have you seen Juan?"

"Not since lunch," recalled Nathan. "Why?"

"Captain Bankowski said he told him about our situation … being in the future I mean. He said Juan took it pretty hard."

"Where did he go?" asked Nathan, anxiety starting to build.

"I don't know. I guess Captain Bankowski told him somewhere outside."

Nathan jumped up and ran outside. The air was damp and cool now that the rain had stopped.

"Juan!" he called. "Juan, where are you?"

Jake informed Mason and Manny, who followed him outside. They split up, each standing outside one of the perimeter pods. All called out for Juan, but to no avail. Jake wondered if Juan could even hear them over the crickets, or whatever was making such a racket. After rejoining on the ocean side of the house, Mason suggested searching for him.

"It's pretty dark," observed Manny, "Do we have a flashlight?"

"I think Juan brought one from *Oblique View*," speculated Mason, "I'll go look."

As Mason hurried inside, Jake suggested they split up with two going north and two south.

"What if there's only one flashlight?" asked Nathan.

"Well," Jake conceded, while peering upward at the clouds covering the quarter moon, "It *is* pretty dark. I guess we should stick together if there's only one light."

Mason soon reappeared with a flashlight.

"Is that the only light?" Jake asked.

"Yeah," answered Mason, "Let's start where I left 'im."

Mason led the way southward along the dune following his and Juan's footprints, now only faintly discernable because of the rain. After a short distance Mason stopped, squatted, and examined the wet sand illuminated by the light beam.

"Here's where I told 'im." stated Mason. "My tracks go back from here." He shined the light along his footprints, and then aimed the light in the other direction along another set of footprints, "And he went off this way. Let's go. Juan! Can you hear me?"

Juan's footprints were difficult to follow; it looked as if the rain had been heavier in this area. A little farther on, Mason suddenly stopped and aimed the light on one area of the sand. The other three caught up and surrounded the illuminated area. The marks in the sand were very clear, obviously made after the rain had subsided, and told a story of struggle. Using the light to examine the surrounding area led to the conclusion that three or four persons had approached from the south, participated in some type of struggle, and then returned southward with one person partly walking and partly being dragged.

"What are we going to do?" Nathan asked, thinking Juan had been the only one to try to reach out to him on this trip. "We have to go after him!"

Jake mentally calculated the distance they had come following Juan's tracks, about a hundred yards. He weighed the options; should he send Nathan back to the house or let him accompany them into ... into what? Danger? As much as he wanted to protect him by sending him back, he wasn't sure he would be in less danger there. At least, Jake reasoned, he could try to watch out for Nathan if he was along.

"Turn off the light!" Jake whispered urgently. "Listen!"

Mason shut off the light and they all listened for any sound.

"I don't h ... " Nathan's voice stopped when Jake grabbed his arm and pulled him down to a squatting position.

"Shhhh!" whispered Jake.

Manny and Mason joined them closer to the sand. They listened, but heard nothing other than night sounds.

"What are we doin'?" whispered Mason. "I don't hear nothin' out of th' ordinary. We need to go after Juan."

"Look, we don't know anything about whoever took Juan," Jake explained. "We don't know if they're armed, or even *why* they took him. How do we know they haven't been watching us the whole time since we left the house? We can't continue following the tracks with the flashlight because that just broadcasts our presence, making it extremely easy to walk into an ambush. We need to use our brains."

"How're we gonna follow th' tracks *without* th' flashlight?" argued Mason. "We couldn't even walk through this uneven sand an' scrub without light."

"I agree," whispered Jake, "but I think we might be safer if we split up. Listen, the beach is pretty flat, easier to walk without a light, right?" Not waiting for an answer, he continued, "I propose *you* keep the light and use it to follow the tracks while the three of us head for the beach and follow your progress there. That way, if anyone's watching, they'll see only one person with a light, not four."

"Okay, it sounds all right," Mason whispered back. "I'll give ya a coupla minutes to get there, an' then I'll start."

Jake led the way, crawling over the dune toward the beach. The dune was only about five feet high at this point so they made it to the beach in about three minutes. Keeping the breakers on their left, they crouched along the sand following Mason's light and mirroring his progress. After moving in this manner approximately forty yards, Manny let out a muffled cry, bringing Jake and Nathan around immediately.

"What happened?" Jake asked in a whisper.

"I stepped in a hole; twisted my ankle," responded Manny, and then after trying to put weight on it, "I can walk. Let's keep going."

Not wanting Mason to get too far ahead and with no way of signaling him, Jake replied, "Okay. Try to stay with me." Jake and Nathan then led the way southward on the beach, trying to stay abreast of Mason's light.

Hours seemed to pass as they slowly moved southward. Manny's ankle hurt like hell, but he wasn't about to give up. He realized that, at least for now, he needed these people.

Mason was following the tracks when he heard a sound to his right. He aimed the light in that direction and saw Juan, bound and gagged, moaning and writhing in the sand among some scrub brush. He started toward the figure, when he heard a sound behind him in the grasses. He whirled and his light shined directly into the face of a hooded figure standing about twenty feet away. The figure shrieked, trying to cover his face with one hand as he fired a weapon with his other. The weapon sent a quick light pulse with a *puht* sound, grazing Mason's left shoulder, obviously wide of its mark. Mason swiftly removed the .38 from the back of his waistband, took quick aim and fired off three shots in rapid succession. The figure spun and dropped.

At the same time, other figures jumped the people on the beach. Jake was knocked to the sand and someone jumped on him, striking him on the head. He blacked out.

Manny was likewise knocked off his feet, but using the experience he gained in many street fights he pushed the button on his switchblade as he fell and shoved it into the figure that leaped on him. He rolled the attacker off and started after the figure moving around where he imagined Jake to be. He had trouble seeing the dark figure in the darkness, but had an idea of his location from the sounds of his footsteps on the sand. He swung the knife in the direction of the attacker, but swiped at only air. His mobility hindered by the sore ankle, coupled with the fact he couldn't see, caused him to react more on instinct than anything else.

Suddenly, he was grabbed from behind, arms held tightly against his sides in a bear-hug as he sensed another attacker closing in. He turned the knife in his hand and stabbed backward, the knife finding its mark in the attacker's midsection, causing him to utter a high pitched scream and release his grip. Just then, Manny perceived movement toward his head, but not in time to avoid it.

Mason, upon hearing the scream was torn between releasing Juan and helping whoever was in trouble on the beach. He figured Juan was okay for now, so he climbed the dune and headed toward the ocean. As he crested the dune, his light illuminated three bodies on the beach. Descending as fast as he could through the loose sand, he tripped on something at the bottom, losing his light and gun. He tried to rise and then there was nothing.

Chapter 18

Manny awoke, sputtering as a breaker crashed over him. Pushing back onto his knees in the lace-like spume, he wiped wet sand from his face then looked around, trying to remember what led him to be in the surf. After a few seconds he recalled the fight, but that was at night and now it was dawn, the sky over the ocean was awash with colors of red, orange, yellow, and green. His head hurt, and when he felt the left side above his ear, he found a large lump that hurt to the touch. He brought his hand down and found blood on it.

"Son of a bitch!" he exclaimed.

Scanning the beach, he saw Jake's motionless body farther from the water's edge. He stood and then fell when he put weight on his ankle. He tried again and managed to remain upright, limping slowly from the surf.

Reaching Jake, he saw an open gash with matted blood on the back of his head. He turned him over and felt his neck for a pulse. Finding a pulse, he slapped him a couple of times on the face. Jake moaned and tried to move.

Feeling the sting of the slaps Jake tried to emerge through, what seemed, several layers of consciousness. Finally, he blinked his eyes open and tried to focus. Lying on his back, he was looking at the early morning sky with its colors and dark wispy clouds. Reality suddenly intruded on his first tranquil thoughts and he sat bolt upright, a decision he immediately regretted as the pain in his head throbbed and nearly caused him to pass out. Regaining his faculties while holding the back of his head, he struggled to survey the beach.

"Where's Nathan?" he asked, near panic.

"Don't know," answered Manny as he looked around. "I just came to myself. I don't see him."

Jake looked around, head throbbing.

"We have to go after him!"

"Hold on," Manny replied. "We need to check on the others."

Jake saw Mason lying against a large section of driftwood at the base of the dune, blood on his partial baldhead. "Captain Bankowski!" he shouted, while pointing toward the still body.

Manny looked in the direction Jake was indicating and began limping toward Mason. Before reaching him, Mason moved, raised his face out of the sand, and shook his head. Jake managed to stand, although wobbly, and staggered after Manny.

Manny and Jake arrived and sat on the sand alongside Mason, who jumped up quickly, eyes searching inland. He staggered to the crest of the dune and scanned toward where he had last seen Juan. Relief surged as he saw Juan struggling, still bound, in the same location he had been earlier. As he closed in, he paused to step over a black-clad figure lying face down in the brush.

"Juan!" he exclaimed as he knelt over the bound youth and removed the wadded material from his mouth before untying him. "Are ya all right?"

"Thank God you're alive!" Juan said as soon as the gag was removed. "I thought you were dead when you didn't come back."

"No such luck," Mason responded with a smile as he released the bindings from Juan's hands. "I guess ya're stuck with me for a while yet."

Jake and Manny joined them, Manny stopping to gaze down at the lifeless body of the attacker.

"Where did *you* guys come from?" Juan asked as he rubbed his sore wrists. "I thought Captain Bankowski was out here alone."

"We were following on the beach, in case the guys who took you attacked him. We were following his light because we couldn't see much in the pitch darkness." Jake explained. "We figured we would surprise them, but it seems they turned the tables. How did they know we were there?"

"Maybe they heard you coming when you heard my shots." Mason theorized.

"What shots?" asked Jake, looking confused and still rubbing his head wound.

"I heard them," interjected Manny, just now joining them after checking to make sure the attacker was dead. "But I had my hands full with one of them. When I heard the shots, I thought they had guns. You were probably already out."

Mason walked to the body and rolled it over with his foot, muttering, "They seemed to know we were comin'... an' where we were."

The face of the dead man looked serene, but ashen and his mouth was slightly open, revealing the tips of, what looked like, filed teeth. Mason lifted the man's upper lip then jumped back.

"Holy mother o' God!" He exclaimed, "Did ya see that?"

Manny squatted beside the body and parted the lips to reveal a set of slightly yellowed pointed teeth, canines somewhat longer than the rest. They reminded him of those of an animal, a predator.

"Are those real?" asked Juan, incredulously.

Manny attempted to dislodge them with his thumb and forefinger, but found they were very much real.

"Look at his eyes," instructed Juan, "They all had the same color eyes."

Manny lifted an eyelid on the body and they gazed at the pale blue-violet color of the exposed eye.

"You say they *all* had this same color?" Jake asked.

"That's the only thing I could make out about their faces, but yes, they all seemed to have the same color eyes."

"We need to find Nathan!" Jake said with urgency, "They must've taken him last night."

"Yeah," agreed Mason, rubbing his left shoulder that was suddenly burning. "But I think we better compare notes to see what we're up against. Let's see if we can find my gun. I had it when I went down last night."

As they walked toward the place where Mason had been rendered unconscious, he turned to Juan and said, "Tell us what happened to ya last night. We need to understand who these people are."

"They surprised me and tied me up, then they were taking me that way ... " Juan stopped mid-sentence while pointing south.

Nobody had bothered to glance away from their immediate surroundings until now, but Juan's expression caused them to look up, and to their amazement saw a city a few miles in the distance, a city with skyscrapers interspersed with lower buildings. They stared in silence and awe.

"Where did *that* come from?" wondered Manny out loud.

"I wasn't lookin' that way," said Mason.

"I wasn't either," agreed Jake. "That might be where they took Nathan, let's go."

They resumed their movement toward the dune, glancing occasionally at the city.

"Anyway," continued Juan, "they were strong and kept pulling me, even dragging me sometimes when I tripped. They talked, but so low I couldn't make out what they were saying. When we got here, they threw me down over there and then split up; one hid in the brush and the other three left, I thought toward the ocean. I didn't know what they wanted or why they stopped and separated. Then I saw a flashlight coming and hoped it was all of you. I saw it was only one person, then I got afraid. When you came toward me last night, I knew the guy was hiding and I tried to warn you but I couldn't get the gag out."

Jake thought a moment, then asked, "How long was it until Captain Bankowski showed up, I mean after they separated?"

"A couple of minutes, not more than about three."

"They must've heard us," speculated Manny, "because it was too dark to see us on the beach."

"It's strange, almost as if they were expecting us to be walking in the dark on the beach," Jake remarked thoughtfully. "And why would three of them head for the beach and leave only one up here. It's like they not only anticipated our strategy, they also seemed to know how many of us would be there. One up here to take care of one man and three to handle three men on the beach. It's almost like they could see in the dark."

"You know," Manny said, "come to think of it, during the fight it was like they could see me even though I couldn't see them. I got two of them good but only because I knew where they were. I used my knife on them, but I could never find the other one even though he was close ... like he could see me and kept away."

They reached the place where Mason had fallen earlier and found his flashlight, still on with the light growing weaker. Mason scanned the immediate area and saw tracks and dig marks all around where he had been unconscious, wondering if they had also been searching for his weapon. He found the gun buried underneath where he had fallen.

Juan walked back to the dead attacker and picked up his weapon, which he found to be surprisingly light; it couldn't have weighed more than two pounds. On further examination, it was about 18 inches long, shorter than a rifle but longer than a handgun and resembled a double barreled shotgun, but with the two very narrow barrels arranged vertically instead of beside each other. Two buttons were located on the right side, also vertically situated and presumably one for each barrel. He aimed across the dunes, pressed the top button and the weapon emitted a quick burst of light with a *puht* sound; pressing the bottom button caused a sustained beam to be emitted as long as the button was held in with a *puuuuht* sound lasting until the button was released. Satisfied, he jogged toward the beach to join the others.

Manny waded in the surf searching for his knife. When he was about to give up, he saw a portion of the handle in a small gully left by the receding water from the last breaker. Scooping the knife and a handful of sand, he washed it off in the next breaker, wiped it on his wet pants, and returned the blade to its handle.

While Mason and Manny were concentrating on their

weapons, Jake walked southward on the beach looking for Nathan's tracks, but to no avail. All he found were millions of indentations in the sand and some fairly large holes above the high water mark. While scanning the beach, his eyes caught a glimpse of something, maybe a large piece of dark cloth rolling in the breakers. He waded in, grabbed at the cloth and found it attached to a dead body, one of the attackers. Grabbing the wrists, he dragged it onto the sand. He found blood oozing from just below the sternum, and out of curiosity, lifted one eyelid, exposing the same eye color as the other attacker.

"Well, that's two of the four." Jake said. "That leaves only two more."

"I *knew* I got one of them good," Manny said when the others caught up with Jake, who was standing over the body. "And I know I got another one too, but I don't know how bad."

Satisfied that this attacker had the same physical anomalies as the one Mason had shot, they headed south.

They scoured the beach and spread out to the dunes, finally finding footprints over the dunes, along with occasional pools of blood. A few hundred yards further they found the third attacker lying on his back gasping for breath, foamy blood trickling from his mouth.

Jake fell to his knees, grabbed the man's robe just below the hood with both fists and demanded, "Where's my son! What'd you do with him?"

The dying man opened and aimed his pale blue-violet

stare into Jake's eyes, bared his pointed teeth in a satisfied but painful smile, and gasped his last, slumping into dead weight.

"And then there was one." Manny murmured, while looking straight ahead at the first buildings of the city.

"Or more," added Juan.

Chapter 19

The sun was at mid-morning height as they approached the city. They were now taking increased measures to conceal their presence by staying low and moving behind small sand dunes. When the group was within fifty yards of the first building, they crawled into a trench to determine their strategy.

"What do you say we split up and try to find out where they took Nathan," suggested Juan. "That way we can check in four different directions."

"I don't think that's wise," countered Mason. "Since there's only four of us an' we only got three weapons, I think we should stick together ... for safety."

"Especially since one of those weapons is only good up close," added Jake. "Have you figured that thing out yet?" This question was directed to Juan who carried the weapon taken from the first dead attacker. He aimed it toward some brush and pushed a button on the side. Immediately, a light pulse emanated from it with a *puht* sound; on contact, a branch burned off and fell onto the sand.

"Yep." Juan said to Jake, with a huge grin.

"Good," replied Jake. "That gives us two weapons that are effective at distance. Too bad the other attackers didn't have weapons. How many bullets do you have?"

Mason put his hand in his pocket and retrieved some shells. After counting them, he responded, "I got a coupla boxes on th' boat, but here I got fourteen, an' with ten left in th' clip, makes twenty-four rounds. Hope that's enough."

"Me too," agreed Jake. "I certainly hope that will be enough."

"Are we agreed we should stay together?" asked Mason.

"I guess we should," agreed Jake. "After all, if one or two of us would find Nathan, how could the others be notified to help free him."

Manny and Juan nodded.

"Who's goin' to take lead?" asked Mason.

"I will," volunteered Jake. "He's *my* son."

As they prepared to leave the trench, Juan asked, "Why do you think they left *me* behind and took Nathan? I was already tied up, they could have come back for me."

"Easy," responded Manny. "You were already tied up for transport but there were four of them; we killed two outright, and wounded the third. That left only one to take the prisoner wherever they were going ... and Nathan was closest."

"I guess that kind of makes sense," reasoned Juan. "I was just wondering why I'm here with you and Nathan's the one in trouble."

In climbing from the trench, Mason's foot slipped on loose sand against the trench side, pitching him to his knees. Regaining his feet, he stopped and brushed away more loose sand revealing some well-worn concrete blocks.

"What do ya make of that?" asked Mason, pointing to the blocks. "Looks like somethin' we had in our world."

"This might have been a basement in a previous life," said Jake, "but I think we should go now." Jake left the trench first, running crouched toward the first building, a five-story covered by a stucco appearing surface. Mason followed, then Manny with Juan bringing up the rear. They flattened themselves against the exterior wall, and then crept to the corner. Jake peered around the corner expecting to see a bustling city with black-robed people in the street.

"What d'ya see?" asked Mason, close behind him.

"Nothing," replied Jake. "Absolutely nothing. Look for yourself."

Mason edged past Jake and peered around the corner. The scene was unlike anything he could have imagined. He was looking down what appeared to be a major street in this city and it was deserted; not only deserted, but it looked as if nobody had lived here for many years. The buildings were stained and crumbling, many with broken or missing windows and doors, and so many weeds were growing up through cracks in the street that the surface was only visible intermittently. Trash littered wherever it had been deposited by countless winds. It was as if a new city had been built somewhere else and everybody abandoned this one in favor of the new one. Juan and Manny joined them and also scanned the scene.

"Well, it doesn't look like we'll be able to question anyone about Nathan's location," surmised Manny. "So, what do we do now?"

"We keep going," answered Jake. "We know Nathan was taken toward this city, so I figure this was the destination. God knows he could be anywhere and it could take us days to search him out, but I'll be damned if I leave here without him! I'm going on; if any of you want to turn back, I'll understand."

"*I'm* with ya," volunteered Mason.

"Me, too," said Juan. "I'm with you every step." Manny nodded agreement.

"Okay, let's go," Jake urged and led the way around the corner. "Keep your eyes open for any movement."

Flattened against the building, they ducked into the main door keeping low as they entered. The interior appeared to have been an office building of some sort. They stood in a large foyer with tables arranged in a circular pattern around a larger table, each with at least a few reclining chairs, now torn and weathered. A large window, streaked but still intact, illuminated the room but its curtains hung in rags, resembling tattered sails on a derelict sailboat.

Jake looked around and said, "Let's go; nobody's here."

"How do you know?" asked Juan.

"Look at the dust and sand on the floor. No footprints, no disturbance. Nobody's been here for a long time."

They exited the building, hugged its exterior wall and continued to the next structure, which at three stories was smaller than the first. As Jake moved along the wall he encountered a large window that was devoid of any filling, glass or otherwise. He stopped short of the window and peered in. Again, there was no sign of recent activity, but something caught his interest and he entered through a door after motioning for the others to remain outside. A few seconds later he returned carrying a length of material that resembled a pipe, closed at both ends and between three and four feet in length.

"Got myself a weapon," explained Jake, handing it to Mason. "Feel this thing, hard but very light." Mason pursed his lips, raised his eyebrows and nodded his approval, then handed it back.

They resumed their search. The next building was a small skyscraper, approximately fifteen stories high. The group entered and found some tracks in the floor dust, which they followed up a ramp to the second floor. The tracks continued down a hallway while the ramp continued its upward spiral under undisturbed dust. Mason, with his .38 at ready, took the lead and followed the tracks to stairs at the end of the hallway, then downstairs and out the rear door where the footprints disappeared in wind-blown sand.

Jake stuck his head out the rear door and looked in all directions. Nothing. In the next building, a nine-story, they located an elevator unlike any they had ever seen. The door was clear and the floor was oval shaped. Peering through the clear door, Jake could see that, from the dust on the floor, it hadn't been used in ages. All three stairways had also been undisturbed for an extended period of time, one had partially collapsed. The main room appeared to have been a restaurant with many tables and chairs, most broken and lying askew.

"Move on," directed Jake and they exited the front door.

They continued in this manner into early afternoon with no positive results. Because of this, they had become lax in their concealment methods, walking boldly and not flattening themselves against walls as they searched. They passed, and gave cursory examinations to all forms of buildings, offices and stores alike; so much like a normal city, but without the people. Occasionally, stores still had small amounts of damaged merchandise lying around but most had been cleaned out and apparently looted. The heat was also beginning to take its toll on their energy, and exposed surfaces were showing the effects of sunburn. Jake passed around the sunscreen he still carried.

While crossing a side street, Jake caught movement in his left periphery, probably two or so blocks away. He turned in that direction. Seeing nothing, he motioned for the others to take cover while he continued to search for who, or what, had caught his attention.

"What happened?" grimaced Manny, rubbing a swollen ankle that was becoming more painful with every step.

"I'm sure I saw something move a couple blocks down

that way," explained Jake, pointing. "I think we should investigate."

"Okay," agreed Mason. "Lead th' way."

Jake resumed his original methods of concealment and the other three followed his example, although Manny was limping noticeably and had assumed the rear position from Juan because he was having difficulty keeping up.

Jake located the place he thought he had seen the movement, a fairly small structure that appeared somewhat older than most of the buildings they had visited and only two stories high. A very light coating of sand existed in small patches, and one patch looked to have been disturbed recently. The main door was ajar, so Jake opened it slightly wider and slipped through, followed by Mason and Juan. They were in an atrium with no doors. Manny found a type of stoop by the steps and sat down.

"Where's Mr. Cranston?" Jake queried.

Juan poked his head through the opening and then returned. "He's sitting outside. I think his leg is bothering him."

"Yeah, he hurt his ankle last night on the beach," explained Jake. "But we need him in case Nathan is being held in here. See if you can get him, Juan." The teen left the building and returned a few minutes later with Manny.

"Sorry," Manny apologized. "My ankle hurts, but it'll be okay."

Let's see if we can find a way in," directed Jake, staring at the solid wall.

"Remember the first house we found," reminded Juan, surveying the walls, "Nathan found the doorway by accidentally finding a magic spot on the wall."

"That's right," agreed Jake. "Look very carefully for anything that might indicate a key spot like Juan said."

All four searched much of the wall until Jake found a small, slightly soiled area about four feet above the floor. He placed his palm on the spot and as he removed it, a doorway opened in the wall, taking the other three by surprise.

"You found it!" exclaimed Juan.

"Let's go in. Stay together," ordered Jake.

"Yeah," replied Juan. "In case we find any more of those blue-eyed freaks."

They found a ramp leading to the second floor, and a hallway leading straight ahead on the first floor.

"Which way?" queried Mason.

"Let's try the low road, but leave one here to get anyone that might try to escape from up there," suggested Jake. "Juan, do you think you can operate that thing well enough to take care of any of those critters if they try to escape?"

"Yep, you can count on me, Mr. Myers." He then flattened himself against the hallway wall in a position that provided him the best view of anyone moving down the ramp and readied his weapon.

Satisfied that nobody from upstairs could get by them without a fight, Jake turned his attention to the first floor hallway. Seeing that no doors were visible, he led the way, methodically studying the walls for any smudge or soiled places.

Approximately a third of the way down the hallway Jake heard a muffled noise to his right behind the wall. He raised his hand for the others to stop. He motioned for them to situate themselves, like him, against the left wall facing where he had heard the noise.

Jake very carefully searched for an opening into the room from where the sound had emanated. Then he saw it - a small smudged area on the wall.

Expecting to see more of the creatures that had taken Nathan, he readied his club and motioned for the others to get set and then placed his hand on the smudge. He removed his hand and charged through the gaping doorway that had immediately opened, club ready to swing, Mason by his side, gun aimed at arm's length.

From the hallway Manny watched Jake and Mason barge into the room, then heard a high-pitched scream but no shots. He couldn't see past the two men's backs as they continued to stand just inside the room. Limping across the hall he positioned himself so he could look between them.

He saw a cowering woman, protectively shielding a child.

Chapter 20

Their attention was quickly drawn to the left as they heard a deep measured voice, "Drop your weapons!" The order came from a tall man aiming a double-barreled shotgun at them.

Hesitating, they heard a heavy Scottish brogue to their right, "Ye hairrrd the mon, drrrop yerrr weapons!"

Turning, they saw a barrel-chested bald man, at least a foot shorter than the one with the shotgun. This one had a long barreled revolver that looked like something from a western movie aimed at them. Jake dropped his club while Mason squatted to place his handgun on the floor, a move that caused the tall man to tighten his grip on the shotgun. Manny tried to pocket his knife unobtrusively, which caused the short man to step in his direction, revolver at arm's length and pointed directly at Manny's head. Thinking better of it, he let his knife fall to the floor with a clatter.

Juan, alternately watching the ramp to the second floor and the trio enter the room down the hall had heard the scream and the barked instructions to drop their weapons.

He left his post and crept quickly down the hall toward the action. He stopped beside the doorway and prepared to enter when he felt something poking into his back.

"Drop it, mate," a husky male voice menacingly whispered in his ear. "If you don't, it'll be the last decision you ever make."

"Can I lay it down?" Juan asked quietly. "I don't want to damage it."

"Okay, but do it carefully, no sudden moves."

Juan squatted, placing his weapon on the hallway floor, and then with reflexes honed from years on the wrestling mat lunged, grabbing the man's ankle and lifted while driving his shoulder into his mid-section. He landed on top of the man and heard a *whoosh* as the air was knocked out of his lungs. The man was rendered temporarily immobile, allowing Juan to search for the gun that had been against his back a few seconds before; all he saw was a length of wood against the far wall.

"Thot's enough!" A voice thundered above him. "Staind uup und put yerrr hainds behint yerrr haid!"

Juan turned to see a short bald man with a revolver aimed at his head, so he stood and slowly raised his hands, interlocking his fingers behind his head.

"Cuum in und join yerrr frrriends," instructed the bald man, then to the man struggling to regain his breath on the floor, "Ye okay, Buubby?" The wheezing man sat upright, nodded while continuing to gasp for air, and motioned for them to go on.

Juan walked into the room where his hands were immediately pulled behind him and bound, then he was pushed to the far wall and forced to sit with the other three, all similarly bound.

The tall man sat in a chair with the shotgun resting on his lap while the bald man inserted the revolver into the waistband of his pants, pulled a chair to a location in front of the prisoners and sat facing them. It was during these movements that the prisoners noticed his left arm was gone below the elbow. At this juncture, the third man entered from the hall, holding his stomach and carrying the wooden rod Juan had seen earlier. The woman and child sat on a couch-like piece of furniture out of the way in a corner of the room.

"Now gents, wha' airrre ye doin' herrrre?" the bald man asked very politely with his thick accent.

"We're looking for my son and thought he might be a prisoner here," explained Jake.

"Und wha' made ye think he was herrrre? Why did ye think we would have yerrr suun?"

"We didn't know you were here," answered Jake. "We've been checking out every building we encountered since we arrived here late this morning, but didn't find any sign of life until now. We didn't think there was anybody left in Florida except the ones that took Nathan."

"Und who airrre the ones thut supposedly tuuk yerrr lad?"

"I don't know, except they had sharp teeth and blue

eyes." The two men exchanged glances. Looking back at Jake, he continued the interrogation.

"Und, how do we know yerrr tellin' uus the trrruth? Wherrre airrre ye frrrom?"

"You wouldn't believe me if I told you."

"Well, trrry uus."

"Okay, you asked for it; we're from more than two hundred seventy years in the past."

"Whuut hoppened?"

"We went out on a fishing trip," explained Jake. "We ran into a storm and dense fog. When we came out of it and came to shore, we were in the year 2283."

"When did ye go on yerrr fishing trrrip?"

"2005."

"2005? Ye left in 2005 und rrreturrrned in 2283?"

"That's right. Whether you believe it or not, that's what happened."

"Who was the operator of the boat?" asked the tall man.

"I was," volunteered Mason. "I've been takin' out charters for twelve years an' never had anythin' happen."

"What happened to the boat in the fog?" the tall man directed the question to Mason.

"What d'ya mean?"

"What about your instruments? How did they react?"

"Nothin' worked," explained Mason. "The compass, radios, cell phones, GPS ... nothin'."

"What's a GPS or cell phone?" asked the tall man with a confused expression.

"GPS, Global Positionin' System; it's an instrument that tells ya where ya are by continually gettin' signals from a satellite. A cell phone is a phone ya carry with ya an' can call anybody, anytime."

The two men again exchanged glances.

"Tell us about what happened to your son," the tall man asked Jake.

"This young man," Jake indicated by nodding his head in Juan's direction, "was captured by four men ... uh ... things and when we tried to rescue him they jumped us. We killed three of them but one got away and took my son. We tracked them to this city but haven't been able to find a trace of them since. I need to find him and I can't while I'm tied up here!" His voice rising with impatience.

Again, the tall man and bald man looked at each other, then the tall man nodded and walked over to the four bound prisoners. "I believe you," he said and untied them. "I'm Johnathon MacKensie, friends call me Mack, and he's Angus Campbell, we call him Scotty. The one rubbing his stomach is Bobby Blackhorn, and over in the corner is Veronica Langham ... Ronni, and her boy, Davy. I'm sorry for treating you like this but we saw you coming this way with weapons and had to find out what your motives were."

"Thank you, Mr. MacKensie," said Jake. "But why did you believe me? I hardly believe it myself."

"Because," explained Mack, "I was piloting a commercial flight from Caracas, Venezuela to New York in 1965 when we ran into some turbulence and dense fog over the

Bahamas. None of my instruments worked and we had no idea where we were or even where we were heading. We were in the fog long enough to deplete our fuel, so when we came out we had to find a place to put down quickly. I visually found an airport but couldn't raise the tower on the radio. We had to set down and since there weren't any other planes on the runway, we tried to land. The runway must've been very old because there were broken sections, like potholes. We lost the nose gear and the starboard landing gear; by the time we stopped sliding, we had lost the starboard wing, belly of the plane, and tail section. Fourteen people died out of thirty-six on board. It was terrible."

"How long ago did this happen?" Jake queried while rubbing his wrists.

"We've been herrre overrr thrrree yearrrs," interjected Scotty.

"I think we may be of some help to you," volunteered Mack. "The people that took your son are called *Azujos*, short for *Azul Ojos* or *Blue Eyes*, according to some native inhabitants we met shortly after coming here. Legend says they are born with pale blue eyes which change to pure violet as they age. They've taken lots of people over the years, including my co-pilot and Ronni's husband, along with several others we knew. We all hate them! We were told to avoid an area about two miles west of here, a large stadium, because they seem to be very active around there. None of us have ever been there, tried to keep our distance."

"Thanks," responded Jake. "By the way, I'm Jake Myers, that's Captain Bankowski, Allen Cranston, and Juan."

"Mason," Mason said, extending his hand to Mack. "An' he's Juan Morales."

"Pleased to meet all of you," Mack responded. "I don't want to break up this get-acquainted party, but we'd better get moving if we want to have a chance at getting there in time."

"Thank you for the information," Jake said. "If you'll give us directions, we'll get started."

"Like I said," Mack countered, "We had better get moving. With a couple more men you stand a better chance of finding your son."

"I have a bad leg," complained Manny, eyeing Veronica furtively. "I think I would just slow you down so I'll stay here. By the way, what's the hurry?"

"Scotty, stay here and keep guard," directed Mack, then while gathering shells from a wall drawer and stuffing his pockets, he explained, "We need to get there soon because the Azujos are nocturnal; they only come out at night, and it's now mid-afternoon. Bobby, grab some guns and ammo! We'll go as soon as everybody's ready!"

Mason picked up his pistol, Jake gathered his club, and Juan recovered the light-shooting weapon he had left in the hall, while Bobby went to a room down the hall, returning shortly carrying another long barreled revolver, with two others tucked into his waistband.

"Keep good watch, Scotty!" Mack shouted over his shoulder as he led the party into the hallway.

"Aye Cuptain!"

Manny chuckled because it reminded him of a line from Star Trek.

Chapter 21

The five men moved at a quick rate through the city, Mack's long legs setting the pace. After a few minutes of small talk, Jake's curiosity got the better of him and he fell into step alongside Mack.

"You said earlier that these Azujos had taken some people you knew; what happened to them?"

"I don't know," Mack replied in the quiet and precise way he had spoken back in the room before they left. "They just never came back. We had a few run-ins with them when we first arrived, but not since we learned to stay inside from dusk to dawn. As a matter of fact, one of those light-shooter weapons, like the kid's carrying is what took Scotty's arm off. One burst of light and half his arm was gone. You know, I've often wondered about the Azujos and what they did to the people they took, but was afraid of finding out for sure. I'm sorry, I know you're grasping at as much hopefulness as you can ... and I hope we can find your son, but we know they *are* dangerous."

"I understand, but I think it's important to know as

much as you can about your adversary; it might come in handy later on. Do you have any idea *what* they are?"

"As far as I know they are some type of people; I don't know where they came from or how they seem to be able to see in the dark, other than what we were told."

"What *were* you told, and what ever happened to the native inhabitants you mentioned earlier? I'd like to talk with them."

"I don't know what became of them; they were a nice couple in their sixties ... Martin and Gizela Foreman were their names. They told us how this area used to be a thriving city until the Azujos began to take over, and gradually people and businesses disappeared until nothing was left. They were among the few hold-outs that didn't leave the area when the mass migration started about twenty some years ago. Gizela even started to help Ronni with the basic operations of the computerized apartment. We knew them about two or three weeks and they had mentioned several times that they wanted to travel north to find people. We talked to them one day and they were gone the next. They told us that legend had it the Azujos had been regular people a long time ago and something caused them to change, but I doubt it."

"Why?"

"Think about it, why would only certain people undergo change like that and not everyone? We really don't know much about them, and didn't want to ... until now."

"I can't thank you enough for your help. I just hope we can find Nathan alive."

"Glad to help, but save your gratitude until we find out if we're successful. This may turn out to be a wild goose chase."

Bobby, who was walking just ahead of Juan, slowed until Juan caught up and then matched his pace.

"What did you do to me back there? I thought I was guardin' you tight and then the next thing I know, I'm flat on my back, suckin' air."

"It was an ankle pick into a single leg," answered Juan with a smile. "You were wide open for it."

"Well, what ever it was, you were quick. I guess my reflexes are shot."

"Don't be so hard on yourself; I've been wrestling for six years, placed fifth in states last year."

"Yeah, that and you're a lot younger too." Bobby conceded with a grin.

"So, you survived a plane crash; I bet that was scary."

"Yeah, I wouldn't ever want to go through somethin' like that again."

"Tell me about it … I mean, what was it like? You don't have to if you don't want."

"No problem. I was sittin' toward the rear and the tail section broke off a couple rows behind me; everyone sittin' back there was killed. We looked at it after gettin' out of what was left of the plane. It looked like it had flipped end over end. It should've slid on the runway, but we figured it must have caught a rough patch and started to flip."

"What happened to the dead bodies; did you bury them?"

"Couldn't. They disappeared."

"What do you mean?"

"We didn't know where we were and why nobody came to help us. We couldn't find anyone anywhere. The terminal was totally empty, and the stores inside had been trashed. We went back to the plane and got our luggage out and spent the first night in the abandoned terminal; it was more comfortable than the alternative, an empty hangar. We talked about what to do with the bodies, even had input from survivors whose friends and relatives were among the dead. We decided to try to find people in the morning to help us with them, and if we didn't find any, we would bury them in the evening."

Bobby paused as if concentrating, trying to recall something.

"And ... ?" Juan prodded.

"As we were dividin' up to spread out and search for people, someone checked and found out the bodies were gone. Every single one of them."

"Where did they go? What happened to them?"

"Don't know, we never found a trace."

"Well, what do you *think* happened to them?"

"At first, it was a total mystery, but now we're pretty sure the Azujos took them."

Juan was silent for about a minute, then he asked, "Mr. MacKensie, er Mack, said the Azujos took some of you. How many?"

"Well, there were twenty-two survivors, but two died later from their injuries. That left twenty of us. At first, we didn't know what was happening, but our number decreased through the first month or so. One or two would just disappear; usually they would be out at night and just not come back. At first we lost ... " he paused to recall, "One the first couple weeks, then about three the next couple weeks. Within two months, we lost nine. It was around then we made the connection about night, they all disappeared at night, so after that we made sure to only go out in the daylight. Davy wandered off one evening and some of us got together a search party to try to find him before nightfall. There were five of us in that party. Well, we found Davy, but it turned dark before we got back and we ran into a band of Azujos. We fought and killed two of them, but they wounded two of us and killed two, one was Davy's father. They used those light things, like what you have there. One blast from that thing and Scotty lost his arm ... another and I got this." Bobby rolled back his right sleeve to expose a wide scar from about two inches above his wrist on the outside of his arm, the whole way past his elbow.

"That looks nasty. Why did Scotty lose his arm and you didn't?"

"I guess his was a direct hit and mine was just a graze. One thing, it doesn't bleed when you get hit by one of those light beams; I guess you'd say it cauterizes the wound immediately."

"So how many of you, survivors I mean, are left?"

"There's the ones you met and two others, an older married couple, kinda keep to themselves but live in the same building. That's where I was when you guys showed up, visiting them upstairs. I couldn't get to the room with the guns, so I tried to trick you with a stick. Anyway, we lost one who was careless when she went swimming and drowned, and another... an old guy died in his sleep, probably a heart attack."

"Do you five live together?"

"Naw, we each have our own rooms, except Ronni and Davy, they live together, of course."

"Man, I'm getting hungry, haven't eaten since yesterday."

"We'll fix you somethin' when we get back."

"With everything deserted, there can't be any stores for you to get food, so where do you get yours?"

"The people we found had lived here all their lives and told us where to find some surviving fruit trees, and there are still a few berry bushes. Mostly we fish during the day and eat what we catch. Some days we don't eat much ... others, we feast."

"It's a good thing I like seafood."

"You'd better," replied Bobby, laughing.

"By the way, why were you on a plane coming from Venezuela?"

"I was workin' down there buildin' a plant. I'm in construction and a job's a job, whether it's in the U.S. or another country. I was flyin' home when the job was done. I'd have rather taken a ship than a plane. Flyin' always made me un-easy, and bein' an old Navy man, I prefer ships. Lucky I was never married and really didn't have much family. For me, I guess endin' up here is more of an adventure than a tragedy. Don't get me wrong, there are things from my time I miss," he said and paused, "… but there's nothin' I can do about it, so I try to make the best of it."

"That's quite a collection of guns you have there."

"These?" Bobby swept his hand past the revolvers in his waistband. "These aren't mine. They belonged to Ronni's husband; he was a collector. Matter of fact, that's why he was in Venezuela, buying these from another collector. A couple of them date back to the Civil War and must be pret-ty valuable. But …," he paused for a moment, "but the only thing they're good for here is protection. Lucky for us he also included ammo in the deal, a couple are .32 caliber so they share the same bullets."

They returned to walking in silence, and five blocks fur-ther they were leaving the city. After passing through some brush, they found a well-trodden path that wound through more brush up a slight grade for approximately a quarter of a mile. Mack stopped abruptly, pointing to an impos-ing structure about two hundred yards ahead on the plateau they had just ascended. It was immense in area, but only about three stories high with three huge doorways on the side facing them, each filled with doors constructed of bars much like prison doors.

Chapter 22

Jake stepped forward to face Mack. "Thank you. You've risked enough. We'll take it from here."

"No sir," replied Mack stubbornly. "We've come this far and there's no way we're stopping now. Bobby, give this man one of the guns."

Bobby, who appeared to be around fifty and stocky with a ruddy complexion and short cropped blond hair, stepped forward and held out a revolver and shells.

"Thank you." Jake dropped his club and gladly took possession of the firearm, examined it and then inserted some shells. ".45 caliber?"

"Yeah, good handgun," answered Mack. "Lucky for us, Ronni's husband had these firearms in his luggage. Now maybe we can put them to good use."

"What's our plan?" asked Juan.

"What do you think?" Jake directed to Mack.

"I think we should stay together for now. There's safety in numbers and the sun is going to set in about two hours.

THROUGH THE TRIANGLE

If your son's here, we need to find him and get out quick so we can make it back by sundown."

"Okay, lead th' way," directed Mason.

Mack reached the rightmost barred door first and found it held tight by what seemed a type of padlock. They moved on to the one to its left and also found it padlocked. Checking each one in order, moving in a clockwise direction around the entire facility resulted in the same observation. The walls were sheer and made of some type of smooth substance so climbing the wall was not an option.

"Well, we've wasted a lot o' time checkin' th' doors, gimme yar scattergun for a minute," Mason commanded, and Mack handed over his shotgun.

Mason walked to one of the doors, placed the end of the barrel about an inch from the lock, and fired; the lock exploded.

"There ya go!" he said matter-of-factly as he returned the shotgun to Mack. "Let's check out what's inside."

The shredded padlock was cast aside and Mack opened the barred door. Cautiously, they crept inside, alert for any movement. The five men moved through a large hallway leading toward the center of the stadium. Large beams surrounded them as part of the lattice-like support structure. The beams were a discolored white and felt like plastic to the touch. They emerged from the hallway onto the edge of a playing field surrounded by an enormous number of seats. Jake was taken aback when he saw the playing surface, which was blue and marked with six faded white lines radiating outward from a yellow central circle.

"I wonder what game they played on this field," he said louder than he intended.

"Okay, we're inside, maybe we should split up so we can cover more area in less time," suggested Mack. "Bobby and I'll go left and you three go right; we'll meet up on the other side."

Mason, Juan, and Jake watched the other two men climb a set of stadium stairs and disappear between two sections of seats, and then did the same to the right. They passed between two sections of seats to an interior hallway that appeared to run around the stadium behind the seating area, much like the stadiums Jake had attended. This hallway didn't appear open to the outside, but was enclosed with offset areas where concessions may have been sold. Walking the hallway, their eyes were constantly searching for any sign that might indicate Nathan's presence. One by one, they became aware of an odor; at first barely perceptible, but the farther they walked in the hallway, the stronger it became.

"What's that smell?" asked Juan, wrinkling his nose.

"It smells like Norbert's back in Baltimore," Jake replied quietly. "That was a deli on the block where I grew up. He used to throw out old lunchmeat a couple times a week, usually put it in the trashcans in the alley behind his store. That's it, to me it smells like old lunch meat." In addition to the smell, there was a buzzing, or humming sound that varied in pitch and also seemed to increase with the increasing odor.

They stopped short of an opening to the right that

seemed to be cut into the existing structure, and appeared to be a makeshift hallway. It was a dissimilar situation than they had encountered thus far. The floor and walls were made of various materials, roughly improvised to cover constructed openings in the existing structure. The construction appeared to have been completed rather quickly, with little planning or thought toward the aesthetics of the finished product; it reflected nothing but function.

Flattened against the main hallway wall, Jake held his revolver at the ready and peered into the opening, but saw that this makeshift hallway made a dog-leg turn to the left approximately twenty feet in. It appeared that after the turn, it probably ran parallel to the one they were now in. He told Mason and Juan to stand guard while he checked out what was inside.

Stepping through the opening, he was assailed with the same odor as before, except stronger and the humming increased in intensity. Nearly gagging at the stench, he pulled a handkerchief from his rear pocket and held it over his nose before proceeding. Creeping down this new passageway, the disgusting odor and sound became stronger and louder until he reached the branched opening. Looking around the corner, a short hallway opened into a large area that had been hollowed out from the structure of the stadium.

Proceeding slowly forward with the revolver in his right hand and his left covering his nose with the handkerchief, he visually searched the vast open area. It was approximately forty feet across and had been hewn out of the existing structure.

The room was illuminated by natural evening light entering through a two-foot aperture in its roof that must have opened all the way through the stadium seating above. Once his eyes adjusted to the dim light, he could make out a number of seats on one side of the room, obvious transplants from the stadium above. Then as his focus shifted to other parts of the room, he stepped back in horror. Piles of bones were stacked around the perimeter of the area, presumably sorted by type. He saw a pile of large bones, a pile of small bones, a pile of curved bones, and a pile of skulls ... human skulls!

"My God," he choked. "They're cannibals!"

Something was moving in the room, but it wasn't a person; it was in the air along with another... two of them. One landed on a skull and he had to stare hard in the dim light to confirm what he was seeing. It was a fly as large as his fist! He then noticed more of them moving here and there as others took to flight, and immediately made a connection about the origin of the buzzing sound.

He also observed an area close to the center that contained what appeared to be a scorched metal mesh hammock, stretched between four metal support beams, suspended over and surrounded by ashes as well as some partially burned brush. Lying in the ashes was what looked like a human hand attached to a charred forearm.

"My God!" he gasped and fled the room, stumbling out into the hallway where Mason and Juan waited.

"What happened?" asked Mason. "Ya look white as a sheet."

Jake bent over, hands on knees and head down, trying to keep nausea in check. Not able to talk; he just stared at the floor until he regained enough control to straighten and describe what he had seen.

"Damn!" Mason exclaimed. "Let's get movin', we need to find yar boy quick!"

They resumed searching the hallway, but with a renewed sense of urgency spurring them to increase their pace.

A few minutes later they found another improvised passageway leading to the right, much like the previous one. Again, Jake entered and followed the parallel hallway to another large area. Cautiously peering into the open area, he saw girders that supported the seating section above, and tied to five of them were people who were gagged and blindfolded. He saw that one of them was Nathan and immediately ran to his side. "Nathan!" he said, lifting his son's head. "Nathan, are you all right?"

Nathan, semi-conscious, stirred and moaned. Jake untied him, removed the gag and blindfold, and supported him as he nearly fell.

"I found him!" Jake yelled to the others. "Come and help!" Mason and Juan came running. Quickly analyzing the situation, they rapidly ran to help the other bound captives.

Juan approached a man who looked to be in his seventies. "This one's dead," he reported, then moved on to the next one, a middle-aged woman. "This one's dead too."

Mason moved to a moaning bearded man with straggly looking long hair, and untied him. He then moved on to a young blond woman, probably in her late teens, who looked up at him with imploring blue eyes once the blindfold was removed. Just then, the bearded man tried to stand and collapsed, causing Mason to leave the young woman in order to keep him from hitting the floor.

"Juan, help the girl!" Mason commanded while supporting the bearded man. Juan scooted to the girl and untied her. She stood and threw her arms around his neck and started to cry.

"Let's get out of here!" Jake ordered while helping Nathan to his feet. Mason followed in like manner with the bearded man, and Juan let the girl go ahead of him as they headed out of the room.

Jake and Nathan reached the main hallway first and were surprised by a barked command from their left.

"Stop! Now!" The voice sounded hollow, but menacing.

Jake, still holding Nathan up, turned toward the voice and saw two figures, with black hoods extending beyond their faces that hid their features; each was holding a light-shooting weapon aimed directly at them.

Mason, walking directly behind Jake and Nathan, stopped before entering the hallway and quietly sat the bearded man down, leaning him against the wall. He held his index finger in front of his lips and motioned for Juan and the girl to stay put while he flattened against the wall and waited for his opportunity, pistol ready.

Jake, still supporting Nathan's weight, started backing away from the Azujos.

"Stay!" one of the hooded figures ordered and moved forward. Jake had backed past the doorway, giving Mason the opportunity he required.

As Mason was about to make his move, Mack and Bobby, having made their way around the stadium came into view from behind Jake and Nathan. One of the Azujos fired his weapon and Bobby fell backward with a burned spot on the shoulder of his shirt. Mack flattened against the wall but didn't attempt to fire his shotgun because Jake and Nathan were in the way.

The distraction was all Mason needed. He stepped into the hall, pistol at arm's length and fired two quick shots, surprising both Azujos, one of whom rebounded off the hallway wall before landing face first on the floor; the other lay sprawled on his back.

Mack ran to Bobby and helped him sit up. "Take it easy, Bobby," he soothed, "We'll get you back home. Can you stand?"

"I think so. Help me up."

Mack helped Bobby to his feet and supported him slightly as they fell into line behind the others. Juan stayed close to the girl, who seemed strong enough to walk on her own, although still crying and continually looking around in wide-eyed terror.

They hurried from the stadium and made it to the city limits without further encounters with the Azujos. When they reached the first buildings, they felt safe enough to rest a couple of minutes, even though the last of the sun was already melting into the horizon.

"We need to get moving," urged Mack. "It's going to be dark before we get back and they might have heard the shots."

As they prepared to resume, the bearded man seemed to be gaining strength and tried to stand. He managed to remain upright and took a few wobbly steps before falling to his knees. "I'm sorry, I'm too weak," he said. "The drugs haven't worn off yet."

"Drugs?" Jake responded. Until now, he hadn't thought about why Nathan and the others were so weak and somewhat unresponsive. Now it made sense. He moved to where a semiconscious Nathan was sitting against the wall of a building, head cocked to one side. Jake lifted his head and, as much as he hated to, slapped him. Nathan stirred, opened his eyes and looked up at his father.

"Dad?" Nathan mumbled, "Wha're *you* doin' here? Where'mI?"

"You'll be okay, Nathan. Let's get you out of here."

They resumed their trip in silence, Nathan still leaning on Jake, the bearded man walking with some help from Mason, and the rest able to walk on their own. Their progress was hindered by the weakness of the two prisoners and moving cautiously to avoid detection from any Azujos they might encounter now that the sun was setting.

Mack and Bobby, concentrating on where they were

stepping because of cracked surfaces, debris, and diminishing light, assumed the lead. Reaching a corner about four blocks from their destination, they glanced up to see two Azujos blocking their way and one was aiming his weapon at them.

Chapter 23

M ack and Bobby stopped, four others nearly running into them as a hollow voice demanded, "Drop all your weapons, kick them aside and lie face down!" Jake's grip on Nathan tightened as fear exploded in his mind; fear that he had come this far only to have it all end here.

Juan, walking with the girl and trying to find words to start a conversation, saw the others stop about twenty feet ahead. Hearing the command clarified how dire their situation was. Hidden from the Azujos by the height of the others, he frantically tried to figure a way to use this to his advantage. He looked in the frightened girl's eyes and saw panic about to erupt. He softly took hold of her arm, and with gentle pressure guided her downward into a doorway beside them.

Crouching, Juan crept forward using the other men as a shield, nearly reaching Jake and Nathan as he heard weapons clattering on the sidewalk and being kicked away. He heard a growl and an almost simultaneous cry of pain, and then the six men were lowering themselves to the sidewalk in accordance with their orders; Juan, already crouching behind them, did the same. He figured the Azujos expected everyone to be unarmed, but he still had his weapon. Although the two-to-one odds were against him, surprise could be the equalizer. He flattened out like the others, but continued to hold the weapon strategically aimed toward the hooded figures. Seeing their captives in a submissive position, the Azujos with the light-shooter lowered his weapon slightly as the two approached the prone figures. Juan held in the lower button on the side as he made a sweeping motion across the captors' mid-sections, *puuuht!* The constant light beam severed the hooded captors in two and they immediately fell to the sidewalk, screams still in their throats.

The attack happened so quickly, nobody but Juan realized what was happening until they looked up to see the Azujos fall and heard their weapon rattle on the sidewalk.

"Get up and grab your guns," Juan instructed in a quiet, but confident voice. "I think we should get into that open building across the street." Mack, Mason, Bobby, and Jake retrieved their guns and walked as quickly as possible across the street while helping Nathan and the bearded man. "Let's go." Juan took the girl's hand, and helped her to her feet before following the others.

Once inside, they climbed a ramp to the second floor and positioned themselves by the windows. It was a comparatively small building consisting of two rooms on the first floor and one large room on the second. The ramp rose gently to a landing, turned 180°, rose gently to a second landing, turned 180° and continued upward, emerging onto the second floor through a gaping rectangular opening that didn't have a safety railing around it. The room appeared to be unfinished and was totally open. Nowhere to hide.

Bobby, holding his shoulder, was kneeling over Mack who was sitting, leaning against a wall. "How are you doin'? How bad you hurt?"

"I'll be all right Bobby ... don't worry," Mack answered with a grimace while holding the front of his rapidly darkening shirt.

"It sounded like someone got hurt down there, was it you, Mr. MacKensie?" Juan asked after picking up on the exchange between Bobby and Mack.

"Yeah, one of them clawed me."

"Clawed you, why?"

"Don't know. Maybe we were too slow ... obeying their orders." Mack replied in obvious pain.

The room was becoming darker by the minute; soon they wouldn't be able to see each other, but for now there was a little light.

"Let me see the wound before it gets too dark." Jake said. Mack lowered his hands while Jake knelt beside him and opened his sliced shirt, revealing four parallel slashes running diagonally across his chest. Jake quickly removed his outer shirt and used it to cover the wound, and then said, "Mr. Bankowski, I need your belt." Mason removed his belt and Jake wrapped it around Mack's chest to hold the shirt in place.

"That should stop the bleeding; keep some pressure on it to speed clotting," Jake said before resuming his station by one of the four windows in the room. Mason stationed himself by another, Juan by the third and Bobby by the fourth, each trying to remain hidden while watching the streets below. Jake had placed Nathan beside him and Mason did likewise with the bearded man, who was still attempting to stand.

"Hey," whispered Mason. "You'd best stay down; we don't wanta let'm know where we are." The man complied and resumed his place along the wall and a period of silence followed.

Ronni was worried. Mack and Bobby knew better than to be out after dark, and so far they hadn't returned even though the sun was setting. She wanted them back. The two of them, along with Scotty had kept her sane through the hard times. They were understanding and caring, and had helped her with Davy; they were people she could count on, family. Now there was a growing knot in the pit of her stomach as she watched for some sign of them.

This had been a bad day, starting with Davy's behavior. She thought he was aware of the dangers outside and that he should only go out under her supervision, but he had left the building this afternoon. She was sure that her retrieving him had attracted the strangers' attention, which ultimately led to their arrival. She was frightened when she saw unfamiliar people walking with guns, so she grabbed Davy, hurried into the building, and then alerted Mack. He set the trap that captured the strangers. As much as her heart ached for the man who said he was looking for his son, she still didn't want Mack and Bobby to go out there; it was too dangerous, especially now with the advancing darkness. This was all too familiar, she thought as a shiver ran up her spine, remembering the night Tom was killed. What a wonderful husband and father he was, only to die trying to save their only child. She could see why the stranger was so desperate, but in a way she hated him for putting Mack and Bobby in serious danger.

To make matters worse, one of the strangers stayed behind and was unabashedly flirting with her. He was younger than her, handsome, well built, and intelligent. Allen Cranston was a man most females would fight over, but there was something that made her want to keep him at a distance; his eyes, there was something about his eyes, a coldness that was evident even while smiling. She couldn't help thinking that he was hiding something ... something evil.

She watched Cranston out of the corner of her eye, making sure he wasn't close as she continued to watch the streets below for Mack and Bobby.

"Check this out!" urged Juan quietly. "Look down in the street." Mason positioned himself to unobtrusively look through his window at the street below. Bobby and Jake slid over to Juan's window to gaze over his shoulder. Juan felt a hand on his shoulder, warming the area beneath it and causing him to look up to see the girl. She was leaning on him while looking through the window. In the dark street below several shadows had gathered around the dead bodies, some appeared to be looking around while others lifted the bodies and carried them off. The remaining ones huddled and then slowly dispersed in all directions.

"My God," whispered Jake. "It looks like they're starting a systematic search!"

"What'll we do?" asked Mason.

Jake thought a moment before answering, "It's dark in here. Let's position ourselves around the room facing the ramp. If we remain still, he ... or it, won't be able to see us until it's too late. Juan, you better get him with that light thing you have because everything else we have will make noise and attract others. What do you think?"

Barely able to see each other in the darkness, they grunted their approval and moved to scattered positions about the room, most squatting to provide the least target area as possible. Juan decided to lie down on his stomach, aiming the light-shooter where the intruder would be after ascending the ramp, finger on the side button ready to fire. Jake flattened against the wall to the right of the ramp, revolver ready. Mack, too weak to do much had given his shotgun to Mason, who stood motionless to the left of the ramp. The bearded man, Nathan, Bobby, and the girl sat separated along the wall farthest from the ramp.

Everyone tensed and remained motionless, holding their

collective breath as they heard footsteps approaching from below. Juan wished the room wasn't quite this dark so he could take better aim. The footsteps were cautiously approaching the top, and since there was no barrier or railing around the ramp entrance, he visualized a clean shot to where the intruder should be at that moment. As he was about to press the fire button, a light pulse hit the weapon, propelling it from his hands; he felt a stinging pain in his right hand and forearm. This was followed by the characteristic *puht*, and then another *puht* toward the far wall followed by a grunt of pain. Juan rolled to his left as a light pulse hit where he had been a moment before, followed by the *puht*.

Mason silently stood while moving behind the attacker and swung the shotgun like a baseball bat about head high; a sound that was a combination crack and whump resulted, and the intruder crumpled to the floor. "Take *that* you sonofabitch!" he swore in a barely audible whisper. Everyone remained quiet, listening for any sound that might indicate that the unconscious Azujos was not alone. Hearing nothing, they relaxed enough to assess the damage.

"Is everybody okay?" solicited Jake urgently, fearing Nathan may have been hit.

Juan, trying to regain feeling in his right hand by rapidly shaking it, as if attempting to dislodge a foreign substance, said he was fine.

"I'm okay but I think this guy's not doin' so good," responded a voice that seemed to come from the bearded man.

Jake made his way toward the voice and nearly tripped over him. He knelt and tried to make out who the slumped figure was, finally determining it was Bobby. "Bobby, can you hear me?"

"Uhhnn," came the weak reply.

"Where are you hit?" Silence.

"Bobby, can you hear me? Where were you hit?" Silence. Jake felt his neck and found no pulse. "He's dead. Anyone else hit? Nathan?"

"I'm okay," replied a voice to Jake's right.

"Me too," echoed a female voice.

Mack lamented in a weak voice, "Bobby, aw Bobby..." but he didn't finish what he intended to say as one hand moved from applying pressure on his makeshift dressing to his eyes, thankful for the darkness.

Jake felt his way to the prostrate Azujos. He pulled the figure's hands behind his back and used his belt to tie them, and then forced a handkerchief into his mouth. "I need another belt, any volunteers?"

Juan handed Jake his belt and then felt around for the intruder's light-shooter. Figuring his previous one was damaged, he wanted one that was definitely in working order in case of any further confrontations. He then slid across the floor to his station by the window where the girl joined him, sitting against the wall. Jake used the additional belt to bind the intruder's legs, removed his t-shirt and tied it around the intruder's head and mouth to keep the gag in. Satisfied that the unconscious figure would be rendered immobile when he came to, Jake scooted to his window station. Mason returned to his station to find the bearded man already there.

"Give me a gun," the man whispered. "I feel strong enough now." Mason felt around on the floor until he found Bobby's revolver and held it out for the man, grip first. "Thanks." He said, then moved to the next window and assumed Bobby's station.

During the next hour several shadowy figures were observed passing through the street below their vantage point, seemingly in the direction of the stadium, but none showed the least overt interest in searching any of the surrounding buildings, allowing those on guard to relax a little.

Breaking the silence that permeated the room since the attack, the bearded man spoke quietly, "I want to thank you for rescuing me earlier. I thought I was a dead man."

"Don't mention it," responded Mason not turning away from the window, "I'm glad ya're feelin' better. By the way, my name's Mason Bankowski."

"Mine's Callahan, David Callahan, and the girl's Skye Delaney. The other two people back there, the dead ones, they were captured with Skye and me; all four of us at the same time."

Mason thought a few moments before responding, "Callahan, where've I heard that name? Wait a minute, yeah, that's the same name as a pleasure boat captain I talked to on th' radio a coupla days ago; yeah, captain of th' *Blue Heron*."

"You the captain of *Oblique View*? I thought you bought it in the storm when I couldn't see or raise you on the radio after the fog lifted. By the way, that wasn't a couple of days ago; it was more like eight months."

Chapter 24

Manny couldn't understand it; his charm and good looks had never failed him before. This woman was different, aloof, not showing the least bit of interest in him whatsoever. A few years older than he, she was very attractive with a nice shape, around five-six, shoulder length hair, and hazel eyes. She could be a knockout if she fixed herself up a little, did something with her hair and wore something better than the plain faded dresses that seemed to be the staple of her wardrobe. If she would just give him a chance, he knew he could show her a good time, but she wouldn't permit him the least foothold, nothing. He even tried playing with her son to show what a good guy he was, but she kept calling Davy over to her as if she was afraid he would do something to him. She was so occupied, always looking out the window, and the old Scot was asleep in the corner or else he would show her how good he could be. Well, sometime in the near future he *would* have her, and the bitch would damn well enjoy it. That was a promise ... and Manny *always* kept promises he made to himself.

Jake awakened, but had trouble focusing because of the brightness. Shielding his eyes, he realized the sun was blazing through a window into his face. He quickly surveyed the room and saw that, with the exception of Bobby, they had survived the night and it looked as if everyone was sound asleep. He rose to his knees and peered out the window on empty streets.

"Hey, everyone," he called loud enough to wake them. "It's morning, the sun's up and we're safe." There was moaning and stretching, yawning and scratching, and finally most of them rose to their feet.

Jake was relieved to see Nathan stand and stretch. "How are you feeling?" he asked.

"I feel pretty good now," answered Nathan. "I don't want to go through that again!"

"Don't worry, that *won't* happen again; I promise. I'm just glad we found you in time. We'll talk about it later." He then scrutinized the room, which looked different, smaller than he had imagined it in the darkness last night. He observed Mack trying to stand and Bobby's body with a burn mark on the front of his shirt, just below his heart. Jake felt deep sadness, seeing how this man who had been a stranger a few short hours ago had given his life helping to rescue his son. He offered up a silent prayer on Bobby's behalf.

The prisoner still appeared unconscious, but Jake wanted to get some answers from him now that he knew they spoke in English. Walking over to him, Jake rolled him onto his back expecting him to thrash about, but he was limp. Feeling for a pulse and finding none, he swore to himself.

"Our prisoner is dead," he said, standing. "He must have died sometime during the night because I was sure he was alive when I tied him up."

Juan walked over to the body and suggested they have a close look at him. Removing his shirt, gag, and both belts, Jake threw them aside and helped remove the hood. The Azujos' face was long and narrow, with a slightly open mouth exposing the characteristic pointed teeth they had witnessed before. Rolling back an eyelid exposed a pale blue-violet eye, but they saw no eyebrows. His skin was a pasty light gray and his head was covered with patches of thin straggly long hair, reminding Jake of his Aunt Marjorie when her chemotherapy caused huge clumps of hair to fall out. His hands had four fingers and an opposable thumb like their own, but the digits were thick, scaly, and ended in fingernails that resembled short thick claws.

"I don't get it," pondered Jake quietly to the few standing close while pulling on his t-shirt. "These are obviously humans with a language, but they have animal characteristics, seem to be able to see in the dark ... and they're cannibals. How could something like this evolve?"

Juan agreed, "Yeah, this guy sure *could* see in the dark. Do you remember how dark it was in here last night when this freak showed up? He didn't hesitate at all; he made three quick shots, the first one knocked the weapon right out of my hands, the second hit Bobby dead on, and the third was right where I had been a moment before. Three shots, two hits and almost a third, and it wasn't like we were standing next to each other and he just lucked out; Bobby was half way across the room! Besides, why would he shoot at me a second time unless he knew he didn't get me the first time; he had to see me moving."

"You're right, come to think of it," agreed Jake. "But is that the reason they only emerge after dark? Maybe the light *hurts* their eyes." He paused for a moment lost in thought, and then continued, "But what about the two that Captain Bankowski killed at the stadium? It wasn't dark yet and they were there."

"Maybe it had somethin' to do with th' goggles they were wearin'." suggested Mason, overhearing the conversation.

"What goggles?" asked Jake.

"When I shot'em, I saw one was wearin' dark goggles an' when I stepped over 'em, I saw th' other one was wearin' 'em too."

"So," surmised Juan. "The light *must* hurt their eyes. That's good to know; makes things a whole lot easier to move in the daylight. Let's take his hooded robe; you never know, it might come in handy sometime." They rolled the corpse in order to free up the garment for removal. Beneath the robe was a jumpsuit type of garment made of a charcoal-colored elasticized material.

"Well, just when you think they're more animal than human, you find out they have tailors," remarked Jake. "What will they surprise us with next?"

Mack stumbled toward them. "I suggest we get back to the apartment. Ronni and Scotty will be worried."

Jake turned toward him and asked, "How's that wound?"

"I'll survive. The bleedin' stopped. Let's go."

Mack led the way down the ramp, Mason followed with Bobby over his shoulder, Jake waited for Nathan and fell in beside him while Callahan, Skye, and Juan brought up the rear.

"Thank you for protecting me," Skye said bashfully to Juan as they walked down the ramp.

It was the first words she had spoken to him, and for the moment he felt better than he had for days. "I didn't do much, and besides you're worth it." As soon as the words escaped his lips he wanted them back; what he said was stupid, and he was suddenly flustered.

She smiled at him and said, "What a nice thing to say. Thank you." He felt a little better.

"There they are!" exclaimed Ronni as she first glimpsed the figures heading toward her on the street below. Then as she ran from the room, "They're back, Scotty!"

The sudden calamity jarred Scotty from a deep sleep and he dropped the long-barreled revolver that was resting on his lap. Shaking his head to clear the cobwebs, he picked up the weapon and started after Ronni, murmuring to himself, "Tho's na way to wakin' suumwon, Lossie."

Davy was asleep on his bed and heard nothing; Manny

was wakened by Ronni's excitement, but ignored it and pretended to still be asleep.

Ronni ran from the building to meet the party and stopped abruptly, hands over her mouth with fear as she noticed a body slung over another's shoulder. She quickly assessed the group and was relieved to see that Mack, even though apparently wounded, was walking without aid. Her fears were then justified as she realized the body was that of Bobby. She ran to Mason and rubbed her hand over Bobby's back. "Oh Bobby, not you Bobby," she whispered with tears streaming down both cheeks. She buried her face in his shirt.

Mason paused for Ronni's grieving, and then resumed his march toward the apartment building; reaching it, he carefully laid the body on the sidewalk alongside the steps. Ronni had turned her attention to Mack who was seated on the steps. She removed Jake's shirt to reveal four nasty looking wounds.

"We better get you inside and clean those," she said in an even tone, showing none of the emotion she had exhibited a few minutes earlier, although her face was still flushed and wet. "I'm glad you made it back; I was so worried about you."

"Yeah, we were worried too," he responded. "But I think we better bury Bobby before we do anything else."

Scotty, who had remained in the main doorway, volunteered, "I'll get suumthin' to dig with," and retreated into the building. A couple of minutes passed before he returned with a piece of driftwood, shaped into a scoop at one end.

Mason again hoisted Bobby onto his shoulder and followed Mack, with the others close behind. They were closer to the ocean than any of the newcomers had realized, and after only two blocks found themselves at the base of the nearest sand dune, this one approximately ten feet high. Mason started to dig and before long was sweating profusely and wiping his head with a handkerchief. "Let me help with that," volunteered Callahan. "After all, this man helped rescue me and it's the least I can do for him." Mason gladly handed him the shovel before walking a short distance to the nearest building, searching for shade.

Callahan dug for a while and was relieved by Juan, and finally by Jake. Nathan stood by, arms crossed and watched with Skye, Ronni and Mack. When the hole was considered deep enough, Bobby was lowered carefully to Juan and Jake inside the hole. They placed him gently on the bottom, folding his hands across his chest, and then crawled out.

Mack stepped forward and bowed his head, all those watching followed suit. "Lord, none of us know why, in your infinite wisdom you brought us to this fearful place; this place of hardship and loneliness, this place of strife and heartache, but we understand it must be in your plan. Please take care of Bobby; gather him into your eternal arms. He was a good man, a warrior, a friend to all. We loved him like a brother, so welcome his spirit into your loving home. Amen." After a pause, he added, "We'll miss you Bobby

Blackhorn ... We'll miss you." He and Ronni turned away as the others began to bury the body.

"Are ya gonna put up a cross or somethin'?" asked Mason as Mack and Ronni started to walk back to the apartment.

"No," answered Mack over his shoulder. "We don't want the Azujos to know where the body is." They continued to walk.

Chapter 25

Once in the apartment, Ronni cleaned and dressed Mack's wounds with some medical supplies remaining from the plane. While she was treating Mack, the others tried to sort out what brought them to this juncture. Callahan told of a couple of his passengers who just had to look for a certain item one evening on *Blue Heron*, so he and Skye accompanied them. They stayed too long and night fell before they could make it back to camp, an apartment building similar to their present setting. They were captured by the Azujos and taken to the stadium, where they were forcibly drugged. They didn't know much more until the rescue, even though Skye's drug had pretty much worn off by that time.

Mason listened intently and waited until he finished his story before asking, "What 'bout th' rest o' yar passengers? I remember ya sayin' ya had maybe 'bout ten or so on board."

Callahan looked toward the ceiling as he tried to picture each one, "Well, the two dead ones were married, Toni and

Stanley Pulham; everyone else is still alive. Stanley was a pain in the ass but his wife was nice, sorry to lose her. There are, let's see, four females remaining, Amy Kaufman, a teacher, and three college students: Kesha Woods, Audryan Heppbrun, and Skye, who you've already met. There's one remaining male passenger, Carl Fontaine; he's a little strange..."

"He's not strange," interrupted Skye. "He's just kinda shy. I don't think he ever did much before the trip. He was some kind of banker or accountant or something."

"Okay, but he seems strange to me, always keeping to himself. Anyway, I still have two crew members: Veni Fassenetti and Darryl Johns, my first mate and engineer, respectively."

"Ya made mention last night that ya came outta th' fog 'bout eight months ago, right?" continued Mason. "What happened when ya came out?" The mention of when *Blue Heron* emerged from the fog caused Jake, Nathan, Manny, and Juan to exchange glances.

"That's right. It was what, two hundred fifty one ... two hundred fifty three days now. I needed to add the day spent in captivity and today. We kept count by putting marks on a wall. I remember because I counted them before we went back to *Blue Heron* that afternoon."

"*We* came out of the fog two days ago," interjected Juan incredulously. "How can we both be out there at the same time in the same fog, and yet come ashore eight months apart? It doesn't make sense!"

"None of this makes much sense," said Jake. "First, both boats are mysteriously transported two hundred seventy-some odd years into the future."

"How far did you say?" Callahan interrupted with a quizzical expression.

"We're in the year 2283," explained Jake. "So that means we jumped two hundred seventy eight years into the future, why?"

"We knew something like that happened, because nothing was the same as before the trip, and there were no people, as if the entire state of Florida had been evacuated, but we didn't know how *far* into the future. I had no idea it was *that* far. How do you know the year for certain?"

"We found how to operate the computer system in a home where we stayed after coming ashore. Anyway, as I was saying, two boats leave the same area at the same time and are both transported through time into the future, but arrive eight months apart. No, it doesn't make sense. The only explanation I can think of is that we came through two different rips in the fabric of time to the same location. Maybe the storm and fog opened wormholes, you know, momentary pathways to a different time and place. If that happened, then we came through separate ones that opened to the same place but different time. A physicist could probably explain it better, but since there isn't one present, I guess that will have to do." After a few moments of silence, he continued, "And look at *these* people who boarded a plane in 1965 and ended up here about three years ago. It happened, for whatever reason; now we all have to live with it."

A full minute of awkward silence followed while most in the room tried to digest Jake's explanation. Skye and Juan then started their own conversation in one corner of the room while Mason continued to prod Callahan for information.

"Tell us 'bout yarself, I mean b'fore gettin' lost here."

"I'm a retired policeman, detective to be precise from Pittsburgh. I got shot, off duty no less, when I happened to walk in on a convenience store robbery; just stopped in for a paper and almost bought the farm. After that, I just wanted out, took my pension and moved to Fort Lauderdale, bought *Blue Heron* and started a charter service. And you?"

Manny's idyllic situation began to crumble into panic when he heard the Pittsburgh policeman part. Had the ex-cop recognized him; after all, he had problems with lots of cops there. He figured it best to become as scarce as possible until this guy left. Standing quietly, he unobtrusively left the room as if to stretch his legs, and stood in the hallway just outside the door, listening.

"I was a welder," Mason responded to Callahan's question. "Joined th' union when I was sixteen, never finished school. Did alright for m'self, though; bought *Oblique View* an' had a good charter business goin'."

As the two captains continued to get acquainted, Jake migrated to Davy, quietly listening wide-eyed to the grown up conversations. This struck him as very uncharacteristic for a child of Davy's age.

"How you doing, sport?" he asked.

"Okay sir, and how are you doing?"

"Wow," said Jake. "You're quite the little man, aren't you? How old are you?"

"I'm six, sir."

"Six? See that young man sitting over there?" Jake asked, nodding his head toward Nathan, sitting alone on the other side of the room. "He's my son and I remember when he was your age. He was a good boy then, just like you are now." Davy smiled at this and shyly lowered his eyes.

"Davy, come here," ordered Ronni and the boy immediately left Jake and walked over to her. "Sit here by Mommy."

"But I want to talk to the man. He's nice."

"That's okay, leave the man alone and sit here."

Jake heard the exchange and felt awkwardly uncomfortable. She couldn't be blamed for being protective of her son, especially after recently losing her husband, but there was no threat here. Moving to another chair across the room, he sat beside Davy. "That's okay, little man; I'll sit by *you*." The move caused Ronni to become noticeably nervous, which Jake perceived immediately.

"Relax Mrs. Langham, I mean no harm. You have a remarkable son here and I just wanted to make his acquaintance."

Her tension seemed to subside a bit and she responded,

"I'm sorry; just a little overprotective, I guess." It might have been his imagination, but Jake thought she almost smiled.

"I was thinking about our situation here," he said, trying to find some neutral ground. "I would like to find out about the Azujos, what happened to the people that used to live here, and what happened in history between the time we left until now. I'm also curious about the news coverage concerning our disappearance; surely there was some kind of news coverage. Do you have any idea, or information on any of this, or where I can access that information?"

"I don't have much of an idea about that stuff, but I've sometimes wondered some of the same things," responded Ronni absently while getting out some dishes. "Trouble is, I don't know how you can get that kind of information."

"I bet we could learn a lot from a library; unless they've changed, they usually offer all kinds of information."

"I don't know of any libraries around here. Sorry."

"Excuse me, but I couldn't help overhearing," Skye apologized for intruding on the conversation. "There's a college close to our camp; if there's any place you could find what you're looking for, it'd be there."

"Yes, it would. Thanks," Jake said sincerely. "Can you take me there?"

"Make that us," Ronni volunteered, totally surprising Jake. "It would do Davy and me good to get out for awhile, as long as we're back long before dark."

"Be glad to," responded Skye. "I don't think it's too far away. What do you think, Captain Callahan?"

"What's that?" asked Callahan, hearing only the question but not the conversation that preceded it. "What isn't too far away?"

"The college that's close to our camp, how far from here?

"Don't rightly know," he pondered. "I haven't been in this part of the city before. Do you want to go there?"

"I do, er, we do," volunteered Jake. "I want to check some information about all this, and a college library would be the best place."

"Yeah, I can see that. Tell you what, we'll see about finding it this afternoon and if it gets too late to make it back by dark, you're welcome to stay the night in our camp."

"Fair enough."

"Let's eat first," Ronni said, a welcome suggestion to all.

Chapter 26

Ronni was preparing a meal of fried fish and roasted fowl, a bird of some type that happened to be in the wrong place at the right time yesterday morning and had to be used before it spoiled. Bread was also being computer prepared, and Ronni explained that it had been four months before she discovered how to use the computerized kitchen, even with basic instruction from Mrs. Foreman; one of the choices she found was *Baked Goods*. She had been apprehensive at first, not trusting the freshness of the ingredients, but after gathering the courage one day when other food was scarce, she found the bread to be not only palatable, but extremely flavorful. Without exception, the plane crash survivors living in the apartment building came to look forward to having the computer-prepared bread with their meals.

Hearing Jake describe the computer system in the house they occupied a couple of days ago led Ronni to demonstrate how *this* system worked. Jake was amazed at how easily she worked the system, which seemed similar to the one he had experience with. To begin with, the room didn't appear to have any food preparing apparatus, but as Ronni pressed a couple of lighted panels, shelf-like protrusions extended from the wall. She showed him the LED panel on the outside edge of each protrusion that permitted the cook to enter information about what food was to be prepared and the cook's preferences on how it should be done. The food item was set in the recessed top of the protrusion, which returned to its original position within the wall; when cooking was done, it extended from the wall to provide its offering. The system regulated cooking time and temperature through sensors. Another combination of pressing the lighted panels produced a small wall screen that Ronni explained was for baking. Touching strategic places on the LED panel instructed the system as to what baked good was being requested. She had yet to determine where the ingredients came from, but so far they hadn't run out. Jake said he regretted not having time to investigate his system further to determine if *it* could have supplied food of some type.

While the meal was being prepared, Scotty offered to let Callahan use his scissors and straight razor. Callahan jumped at the welcome offer, explaining that nobody packed any toiletries for a one-day ocean excursion. He and Mason followed Scotty to his room after being assured by Ronni that they had plenty of time until lunch would be served. Mack retired to his room to rest.

Jake looked around the room and saw Nathan sleeping on the bed while Skye and Juan entertained Davy with information about themselves.

"Where's Mr. Cranston?" questioned Jake.

"I don't know," responded Ronni without looking up. "He left a while ago, shortly after we came in."

"Did his ankle heal any?"

"I don't know," she replied, showing a total lack of interest. As much as she distrusted Cranston, she was beginning to like Jake; he seemed honest and his eyes weren't cold like Cranston's. Besides, he was demonstrating a genuine interest in Davy and her, and her interest in him was involuntarily growing, almost as if it had a mind of its own. Suddenly she realized where her thinking was headed and chastised herself; she couldn't have feelings for anyone, especially someone she knew nothing about, who showed up only a day ago, and had ultimately caused the death of a close friend. How stupid could she be! She was fine before he came and she would be fine long after he was gone. She had no idea what the future held, but she and Davy would do just fine without anyone else, especially this man.

Jake noticed a change in Ronni's demeanor, coldness that he hadn't seen since earlier when she didn't trust him with Davy. He studied her in silence for a few minutes and when he was sure it wasn't his imagination, asked, "Is something wrong?"

"No. Nothing." The answer was curt, without looking at him. Her voice didn't disclose anything but her body language fairly screamed at him.

"Can I do anything to help?" he asked, attempting to

close the psychological chasm that seemed to be growing by the minute. "With the meal, I mean."

"No. I've got it covered." Again, the reply was spoken to the food and not to him.

"Okay, I'll stay out of your way." Jake walked across the room and sat in a chair, crossed his arms and waited. It didn't matter to him, but for a while she seemed to be receptive to conversation and was even somewhat friendly; he was puzzled about what might have changed. From his present location he was close enough to hear Juan talking to Skye, Davy sitting cross-legged on the floor in front of them, listening with rapt attention.

" ... and I was supposed to help him move to Pensacola the next day. I feel like I let him down."

"You didn't let him down. You couldn't help what happened to you anymore than I could help what happened to us."

"So, how *did* you end up here?"

"My close friends, Kesha and Audryan and I were accepted to different colleges for the fall, so we decided to take a trip to Florida before starting classes in September. My parents were really against the trip, but Audryan helped me talk them into going along with it. She can be quite persuasive when she wants to. Once we got here the ocean trip was first on our agenda, just a time to relax and plan the rest of our vacation while soaking up some sun. Well, we've certainly had enough time to talk, so much that we've even gotten on each other's nerves at times. So you see, I could say I let *my* parents down, but I know better. Unfortunately, I've thought long and hard about what they went through thinking we were lost at sea.

"Yeah, and without a trace; I've thought about that too. It had to be terrible on them."

After a brief silence, Skye continued, "So, you said you were going to be a junior next year; you seem older."

"Yeah, I'm sixteen, and I suppose you're eighteen or nineteen since you graduated in June."

"Actually, I was one of the youngest in my class; I won't be eighteen until next week. I think so, depending on what date it really is now."

"In fact, if you really think about it, we're both around three hundred years old." The unexpected absurdity of their situation caused both to chuckle.

Skye abruptly stood and walked to Ronni who was continuing lunch preparations, and when she was close enough, whispered, "Where is the bathroom? I need to go."

"It's over there in that corner." Ronni indicated the far left corner of the room. Noticing the concern on Skye's face, seeing that the area indicated was totally visible from everywhere in the room, she smiled, "Don't worry, all you have to do is press the triangle on the wall and you'll have all the privacy you want."

Skye walked self-consciously to the corner and found a black triangle on the wall that was about an inch on each side. She pressed it and watched in amazement as opaque walls appeared and a low toilet and sink rose through the floor. She prepared and tentatively lowered herself onto the toilet, feeling much better when she found it to be sturdy and unmoving. After finishing, she searched for paper only to be surprised by a quick burst of fresh water from below, followed by forced warm air, which lasted until she was dry. Feeling much better, she rose, re-dressed and placed her hands under the sink faucet. Water and soap streamed onto her hands, changing to just water. The water stopped and warm air poured from the faucet as she rubbed her hands until dry and then removed them, which shut off the air. She prepared to leave but the walls blocked her exit. She touched the triangle and watched the toilet and sink lower into the floor and the walls disappear.

"That was amazing! Anybody else need to use the bathroom?" Juan and Jake took turns, followed by Nathan who was now awake. During Jake's turn, he recalled the black triangles set in the wall at their previous house and realized bathroom facilities had been available there too, if only they had known.

Scotty re-entered the room followed by Mason and Callahan, both with fresh haircuts and clean-shaven. Callahan's deeply tanned and craggy-featured face stood in contrast to the clean white shirt obviously loaned by Mack. "Wow, you guys look handsome!" Ronni complimented both with a huge smile, causing a slight twinge of jealousy from Jake. He quickly regretted this irrational emotion. "Lunch is ready; let's eat!" she announced, and pressed the lighted panels prompting a large table and ten chairs to rise from the floor. About that time, Mack wandered in, yawning.

Ronni sat at one end with Davy to her right; continuing counter clockwise was Skye, Juan, Mason, Callahan, Mack, Scotty, Nathan, and Jake. "Where's Mr. Cranston?" inquired Juan.

"Maybe he's takin' a nap," speculated Mason. "I'll get 'im." He left the table, walked into the hallway and yelled, "Hey, Mr. Cranston! Lunch is ready!" After about ten seconds of silence he tried again, "Mr. Cranston? You hear me? Food's on! Come an' get it!" Still no answer.

"He musta stepped out; let's eat," Mason remarked upon re-entering the room and took his seat.

They were about to eat when Jake asked if he could say grace, which caused some to self-consciously lower their eating utensils while exchanging glances to verify others were doing the same. After bowing their heads, Jake prayed, "Dear Lord, I want to thank you for helping us to free Nathan, David, and Skye from the clutches of these evil creatures. We thank you also for delivering us safely and acquainting us with these wonderful people. We ask that you have mercy on Bobby, who unselfishly gave his life that others would survive, and finally we ask that you continue to guide us in this difficult time. We also ask your blessing on this food, so thoughtfully and graciously prepared, and on those who prepared it. We ask in Jesus' name. Amen."

Ronni, with moisture welling in her eyes reached over and squeezed Jake's hand, whispering, "Thank you." A few others seated around the table nodded their heads in agreement while Juan, Callahan and Mack crossed themselves. They began to eat, some ravenously.

Manny remained hidden in the room he commandeered earlier, a room that already had a bed and a couch. He was hungry but didn't want to be anywhere around the Pittsburgh cop, who he was sure would recognize him if given enough time. He heard Captain Bankowski calling, but decided it was best to stay put and remain quiet. It wasn't the first time he had gone hungry, and he could eat later; right now it best served Manny to hide and listen to what was going on with the others. His time would come; he would survive.

Chapter 27

The meal was a hit; Jake, not a seafood fan, couldn't remember when fish tasted so good. As the diners finished, small conversations broke out.

Callahan turned to Mason and asked, "Where's your boat now?"

"North, 'bout ... " Mason concentrated, "I don't know. It took us 'bout five or six hours but we were walkin' at night; I figure maybe three, four hours in daylight. Why?"

"I don't think it's a good idea to leave it there. I think it would be best if we brought it down here."

"Yeah, I agree, but we don't have time since ya're goin' to head to that college."

"Can I have everybody's attention?" Callahan asked, interrupting the individual conversations. "I have a suggestion. I don't really know how far it is to our camp and the college nearby, but I can readily find *Blue Heron* from the sea. I think Captain Bankowski and I should hike back to his boat and sail it to where mine is moored, stopping on the way to pick up whoever of you that wants to go along."

"That sounds like a good idea," agreed Jake. "But I don't think you two should hike it alone. I'll go too."

"Me too," volunteered Juan. "I'm with you."

"Okay, that makes four," counted Callahan, standing. "If we leave now, we'll be back before dark. When we return we can make the decision to continue south or to spend the night and make the trip in the morning. Agreed?"

All three nodded in agreement and rose to join him.

"Skye turned to Ronni, "If it's okay with you, I'll stay and help you and Davy?"

"I'd love to have you."

Jake also addressed Ronni, "Could you please watch out for Nathan while I'm gone? I lost him once and I don't want to lose him again."

She smiled and said, "Sure, I'll watch him." Thinking further, she added, "And please be careful … I mean, he needs his father so make sure you come back for him." As soon as the words were out, she realized that might not be the only reason she wanted him to come back.

He nodded, and turned to join the other three who were gathering weapons in preparation for the trip. Mack and Scotty agreed to remain behind to guard the apartment and watched the four men leave.

Manny, listening from inside his room, heard Callahan's proposal, and in a few minutes heard some of them leave. After they passed his room, he poked his head out to make sure Callahan was among those who left. Content that he was safe for a while, he walked to the room where the remainder of the group was talking and cleaning up after the meal. Entering the room, he yawned widely. "Oh, I'm sorry, did I miss lunch?"

Skye was surprised at his entrance and said, "Yes, but there are some leftovers; you're welcome to them. Have a seat and I'll get something for you." Ronni turned away and rolled her eyes; *she* wasn't going to offer him *anything*.

"Why thank you; I'll take you up on that generous offer," he said, sitting down at the table. Skye gathered some of the fish and looked around for some bread, not noticing Ronni quickly hiding it in a compartment.

"Here you go," Skye said with a smile, placing a plate of fish in front of him. "I guess we finished the bread, but at least there's some fish left. Eat up."

Manny had to restrain himself from shoveling the food; he didn't want them to know how hungry he really was. The food was very tasty and he ate his fill.

"Thank you for the magnificent feast," he exaggerated, but thought he was being gracious. "I think I'll go rest for a while." Quickly exiting the room, he was relieved to be alone again; the past couple of hours had reminded him how much he didn't really like being around these people. He had gone along with them only because of circumstances, but he was tired of pretending. Soon it would be time to claim his prize; he was sure she would grow to like being with him.

Scotty and Mack paused their conversation long enough to observe Manny's entrance and the ensuing drama of Skye attempting to be the perfect hostess; they also witnessed Ronni's obvious indifference, something totally foreign to her character. Scotty chuckled silently and raised one eyebrow in Mack's direction, to which he acknowledged, smiling slightly.

After his departure, Scotty waited an adequate time to make sure Manny wasn't in earshot, then called to Ronni, "Lossie, would ye cuum herrre forrr a wee minute."

Ronni put the last of the plates in a compartment, closed it and approached her friends. "Yes, and what can I do for you, you grouchy old Scotsman?" she asked with a warm smile.

Looking to make sure Skye and Nathan, who were engaged in conversation weren't close enough to hear, he stated quietly, "Ye don't much like Misterrr Crrranston, do ye?"

"I don't really *dislike* him, but there's something about him I don't trust," she said. She considered leaving it at that, but decided to confide in her friends. "He seems friendly and a nice enough guy, but I don't like his eyes ... they don't match his demeanor. In a way, he gives me the creeps."

Scotty and Mack exchanged knowing looks and then Mack confessed, "I haven't been close enough to see what you have, but I *did* notice how quickly he left this room earlier. It was like he was afraid of something. I agree, we should keep an eye on him."

"Thank you; you're both very dear friends," she offered. "And Bobby was too; I'm so sorry he's gone."

"Aye, Lossie, we arrre too."

The quartet of hikers left the apartment and retraced the path all but Callahan had taken about thirty hours previously. After about three quarters of an hour they located where they had left one of the dead Azujos; the body was gone and several sets of footprints desecrated the area. Jake walked toward the ocean, climbed the dune and scanned the beach as far as he could see.

"No body on the beach; either it was carted off or the tide took it."

"How would they know about the dead bodies?" queried Juan. "I mean, so they could come and get them."

Jake rejoined the group in time to field the question, "The one that got away and took Nathan might have communicated the location to them. These creatures are pretty intelligent; we have to be wary. And who knows, even though we haven't seen evidence of communication devices doesn't mean they don't use them."

"Well, let's get going," urged Callahan. "We need to find your boat and get back as soon as possible."

"Ya're right," agreed Mason, resuming his trek. "Let's go."

Two hours later they reached the domed house that had briefly served as their home. Seeing many sets of tracks around the house and the open doorway caused Mason and Jake to bring their handguns to the ready; Callahan, sensing their tension, raised his weapon also. Juan readied his light-shooter and turned his back on the house, alert for any unusual motion in the surrounding area.

Callahan stepped in front of Mason as he was about to enter the doorway. "Let me take this one." His police training kicked in as he entered the house, alternately peering around corners into unchecked rooms and extending his weapon at arms length as he entered. After about five minutes he emerged, holding his weapon loosely by his side. "It's clear."

Mason and Jake entered and found the empty coolers in disarray. "Looks like they were hungry," Jake stated simply.

They exited the building and joined Juan as he started toward the beach. Mason crested the dune and was thankful to see *Oblique View*, still at anchor. A few minutes walk along the beach brought them to the raft that remained hidden in the dunes, exactly where Juan had left it. They dragged the raft into the surf, and crawled over the side one at a time until all four were aboard. Juan rowed them to the anchored vessel. Once aboard, Juan raised the anchor while Mason started the engines. Juan checked on the marlin, but found only shredded remains.

"Looks like Nathan's marlin was shark bait. Too bad, I bet Ronni could have made many meals out of it," he said. Jake examined the carcass, recalling Nathan's pride on landing it, and felt remorse … on many levels.

The sky was overcast as *Oblique View* moved along the coastline, presenting a different perspective for Jake as he recalled what had occurred while trailing Juan's captors, the attack on the beach, and Nathan's abduction. The land seemed so serene, and what had transpired there now seemed surreal. He was thankful that Nathan had been rescued and was safe, now under the watchful eyes of Mack, Scotty, and Ronni.

Ronni's face entered his mind, but he deliberately suppressed the vision. Another time and different circumstances might have permitted him to savor the image and the thoughts that accompanied it. He *did* allow himself to shift his focus to Davy. Such a young man at such an early age; what kind of future could he look forward to? Living in a desolate area with intelligent cannibals roaming the streets was not a comforting thought. Maybe there were options however, that Jake wasn't aware of; but then again, maybe not.

They passed the first parts of the city and soon located their destination. Juan dropped anchor and the quartet rowed to shore in the raft. After beaching the raft, they made their way to the apartment building and went in. Knocking at Ronni's door, they were greeted by Scotty. "Cuum in," he invited with a huge smile. Jake couldn't help reflecting on how much had taken place since the first time he entered this door … and how different the reception was now.

They entered and Jake immediately searched for Nathan, who was watching Skye talk with Davy. Ronni gave a brief smile on seeing him and reported, "All's fine here, glad you all made it. Any trouble?"

"No," responded Jake. "But we found evidence of a prolonged visit from our snaggle-toothed friends. Luckily, nobody was home at the time. It looked as if they were searching for us."

"I don't want to interrupt this cheerful homecoming, but we need to decide whether we're going to continue south to our camp now or in the morning," suggested Callahan.

Jake responded quickly, "I really want to get a handle on what's happened here so I vote to leave now." Mason and Juan agreed, and together with Callahan and Skye, started for the door. Jake turned to Ronni, "You and Davy coming?"

She replied, "No. Davy's not feeling the greatest so we better stay put."

"Okay. Take good care of him."

Nathan stood and said, "If it's okay I'd like to go too."

"Sure. I was hoping you would."

As Jake turned to leave, Ronni said, "Wait a minute." Retrieving a piece of paper and the nub of a pencil, she wrote a long number and handed it to him. "That's my videocom number; call me with what you find out. I really want to know."

Jake looked at the number, 344725487021, and saw it contained the required twelve digits Nathan had told him about. At least he knew where this number would connect him. "Thanks. I will." Then he left the room to catch the others.

Chapter 28

The mid-afternoon sun was hazy hot when it occasionally peeked through low-lying clouds during the fifteen-minute ride to *Blue Heron's* mooring; Jake realized it would have taken much longer on foot. Callahan was right about this being the best way to find his camp because *Blue Heron* was easy to locate, moored to the remnants of a sturdy dock. As *Oblique View* glided into a nearby slip, Juan scrambled onto the dock and proceeded to tie off fore and aft. After disembarking, Callahan prepared to lead everyone to the rest of his party, but Jake hesitated.

"Skye, you said the college was close by, didn't you?"

"Yes, it's just over there, why?"

"Would you be willing to take me there and then lead me back to your camp later? The sun's past its zenith and I want to finish before dark."

"Sure, I'd be glad to. Captain Callahan!" she called, and when he turned toward her, "I'm going to take Mr. Myers to the college; we'll meet you back at camp before dark. Tell my friends I'll see them later."

"Okay, be careful." He resumed his trek with Mason and Juan while Nathan held back with his father.

"This way," Skye directed as she headed off. Seven minutes later they arrived on the campus of Southeast Coastal University and headed for the library, as indicated by a marquee containing a large faded campus map located at the entrance.

Once inside, they located the area housing historical documents but were faced with a new dilemma: how to retrieve information with technology that was foreign to them. Jake was dumbfounded, but Skye and Nathan set to work trying one thing after another. Finally, a message screen appeared, seemingly suspended in mid-air. Choices were presented and with Jake's input they chose *World History: Twenty-first and Twenty-second Centuries*.

In the first eight decades, *2001-2080*, history was about what Jake had expected: tensions between countries worsened, governments created and changed allies, and wars broke out between nations he expected and some that surprised him. One development that caught his attention was that within a mere fifteen years of their disappearance, newspapers had all been phased out and replaced with electronic distribution directly to homes. The next two decades, however, were vastly different. In the decades *2081-2100*, he discovered that tensions had escalated to the point where nuclear weapons, in conjunction with something called *Bio-Sonic Distribution Systems* were used with devastating results in 2086, obliterating

London, Moscow, Cairo, Jerusalem, Seoul, and several U.S. cities, including New York, Washington DC, Chicago, Los Angeles, Seattle, and Houston. The abundance of nuclear shocks on the fragile earth's crust caused numerous earthquakes, volcanic eruptions, and tsunamis along with a proliferation of other natural disasters. Between the explosions, radiation, natural disasters, and thirteen years of nuclear winter, fully two thirds of life on earth, both flora and fauna perished.

"That's scary!" exclaimed Nathan after he and Skye had watched the presentation wide-eyed. "So, we just zipped by all that?" he asked tentatively.

"It seems so," replied Jake. "I'm glad we didn't have to try to live through it."

"Yeah, me too," added Skye.

"Let's continue," suggested Jake. "I still haven't found the answers I'm looking for." Nathan glanced at Skye, and followed her lead as she nodded agreement.

The decades *2101-2120* showed events had calmed down, the only memorable incident coming in April 2104 when all governments, needing so much help following the worldwide disasters, were merged into one government for the entire world. There were no longer separate nations, just the *United Nations*. Although individual governments ceased to exist, local languages persisted in their original locales. Each former country contained one central governmental agency, subservient to the world's government headquarters in Rome. The former United States had its main government facility located in St. Louis with regional branches situated in New Hampshire, Georgia, Texas, and Oregon.

Skye pondered this information and murmured in amazement, "The United States ceased to exist almost one hundred eighty years ago. Unbelievable."

Feeling apprehensive about what was yet to be revealed, Jake let the comment pass without acknowledgement and continued with the task at hand. In 2110, due to the vast depletion of vegetation and meat producing animals, a genetic engineering company, Genetic Technologies, or GenTech, was awarded a huge worldwide government grant to develop methods of increasing food production.

"I wonder if they succeeded," pondered Nathan. "It sounds like the world could have used something like that."

"I agree," replied Jake. "But we may never know."

"I could use some of that food. I'm getting hungry."

Skye agreed, "I could use some of Ronni's bread right now."

Jake heard the comment and had to force Ronni's image from his mind before continuing into the *2121-2130* decade where they discovered that construction on an underground transportation system was implemented in 2125 after fourteen years of research. The underlying reason was to make transportation quicker and safer while freeing the environment from the existence of concrete highways. Cars were to be replaced with *Transcaps*, individual vehicles using magnetic levitation technology and resembling capsules. An operator would enter the vehicle, program the destination, and then sit back and relax. Sensors surrounding the vehicle were designed to control speed and distance between adjacent vehicles. The only physical evidence aboveground would be a fiber optic cable, supported one meter above the surface that would transmit environmental images to the walls surrounding the system, enabling riders to experience the same sights they would if traveling above ground.

The *2131-2140* decade produced one extremely surprising development; TELTRAN, a teleportation system was approved in 2133 for international use after twenty-three years of research and development. TELTRAN portals began appearing in most large cities worldwide. "Well, that would make traveling great distances more attractive," Jake mused. "I'm just not sure I want to have my body disassembled and reassembled somewhere else. Sounds risky."

Looking further, he located information concerning construction of space colonies. Closer examination revealed construction on the first colony, a manufacturing station, began in March 2135 and was completed in September 2137. Materials for the colony were mined from the moon's surface and launched into space by mass drivers to be collected and transported to the construction site by ion-engined shuttlecrafts. The raw materials were refined, shaped, and assembled in the colony while it was being built. Utilizing huge solar panels always aimed at the sun for power, the manufacturing colony was then used to create all components for two additional colonies, both residential. All colonies were constructed at Lagrange points; the largest was cylindrically shaped, measuring three kilometers in diameter, fifteen kilometers in length, and housed 1.2 million people.

"What's a Lagrange point?" asked Skye.

Jake paused to recall something he had heard while still in high school, then replied, "I seem to remember that it is a spot in space where the gravitational pull by the sun is the same as the earth's. Something located at one of these points would remain stationary in space."

"Oh," Skye responded, not totally understanding, but also not willing to pursue the subject further.

Moving into the *2141-2150* decade, bombings were reported in November 2141 at GenTech facilities. Jake went backward to the beginning of 2141 and scanned the information slower. A group of protestors calling themselves SOP for 'Save Our Planet' was opposed to GenTech's development of what was dubbed *The Ultimate Growth Factor* and the company's supposed clandestine forays into gene-splicing and synthetic stem cell production. By 2141, eleven GenTech facilities were operational; because of their environmental requirements, all were located between altitudes of 3000 and 6000 feet and on large bodies of water. SOP claimed responsibility for a coordinated series of bombings in which all eleven facilities were destroyed within a total span of fifteen minutes.

Jake scanned a list of the destroyed facilities.

Lake Mackay, Australia
Lake Wanaka, New Zealand
Chingwang Lake, Inner Mongolia
Beysehir, Turkey
Lake Dow, South Africa
Batak, Bulgaria
Montreux, Switzerland
Vidda, Norway
Piraju, Brazil
Sled Lake, Saskatchewan
Flathead Lake, Montana

"These were scattered throughout the world," Jake said, not sure of what actually happened, but feeling strangely apprehensive about the possible ramifications. Scrolling on, he found reports of mutations in February 2142, and by summer 2142 widespread mutations were being reported. It seemed that different species were affected in different ways; rapid growth from ten to over a hundred times normal size was exhibited by insects, arthropods, and arachnids. This fueled a great deal of discussion between physicists and zoologists, arguing the impossibility of such an occurrence due to the effected species' skeletal, respiratory and circulatory systems. Some mammals exhibited bizarre effects, such as herbivores demonstrating carnivorous traits; included were reports of some cattle attacking people while the rest of the herd contentedly grazed on grass. Some normally shy or docile animals such as house pets, owls, raccoons, woodchucks, and squirrels, exhibited overtly aggressive tendencies. Some humans were also affected, in particular their carnivorous cravings, aggressive behavior, and eyesight.

"Azujos," whispered Jake. "So that's what happened to them."

"What" asked Nathan, who by this time was getting bored of the research and had tuned out the information. "What about the Azujos?"

"That's how they changed."

"What's how they changed? I don't follow you."

"A genetic manipulation company had eleven labs scattered throughout the world. A terrorist group bombed all eleven, causing the results of their research to escape into the atmosphere; this affected some species more than others. Some exhibited rapid and effectual growth and others had their characteristics and behaviors change."

"Well that would explain the big ant I saw and the huge crabs Juan saw."

"Yes, that would explain it," Jake responded absently while continuing to scan for further information. He found that between 2142 and 2144, the large insects had become resistant to spraying, were intimidating the birds that normally kept their numbers in check, and had defoliated vast amounts of vegetation. The loss of vegetation created an immediate market for meat, causing meat prices to soar, eventually rivaling precious gems, more so because the lack of vegetation reduced the number of meat producing animals. In most places pork was more plentiful than beef. Also affected was the atmosphere, which measured a considerable depletion of oxygen and an overabundance of carbon dioxide, killing scores of very young, very old, and infirmed. The ozone layer's depletion was extensive resulting in a significant rise in the average global temperature, which caused major ice fields to melt. This, in turn, increased the amount of water in the oceans and caused extensive coastal flooding. Because of the lessened protection from the sun's ultraviolet radiation, huge populations migrated northward to more moderate climates. Through time, many of the large insects vanished due to lack of food and the existence of large spiders.

The remaining decades, 2151-2283, displayed nothing more notable than an obscure report in February 2182 of four pilots coming ashore in rafts, claiming to have crashed their Navy Avenger aircrafts in 1945. They reported the remainder of the crews from the five original planes lost their lives when they ditched at sea after running out of fuel. "Flight 19," whispered Jake. "No wonder they were never found in our time. Wow, what an incredible amount of information; I guess I know enough about our situation now ... maybe too much. Let's go."

"Wait a minute," urged Nathan. "I want to see what the local papers and news broadcasts said about us ... you know, in 2005."

"I forgot about that, but it's getting late so we need to hurry."

Nathan and Skye located the files for news from the week of August 13, 2005. Scrolling the information on the display screen, they found a report about the two missing boats. The Coast Guard had sent vessels to search the entire area with help from naval ships and aircraft; the search had lasted six days before being called off. Officials reported that no debris or any other trace of either vessel had been found, and they were both declared missing at sea. Interviews with family members were interspersed throughout the six days, including Juan's family, Captain Bankowski's wife, and the parents of the three college girls on *Blue Heron*. Tears streamed down Skye's face as she read her parents' interview, pleading with officials to continue the search. Nathan put his arm around her and she laid her head on his shoulder. As he was about to shut down the display, a picture caught his attention.

"Hey Dad, look at this," he urged. "It's a separate picture of Mr. Cranston; he must've won some award or something. Let's see, he ... " Nathan's expression changed from detached interest to wide-eyed agitation. "He's wanted for murder... and his name's not Cranston, it's Contraldo ... Manford Contraldo!"

Chapter 29

J ake hurried to Nathan's side and scanned the information. The urgency in his demeanor shook Skye from her emotions.

"Damn! Where's a telephone, er ... a communication device? I have to call Ronni now!" Nathan searched the room they were in but found nothing that indicated communication. The three of them spread out to search other rooms, finally finding a communication system on the next level.

Jake hurriedly started the system and a wall screen appeared.

DIRECTOR SYSTEM J439FH*
SYSTEM AUTHORIZED FOR USE BY SOUTHEAST
COASTAL UNIVERSITY
ARE YOU A VISITOR?
STATE CLEARLY: YES NO

"Yes." He gazed out a window and saw the gathering darkness; they had stayed too long, but that didn't matter now.

WELCOME VISITOR
STATE CLEARLY: COMMUNICATION
ENTERTAINMENT

"Communication," Jake said impatiently.

YOU CHOSE COMMUNICATION
STATE CLEARLY: YES NO

"Yes."

DO YOU WISH TO CONTACT SOMEONE?
STATE CLEARLY: YES NO

"Yes." Impatience forcing an edge to his voice.

STATE CLEARLY THE PERSON'S NAME
OR
STATE CLEARLY THE PERSON'S VIDEOCOM
NUMBER

Removing the piece of paper from his pocket he read the numbers written there, "Three, four, four, seven, two, five, four, eight, seven, zero, two, one." As each digit was pronounced, it showed on the screen and an underline space appeared to the right, indicating another digit was being requested until all twelve digits were displayed.

THROUGH THE TRIANGLE

3 4 4 7 2 5 4 8 7 0 2 1

A room, quickly recognized as Ronni's apartment appeared and she suddenly emerged into view. "Hi there," she greeted him with a smile. "I didn't expect ... "

Jake cut her off abruptly, "Ronni, is Mr. Cranston in the room with you?"

"Nice to hear from you too," she responded with a mixture of disappointment and frustration. "And no, he isn't."

"Good. Now listen carefully. Take Davy with you and get Scotty and Mack. Cranston isn't who he says he is; he's a wanted murderer. Be very careful but get them quickly. I'll stay on the line until you're safe."

"Okay, be right back. Davy, come with me! Now!" She left the viewing area and almost immediately Jake's blood ran cold as he heard Cranston's voice, but couldn't make out what he was saying.

"Goin' somewhere pretty lady?"

She pretended her exit was routine, "Just going over to see Scotty, be right back."

"I don't think so. I heard what your boyfriend told you. Too bad you had to find out, now you're coming with me," he growled while clicking open his switchblade.

Davy looked from Manny to his mother and back again. Suddenly, she screamed and kicked Manny in the shin. "You bitch!" he yelled in rage, and grabbed her arm. She pivoted and kneed him in the groin, doubling him over in pain.

Jake was listening to the unintelligible sounds of the fracas in a panic when a message appeared across the middle of the screen, with the room still in evidence behind it.

DO YOU WISH TO CONTINUE WITH THIS LINK
STATE CLEARLY: YES NO

"Yes!" he shouted.

WHEN YOU WISH TO END THIS LINK
STATE CLEARLY: CLOSE

The sounds of the scuffle had diminished. "Ronni! What's happening?"

"Run Davy, run!" she shouted, and as Manny looked up, she caught him square in the face with her knee, knocking him to the floor, then ran to Scotty's room where Davy waited, watching what had transpired.

"Scotty, open up! Quick!"

The door opened and Scotty appeared, revolver in hand. "Wha' is it, Lossie? I hairrrd noises!"

She pushed Davy into the room and quickly joined him. "Jake just called and said Cranston isn't really Cranston and he's wanted for murder!" she reported while rubbing her knee. Scotty ran to the hall just in time to see Manny's back disappear out the main door. He gave chase as fast as he could, but Manny was nowhere in sight by the time the old Scot managed to exit the building.

He returned to his room and said, "He's gone, Lossie, I chased him bu' couldna catch 'im."

Mack joined them, "What's the commotion?"

"Come with me, both of you!" Ronni ordered, limping back to her room and entering to the sound of Jake's frantic voice.

"Ronni!" Can you hear me?"

"Yes, I can hear you," she reassured him, stepping into the viewing area, "We're okay, Davy and me."

"What happened?"

"Cranston, or whatever his name is must have been listening outside my door and heard what you said. He wasn't going to let me get help, said he was going to take me with him."

"Where is he now?"

"He's gone, Scotty saw him leave and chased him."

"Why did he leave without you? Don't get me wrong, I'm glad he did, but why? It sounded like there was a fight."

"You might say that," she chuckled. "Let's just say he'll be holding his nose and walking funny for awhile."

"Good for you! Stay close to Scotty and Mack and I'll be back tomorrow."

"Okay. See you then."

Jake enunciated, "Close." The display disappeared. "Let's go," he urged Nathan and Skye, both of whom had witnessed what had taken place.

"She's some woman!" said Skye.

"She certainly is," agreed Jake as they headed for the exit.

Manny managed to scramble around the corner before Scotty emerged from the building. He was counting on the Scot's slowness and reluctance to continue the chase once outside; the old man didn't disappoint. The bitch, on the other hand was going to pay, and pay dearly, he vowed while wiping blood from his mouth. She had taken advantage of his good nature, attacking him when he was trying to be careful with her. Well not anymore, next time she wouldn't surprise him and he *would* have her. He tried to walk, but could only manage a bent-over limp. She would pay!

The sun had set and darkness was advancing rapidly; he knew he had to find shelter soon. About two blocks from the apartment, his worst fear was realized as three Azujos blocked his path. He turned to run and stopped, facing two others. Strong arms grabbed and threw him down; he felt the world evaporate.

Chapter 30

Skye led Jake and Nathan to her camp, an apartment building even more aged than the one they left hours ago. One wing was in ruin, as if a hurricane had homed in on part of the building while the rest escaped harm. On the way, they had one close call when they spied four Azujos a block away, moving parallel to their path in the opposite direction. They ducked behind the corner of the nearest building until the cloaked figures had moved out of sight, and then hurried the remainder of the way

"Skye!" a female voice shrieked as they entered the apartment building and a figure rushed to hug her. "You had us so worried! It's so good to see you again, girl!" After hugging Skye tightly for a few moments, she moved back to arms length while continuing to hold her at the elbows. "You look good. Captain Callahan told us what happened. I'm so sorry about the Pelhams. Ohmygod, it could've been you. What would we have done? We were so sca ... "

"Easy, Kesha!" Skye interrupted. "Easy girl. Calm down and take a breath."

Nathan watched the girl with interest - she was a couple of inches shorter than he, had a complexion resembling very weak chocolate milk, a smile with bright white teeth, and was the most gorgeous creature he had ever seen. He had never experienced anything like this before; it was as if nothing existed at that moment, but her.

Kesha breathed deeply in response to Skye's suggestion, an act that seemed to relax her somewhat. Skye took her hand and said, "Kesha, I'd like to introduce you to Mr. Myers and his son, Nathan."

Kesha smiled broadly, extending her hand, "Hi, I'm Kesha Woods; I'm pleased to meet you." The words bounced from her in a lilting, songlike manner.

"My pleasure," Jake smiled and shook her hand.

"I ... uh ... it ... it's nice to meet you," stammered Nathan, shaking her hand and feeling more embarrassed than he could remember. And then she was gone, returning her attention to Skye.

"I'm so glad you're here. Audryan was so upset ... "

Jake walked away from the girls' conversation and then stopped, turned, and motioned for Nathan to follow him. Nathan seemed mesmerized by the exchange between the girls, but noticed his father's motion and caught its meaning. He walked toward Jake, looking back once before reaching him.

"She's pretty," Jake stated simply. Nathan nodded.

The sound of conversations wafted from one of the rooms. Entering, they saw Callahan, Juan, and Mason talking with a tall, pencil-thin bespectacled man around Jake's age. Next to him sat a middle-aged slim woman with rather plain features; continuing clockwise was a young man of obvious Italian descent, a red-faced heavyset man in a soiled undershirt who was sweating profusely, and a stocky girl of African-American descent who must be Skye's other friend. Callahan rose, moved forward, and introduced them to the others, indicating each in order, "Jake and Nathan Myers, I'd like you to meet Carl Fontaine, Amy Kaufman, Veni Fassenetti, Darryl Johns, and Audryan Heppbrun." Amy and Darryl nodded when introduced, the other three stood and extended their hands to both strangers. Audryan then excused herself and left the room, immediately thereafter was the sound of running followed by excited squealing as she joined her friends down the hall. "Now, tell us what you found out about our future that suddenly became our past."

After seating themselves, Nathan spoke first, excitedly, "One thing we found was that Mr. Cranston isn't who he says he is; he's wanted for murder!"

"Ya're kiddin'!" exclaimed Mason. "Ya mean we had a murderer on my boat? Damn! I can't believe it!"

"Yeah, it's hard to believe," added Juan, then after a pause, "But thinking back, he did act kind of different on board. It was like he was on the fishing boat but didn't want to fish."

"Come to think of it, ya're right. When he called to make his reservation, he talked a lot 'bout wantin' to fish; kept talkin' 'bout how much fun he had fishin' with his grandfather when he was a kid. I wonder what he really wanted … goin' with us an' all? I guess ya was right, Mr. Myers, when ya said we should keep an eye on 'im."

"So if this guy wasn't the same one who called originally," summed Callahan, "Then he probably killed the guy and assumed his identity. Too bad for the real Cranston."

"I wonder what happened to the real Mr. Cranston," pondered Nathan. "I mean what did he do with the body?"

"Most likely disposed of it," surmised Callahan. "He might never be found."

"Anyway," Jake continued, "When Nathan found his picture and the information, we called Ronni to warn her. He tried to attack her and apparently she hurt him but he escaped. He's out there someplace, so now we have to watch out for *him*, in addition to the Azujos."

"Don't worry, we will," promised Juan. "What else did you find?"

Nathan spoke again, "I found news articles from when we went missing; they searched for us six days before giving up. The Coast Guard and Navy used ships and helicopters but said they couldn't find any trace of us."

"Figured as much," concluded Callahan. "They didn't know it, but they could have spent their lives searching and never found us." Mason sat, staring at the floor.

"In other matters," Jake began, "I didn't have anything to write with but I'll try to remember what I read. The big nuclear war happened in the twenty eighties and we lost some big cities, like LA, New York, DC, Seattle, and ... " he looked toward the ceiling while trying to recall others.

"I remember Houston was one of them," added Nathan.

"You're right. Anyhow, the explosions killed two-thirds of all living things."

"Why?" asked Callahan. "There couldn't have been *that* many bombs!"

"Apparently the explosions caused earthquakes, tidal waves, and other natural disasters, and the nuclear winter lasted for, I can't remember for sure, but I think it was around twelve or thirteen years."

"What's a nucular winter?" queried Mason, now focused again on the exchange.

"It's pronounced nu-cle-ar, and scientists predicted it would happen if there was a nuclear war. Dust and debris from the explosions is lifted into the atmosphere where it blocks the sun for years, causing cold temperatures and the loss of plants due to lack of sunlight. So, between the disasters, nuclear winter, explosions, and massive radiation, it's easy to understand extensive loss of life."

"Yeah, I guess ... when you put it that way," Callahan conceded as he sat back on his chair, crossed his arms and stretched his legs, crossing them at the ankle.

"Sometime later, because of so much loss of life and resources, all countries became one government, *The United Nations*. Other things happened, such as space colonies, teleportation and an underground highway system, but..."

"What?" It was Callahan's first mate, Veni, who interrupted. "Excuse me, but did you say teleportation?"

"Yes I did," responded Jake. "It reported that ... " looking to Nathan, "What did they call those places at each end of the teleportation process?"

"Portals," answered Nathan.

"Yes, that's it. They said portals were being established in many of the major cities worldwide."

"Man, that would be great!" exclaimed Veni. "Just step in, set your destination, push a button, and step out where you want. I never thought they would be able to do it."

Nathan regarded the stranger with disdain after his interruption; he seemed to be arrogant and too self-assured. He was tall, about six-two and muscular with classic Italian features and spoke with a slight Italian accent. He needed a shave, as did Callahan when Nathan first saw him; he was sure all the girls would want this guy once Scotty loaned him his scissors and razor. It was then that he realized he was jealous, but it didn't matter, he still didn't like him.

Nathan was roused from his thoughts by Mason's voice, "Go on Mr. Myers; as ya was sayin'?"

Jake continued, "What I was about to say impacts us all; it's about the Azujos. Apparently, a genetics company had eleven research facilities and they were all blown up at the same time by a group of protestors. Their genetic experiments on a super growth factor were released into the atmosphere and caused genetic mutations. Some species experienced huge growth and others had their behavior and eyesight changed, some even changed from being herbivores to carnivores."

Nathan interjected, "Like the ant I saw that was a couple inches long and the beach crabs Juan saw that were ... how big, Juan?"

Juan spoke up, "They averaged about two feet I estimated."

The man identified as Carl Fontaine showed sudden interest and spoke, "Excuse me. I haven't been on the beach a lot but I know beach crabs aren't nearly that big. Are you sure they were that large?"

"Let's just say that I saw them in early dawn from our boat that was anchored about a hundred yards off shore, and I *thought* they were dogs. From that distance, you normally would have trouble seeing beach crabs."

"I can't believe it, just thinking of them growing that large scares me. I can imagine an ant a couple inches long, but that *is* big for an ant. Are those the only examples you witnessed?"

"There *was* another example," said Jake.

"Huh?" Juan asked. "I don't remember any other large things, what do you mean Mr. Myers?"

"In the stadium," explained Jake. "When I explored the first offset room, there were flies three to four inches across. They were flying around the bones that were stacked in there."

"Bones?" Now it was the woman, Amy, whose eyes suddenly widened expressing obvious terror. "What ... what bones?"

"I don't want to alarm you, but I think everybody should be aware that the Azujos appear to be cannibalistic, and as our limited experience with them has shown, possibly able to see in the dark."

"Cannibals!" she screamed. "Oh God, not cannibals! How do you know?"

"Well, for starters there was what looked like a barbeque pit, or grill, in the center of the room, along with evidence of prolonged fires around it. Also, the bones I saw were piled according to type: long bones, short bones, curved bones, and skulls ... unfortunately, they were human skulls."

She visibly shivered and crossed her arms. "This is a dreadful place! Why did this have to happen to us? Why?"

"Sorry to say," Jake responded, "we've all wondered that very question, but instead of questioning our circumstances, we need to focus on survival. I suggest we move everyone to the other camp; there's safety in numbers and that place seems more secure than here. Tomorrow would not be too soon."

"I have a question," inserted Veni. "In my college physics class we were taught that we only see reflected light, so do they actually see in the dark or do they see very faint reflected light?"

"That's a good question Veni, I'm not sure. We had an experience in a very dark room but I can't say it was totally dark, probably not. I need to pay another visit to that library and take more time examining the records; I'll do that before we leave tomorrow."

Nathan, who had been fidgeting in his chair finally found the opportunity to address his father, "You didn't say anything about human bones being near where we were being held. Do you mean they were going to ... " he glanced around the room at the expectant faces before summoning the courage to finish. "Do you think they were going to *eat* us?"

It was a question Jake didn't want to answer, but he also didn't want to lie to his son. After a few moments, he finally said, "I don't know what their ultimate plans were for you and the others in that place, but it can't be ruled out as a possibility." Nathan shivered.

Silence followed, and then smaller group conversations began that lasted far into the night; individuals gradually moving off to their respective quarters.

Chapter 31

Morning brought preparations to break camp and move northward to the other apartment building. Nobody had many possessions to gather, other than any items they happened to acquire after arriving on shore approximately eight months ago. As Callahan's group packed, Jake set out to visit the college again. This time Nathan expressed a desire to stay behind, probably because Veni had volunteered to go, his curiosity getting the better of him. Juan also wished to join them and see for himself what the library archives had to say about the large animals. Skye and her two friends had stayed up very late and were still sleeping. Jake wondered how females needed to catch up that much when they had only been separated a couple of days.

The three men made it to the library in five minutes and found their way to the Archives section. Once faced with operating the system, Jake wished he had paid more attention to how Nathan and Skye managed to activate the display. Everything looked foreign but he tried a few things, regrettably without success. He was feeling frustrated when

Veni offered to help. After a few minutes, Veni had the display screen operational to Jake's profound gratitude.

"What are you looking for?" asked Juan, studying the information on the screen.

"I'm not sure just what I'm looking for, but I think I'll know it when I see it." He chose *World History: Twenty-first and Twenty-second Centuries*, accessed the *2141-2150* decade and scanned the information slowly with Veni and Juan watching over his shoulders. "I think this is it," Jake stated quietly while reading one of the sections. It included this news article from September 2142:

Liebold, Kansas. A report of strange bovine behavior Thursday in which a local farmhand lost his life was confirmed by Regeana Cookeswain, spokesperson for the Liebold Police Department. According to witnesses Kyle Wissinger and his son Kevin, owners of the property where the attacks took place, Gilbert Faines, a worker on their farm was fatally injured by three cows as he attempted to chase them away from a dead cow being devoured by the three. The Wissingers reported they had finished harvesting corn when Faines saw a Holstein cow attack another cow while heading toward the barn at dusk; two other Holstein cows joined in the attack, killed the cow and began to devour it. When Faines ran to the site of the attack the three cows turned on him. He was transported to Memorial Hospital in nearby Johnsonburg where he died four hours later. All three cows were destroyed by police. According to Cookeswain, the Wissingers had been watching the three cows for weeks, noting behavior changes including a tendency to remain in the barn during the day and graze after dark. The attack is just one more example of the increasing number of strange animal behaviors cropping up throughout the Midwest. This was the third death attributed to unexplained animal attacks in the last month. All of the violent attacks were made by animals that are normally docile and domesticated. In most cases, an affinity to darkness was also reported for the offending animals.

"Why were you interested in that article?" Juan asked.

Jake thought a moment before answering, "I wanted to see if there was a link between the acquired aggressive behavior and changes in eyesight. This article indicates a connection between animals that are normally docile, becoming aggressive killers and a penchant for darkness."

"So?"

"So, it seems to prove the genetic changes didn't cause these animals to want to exist in darkness, they *had* to."

"What do you mean?"

"Well, animals don't normally plan, so their living in darkness indicates that daylight probably hurt their eyes. Why would aggressive behavior go hand in hand with light hurting eyes? We have cows, of all things, definite herbivores attacking and eating other animals and humans, which is carnivorous behavior ... and light hurts their eyes. Remind you of something?"

"Azujos," answered Juan. "But I still don't see what you're getting at."

"I think the genetic transformation might somehow

cause a shift in what their eyes can see. Think about it, they see things we don't and their eyes are affected by something in the light that doesn't bother us."

Veni, quiet until now speculated, "May I put forth a theory?"

"Sure," responded Jake. "I'm open for any suggestions at this point. We need to understand the enemy in order to survive."

"There was something else I recall from my college physics class, the visible spectrum. Electromagnetic waves that we can see vary from long wavelengths - red, to short wavelengths - violet. Since we see only reflected light, the light has to fall within that narrow band of wavelengths between red and violet, all other colors falling between. What if the genetically mutated species has a visible spectrum different from ours."

"I think you may be on to something." Jake thought for a moment and then measured his words, "I picture it this way, we see from violet to red and just outside that range on the violet side is ultraviolet, which has so much energy it causes sunburn; beyond the red side is infrared, which is heat. If their eyes have a shifted visible spectrum toward the red side, the higher energy of the violet end could hurt their eyes and that would possibly move what they *can* see into the infrared range."

"So they can see heat," finished Veni.

"It sounds reasonable," said Jake. "But it's only a theory. It is, however, a theory I think worth testing."

"Excuse me," interjected Juan. "I had science and was supposed to take physics this year. What are you talking about, electro something spectra and seeing heat? It doesn't make sense to me."

Jake walked to a desk and retrieved a writing instrument and paper. "I can see why you're confused, so let me show you." He wrote across the paper, explaining as he wrote, "I'll use IR for infrared, R for red, O for orange, Y for yellow, G for green, B for blue, V for violet, and UV for ultraviolet."

(IR: heat) R O Y G B V (UV)

He then underlined everything starting with red and ending with violet.

(IR: heat) <u>R O Y G B V</u> (UV)

"Now the underlined part is what *we* can see, *our* visible spectrum." He then made some notes underneath.

(IR: heat) <u>R O Y G B V</u> (UV)

Long wavelengths	**Short wavelengths**
Low frequency	**High frequency**
Low energy	**High energy**

"Now," explained Jake slowly, "the Azujos seem to have trouble with sunlight, which includes everything including

IR and UV. We think their visible spectrum could be shifted toward infrared which would be something like this." He drew another line below the first.

(IR: heat) <u>R O Y G B V</u> (UV)

Long wavelengths	Short wavelengths
Low frequency	High frequency
Low energy	High energy

"If this is *their* visible spectrum, they won't see all the colors we do, such as blues, *but* they will be able to see some parts in infrared that we can't; in other words, they would be able to see heat. This would explain how they could see us in the dark … we're warm bodies. Also, since violet and ultraviolet have higher energy, it could be *that* part of sunlight that hurts their eyes."

"Don't forget that sunlight also contains infrared," interjected Veni. "So, if they can see infrared, that means they could possibly see the sun's rays in daylight, along with all heated surfaces causing them to be partially blind because of not being able to distinguish details."

"That's a good point," responded Jake. "It's another reason for not coming out in daylight."

"Do you think their eye color has anything to do with it?" asked Juan.

"It's very likely, possibly acting as a filter of the blue end of the spectrum."

"But, if that's the case, why didn't the cows you read about have violet eyes?"

"Remember, the incident with the cows happened when the mutations were just beginning, whereas the Azujos we're dealing with are the result of about a hundred forty years of evolution. I'm sure the first and probably second generations looked more like us, but avoiding sunlight through subsequent generations would eventually cause their skin to become sallow. Acquiring aggressive meat-eating characteristics would cause their teeth to become more adapted to tearing flesh, and the same with the claws. It just seems to make sense."

"You're right, it does make sense, but where does that leave us?"

"At least we now understand a little more about our adversary ... maybe enough to keep us alive."

"What do you say we go back now?" Veni asked and prepared to leave.

"Wait a minute," urged Juan. "If we can, I would like to see the article about Mr. Cranston, or whatever his name is."

Jake agreed, "Yes, I didn't get a chance to check out the article either. Hold up Veni, we'll be ready in a couple minutes." Veni turned and walked back to them while Jake was setting the display for news from August 10, 2005. They inspected the screens and finally located Manford Contraldo's picture along with an article about his escape resulting in the death of a policeman in Pittsburgh, Pennsylvania. A nationwide manhunt was underway and the public was being warned about him being armed and dangerous.

He then tried August 13, 2005. They scanned the pages until they saw an article about a body being found in the burned remnants of an abandoned restaurant close to I-95 in South Carolina. Missing persons files were being scrutinized to determine the man's identity. Scanning forward, they found an article dated August 25th reporting that the body found in the burned restaurant in South Carolina was identified through dental records as Allen G. Cranston of Morgantown, West Virginia, who had been reported missing by his employer when he didn't return from a vacation trip. A nationwide search for the man's car, a 2004 Mercedes, was underway and anybody with information was urged to immediately contact the Jackson County, South Carolina Sheriff's Department or the FBI.

Farther down the page was one of the articles about the disappearance of the two boats and how all search and rescue efforts had been discontinued a week ago, but the families were still petitioning the Coast Guard to resume the search. A picture at the bottom of the page looked familiar, and upon closer inspection Juan recognized it, "Hey, that's the front of Captain Bankowski's house!" Jake examined the picture and pointed to a Mercedes sitting behind his car to one side of the garage.

Chapter 32

"It's about time you guys got back!" Callahan shouted as he saw the three men returning from the college. "We're packed and ready to go!" He walked down the dock and joined his passengers on *Blue Heron*. Jake and Juan climbed aboard *Oblique View* while Veni quickly gathered his belongings and jogged to *Blue Heron*.

"Okay Captain, lead the way!" shouted Callahan to Mason, who started his engines and backed away from the dock; once clear, he accelerated northward, followed by *Blue Heron*.

The trip was short, Mason surveying the shoreline all the while. Before reaching his destination, he abruptly steered toward the buildings on shore; Callahan did likewise and followed the rapidly slowing *Oblique View* into a narrow inlet to a dock that was all but hidden from sight. The structure appeared solid, but after reversing engines and drifting against it, Mason crawled out and tested its sturdiness while Juan tied off. Callahan waited until Mason gave him a thumbs-up before docking.

"I didn't see this on the way down," said Callahan.

"Neither did I," responded Mason. "But I was lookin' for somethin' like this so we wouldn't have to drop anchor away from shore. I think we're only a coupla blocks from th' apartment."

"Well, however you found it, this is about as good as you could do ... with so much deterioration along here." He turned to his passengers, "This is the end of the line, everybody ashore!"

Jake and Mason led the way to the apartment; Jake entered first and saw Ronni waiting by her door. Smiling, she spoke first, "Hello stranger. Welcome home."

The greeting sounded comforting and he smiled, "Thank you, it's nice to be back. How's Davy?"

Just then a smallish beaming face peered from the doorway, "I'm fine sir, how are you?"

Jake squatted and beckoned, "Come here little man." Davy ran to him and was engulfed in his arms.

"He talked a lot about you while you were gone, especially after your efforts to save me."

Jake released the boy and stood facing Ronni. "I thought about him too ... well, both of you while I was gone. You have to tell me what happened with Cranston, or rather Contraldo."

"Tell you what, I'll fill you in on that if you tell me what you found out; but let's get everyone settled in and have lunch first. Deal?" It was getting rather difficult to talk in the hallway due to the commotion as the rest arrived.

"Deal!" Jake fairly shouted over the din, while stepping back to let the three college girls pass, Skye wiggling the fingers of her free hand as a greeting to Ronni. He saw Scotty and Mack enter the hallway and take charge of room assignments; he and Nathan were the last assigned a room. Mack and Scotty split up, each orienting the new tenants on how to use the computerized facilities; when they were done, they joined Ronni and helped her prepare lunch.

Thirty minutes later everyone was gathered in Ronni's room, introductions were made, and casual conversations followed until they were invited to sit and dine. The other two survivors of the plane crash, the Atwoods, came down and joined the meal, making eighteen diners, twelve at the table and four on the bed. Jake and Nathan sat on the floor, leaning against a wall. Conversations abounded and soon it was difficult to hear over the racket. Finally, after quieting everyone, Mack took charge and suggested each person tell about him or herself because it looked as if they would all be neighbors for a long time. With some reluctance, they agreed and started around the room with Mack setting the example.

"My name's Jonathon MacKensie, with an 's' instead of a 'z'," Mack said in his distinguishing deep voice, "Not that it makes any difference, because I don't expect any of you to send me a Christmas card ... this year." Self-conscious chuckles resulted from some before he continued, "I'm fifty two *and* for those of you wondering, I'm six foot five." This caused more uneasy laughter, and then he said, "I was a pilot for Trans World Airways, or TWA when we crash landed here on our way to New York in 1965. We've been here three years, two months, and fourteen days. I played basketball in high school and college ball at Purdue. I left behind a wife, Marilyn, and two boys, Jon Jr. and Jeremy. I used to enjoy fishing and playing hoops in a rec league … now I just fish." He paused to indicate he was done, then added before the next person could begin, "Oh, and friends call me Mack. Next?"

Juan spoke next and shared about his family and involvement in sports. He ended with, "I had hoped to go to college after graduation and study engineering … but that doesn't seem possible now … maybe college educations aren't needed in this *new* world."

Skye shared that she lived in Charlotte, North Carolina with her parents, two younger brothers, Tim and Perry, and a cat, Snickers. Her mother worked as a bank manager and her father was a social studies teacher. She had graduated second in her high school class and had accepted a four-year scholarship to UNC to study Early Childhood Education.

Kesha, who had been a classmate with Skye, was a cheerleader and played volleyball. She had an older sister, Jessica, who was a flight attendant with US Airways based out of its hub in Charlotte. She lived with her divorced mother, a corporate attorney, and two black labs, Chester and Maurice.

Audryan explained how her parents had enjoyed watching Audrey Hepburn movies when they were young and decided to name their daughter after the actress, since their last name was close to Hepburn. An outstanding athlete, Audryan excelled in softball and field events in track and field -- discus, javelin, and shot put. Being African American, five-two and quite muscular, she stood to illustrate how different she was from her namesake who was Caucasian, tall and slim. She even took some quick poses imitating body builders; her quick wit had some laughing so hard they were wiping tears from their eyes.

Peggy and George Atwood, both retirees, were on vacation when the plane crashed. They lived in the Boston area and left behind three children, five grandchildren, and one great-grandson. They had owned and run two high-end furniture stores before turning the business over to a son and daughter; their other son had become a successful heart surgeon in New York City.

Darryl, next in line to speak, hesitated while scanning the others' faces as if wondering whether someone in the group would pass judgment on what he was about to say.

"It's okay," reassured Callahan quietly, sitting next to him. "You're among friends."

"Well … I … um … I'm Darryl Johns and I came from a small town in upstate New York." Darryl began while rubbing his hands nervously. "Quit school and joined the army. Worked in the motor pool three years until …" He lowered his head.

"Go on, continue," urged Callahan.

"I got in a fight with an officer and landed in the brig. Spent a year there. Got dishonorable discharge over it.

Came to Ft. Lauderdale ten years ago. Did mechanic work until David hired me. Been with him ever since. He treats me good."

Callahan placed his hand on Darryl's shoulder and gave a reassuring squeeze. "You did well, my friend," he said.

Callahan related the details of his near-death experience and how it had cost him his marriage because his wife couldn't take the stress anymore. She left him while he was still in the hospital, and filed for divorce immediately thereafter. After his discharge following months of rehab and therapy, he took his pension and a hefty severance deal, moved in with his brother in Ft. Lauderdale, and bought *Blue Heron*.

Veni was twenty and attended the University of Miami majoring in sports medicine. Living in nearby Stuart, FL, he had worked with Captain Callahan the past two summers to help with school expenses. He had lettered in football, basketball, and track in high school, but said he didn't have the time to participate in college. His mother worked at a Wal-Mart and his father was a salesman at a local car dealership. In addition to his parents, he left behind a younger sister, Sarah, and his dachshund, Snout.

Scotty had been in Caracas to visit his sister who was married to a South American engineer. He had wanted to visit her for many years, so his grandchildren chipped in to send him for a combined sixtieth birthday and retirement present. He had migrated to Akron, Ohio from Scotland and worked as an ironworker until his retirement. He had seven children, fourteen grandchildren, four great grandchildren, and two great-great-grandchildren, at least that was how many he knew of three years ago. He also explained that he lost his arm two years ago in a fight with some Azujos.

Amy Kaufman had taught third grade in Orlando for twelve years and at age forty-three was still unattached. She left behind her ailing mother, suffering with the onset of Alzheimer's. She needed to get away for a couple of days and had left a cousin to care for her mother. She finished by saying, "I guess my cousin got more than she bargained for."

Carl Fontaine was a CPA in a large Ft. Lauderdale accounting firm and had taken this trip on a dare from a colleague. He was told, "You're forty-five and live at this office; it's time you went outside and did something ... anything ... I dare you." He had no family, save a stray cat he fed occasionally. His life was his work ... literally.

Mason told of his welding, Maggie, and *Oblique View*. He had two brothers, both in the building trades, and all three lived within three miles of each other.

Not wanting Davy to think his father's death was his fault, Ronni picked her words carefully, "Hi, I'm Veronica Langham, friends call me Ronni, and this is my son, Davy. Scotty mentioned that he lost his arm in a battle with the Azujos. I lost my husband in the same fight. I left behind a sister, Camille, who was to get married three weeks after the crash ... and I was supposed to be her matron of honor. I hope her wedding wasn't totally ruined by my disappearance. I was raised a little north of Nashville and was considered a tomboy growing up; I even ran track in high school." She looked expectantly to Jake.

Jake cleared his throat and then began, "I'm Jake Myers and have no brothers or sisters. I was raised close to Frederick, Maryland and was big into baseball in high school. I graduated from Towson State University and Penn State University. I was a chemical engineer married to my college sweetheart, Lisa, a pharmacist. We were married for sixteen years and had one son, Nathan," he said while nodding toward Nathan, "... whom I love very much. Unfortunately, things didn't work out and we were divorced. After a couple years we were reconciling, but it all ended two months ago when ... ," he looked at Nathan before finishing, his lower lip quivering, "... when she died." He looked at the ceiling to blink away the tears that began to well in his eyes. He glanced at Ronni and saw her wipe her eyes, as did a few others in the room.

Being last, Nathan self-consciously divulged how much he loved his mother and confided the dislike he had held toward his father for not being there for him or his mother. He then turned toward Jake and started to say something, but couldn't seem to get the words out. To Jake's dismay, he walked from the room.

Chapter 33

W ell, I guess that's all, unless anyone has anything to add." Mack stated after a pause. "Thank you for sharing your lives with us. You're free to do what you want until dinner, which will be in about three hours, right?" He looked at Ronni who nodded agreement. Most had left the room, but Mack and Scotty stayed behind to help with clean up. Jake remained and offered to take Scotty and Mack's place if they wanted to do something else.

Scotty looked at Mack and said, "Hoot mon, we could do suum fishin' for supper." Mack glanced at Ronni, who with a slight smile was picking up a couple of dishes. He nodded to Scotty. "Sounds like a plan; we'll see you later." They exited the room leaving Ronni and Jake alone.

"You don't have to help, just have a seat and we'll talk while I clean up."

"I want to help, just guide me as to where you want me to put these."

"Okay," she smiled, throwing her head to one side to

clear some hair from her face, "You can put those dishes over here on the counter."

A few minutes passed with no communication between them except for furtive glances and occasional self-conscious smiles. Finally Jake spoke, "You promised to tell me about your run in with Cranston. What happened?"

"Well, he must have been standing just outside my door and heard you warn me about him. When we tried to leave, he blocked our way. He asked where I was going, and I told him I was going to Scotty's room to get something and would be right back. That was when he pulled a knife and said I was going with *him*."

After a pause, he prodded, "And ... what happened then?"

"Then ... then I kicked him and he grabbed my arm ... so I kneed him and when he bent over I kneed him in the face," she said smugly. "Got a nasty bruise on my knee, but it was worth it."

"You did great! What happened next?"

"Davy and I ran to Scotty's room; he went after Cranston but couldn't catch him. He escaped, but I *know* he wasn't able to run very fast." Jake chuckled as he pictured Cranston limping away.

"Do you think he might come back for you? It seems like he had a thing for you."

"Never! I think I made it *painfully* clear I'm not interested."

"I want you to be very careful; he's not someone to

take lightly. Before making the trip today, some of us hit the library again and I found out what happened to the real Cranston. His body was found in a burned out building close to an interstate in South Carolina. This Manford Contraldo is bad news and was on the run after killing a cop in an escape. Promise me you'll be careful. It's not like we can call the cops on him here."

She stopped gathering the dishes and turned, looking up at his face. "I promise, and thank you for caring." She gave him a kiss on the cheek and pulled back reluctantly, stopping about a foot away, her stare alternating between his eyes and lips, while gently biting her lower lip. He drew her to him and kissed her full on the mouth as she melted into his arms. After a few moments, he broke it off and pulled away; she opened her eyes to gaze into his.

"I'm sorry, I didn't mean to ... ," his voice trailed away as he looked into her eyes.

She stopped him by placing her index finger on his lips, and said softly, "It's all right. If you wouldn't have, *I* would. I didn't like you very much when you first barged into my room, as a matter of fact I didn't want any part of you and your friends. My life had been altered in too many ways and I think I just wanted whatever I had left to remain unchanged, to allow me some sense of predictability. I had my friends and Davy, but I was willing to take each day as it came, as long as nothing else changed. You were a threat to that relative comfort. Now I have a totally different outlook ... because of you. I am so glad you're here. You're a good man Jake Myers, and I can feel your pain."

He lowered his head, "I'm sorry. I have feelings for you, but it's just too soon. Lisa died almost three hundred years ago, but for me it's only been less than three months, and I ... I don't know *how* I should feel under the circumstances. She was my life and now ... " He turned away so she couldn't see the moisture welling in his eyes.

Ronni gently turned his face toward her and brushed the tears away. "I understand. I was the same when I lost Tom. It'll take time, but I'm not planning to go anywhere." She kissed him gently, then circled her arms around him and stood there, resting her head on his chest. He lowered his head to rest on hers.

During the night, oblivious to all sleeping inside, several black-cloaked figures descended on the neighborhood. For hours, they systematically moved from building to building, attempting to gain access; in some cases they succeeded, in others they didn't. The apartment building was one they couldn't enter.

Chapter 34

"Anyone up for a field trip?" Jake asked, as he and Nathan joined Mack and Scotty at the breakfast table. When Ronni approached with steaming plates of food he said, "Wow … I like your hair. What did you do?"

"I talked to Skye last night about hairstyles in your time, so she and Kesha offered to do a little cut and style," she said, setting a plate before him. Her hair was cut much shorter, tapered, and feathered – it was a great look on her, accentuating her delicate features and large eyes. "Do you really like it?" tapping the back of it with her hand. "It feels so different."

"I like it very much. What about you guys?"

"Aye. We werrre tellin' the lass a few minutes ago tha' she looks verrry differrren', and forrr the beh'errr." Mack nodded approval. "Now wha' werrre you saying aboo' a trrrip?"

Still watching Ronni, he said, "I just want to see what this part of the city has to offer. Who knows, we might learn something useful. After all, it looks like this will be our home for awhile."

Nathan expressed a desire to stay inside and the other two men also declined the offer, Scotty speaking for both, "Ah Laddie, we've been arrround the arrrea a few times and nevairr found anythin' interrrestin' -- but see for yourrrself."

"Okay, I will."

Ronni spoke up, "If you wait until I feed the crew and clean up, I'll go with you. I haven't been away from this building since ... well, too long."

"No problem. I'll even help with clean up."

"You're on. In the meantime, you can help yourself to any of Tom's clothes you want. I think they should fit, you are about the same size as him. I'll clean those later."

"Can I come too, sir?" Davy chimed in.

"You sure can, little man," assured Jake, and then searched Ronni's face for a sign that he hadn't overstepped his bounds. "As long as your mommy approves." She smiled and nodded. "Okay then, you can come."

"Thank you sir." He then resumed his breakfast without further comment.

"Looking for anything in particular?" Mack asked, preparing to shovel in another forkful.

Jake paused before answering, "I don't know yet. In a way, I'm fascinated by the concept of a deserted city, and countryside for that matter. I'm used to sitting in gridlock on eight lane highways totally packed with cars and trucks, and when I finally made it in to the city it was difficult to find parking. This is so different, totally opposite, and I want to experience it. Besides, who knows what we might find out there that we could maybe put to use later. It looks as if we're stuck here, may as well make the most of it. Since you and Scotty have explored the area, what did you find of interest?"

Swallowing his last bite of food, Mack answered as he stacked his utensils on the empty plate and handed it to Ronni, "Well, there are a lot of skyscrapers, and the few we checked out were empty of almost everything. They must have taken what all they could when the owners left. The streets are different than the streets we remember from the sixties; there're no parking meters or any indication that cars or other vehicles used them."

"What do you mean?" Now it was Jake talking between mouthfuls.

"You know, there's nothing on the streets," watching the quizzical expression on Jake's face as he chewed, "Like arrows painted on the streets for left turn or right turn, and there aren't any street signs or traffic lights. It seems like the streets and sidewalks are extensions of each other and are used to fill in the space between buildings. I know there had to be vehicular traffic or how would anyone from the countryside get in to the city? Walk?"

Pausing between bites, "That's a good point. I hadn't noticed those things, but I wasn't looking at the scenery when we were on those streets ... remember?" He continued eating.

"You're certainly right about that. Oh, besides many

buildings that used ramps instead of stairs, we found that most buildings had elevators, but the one we tried was screwed up and didn't move. They might be all shut down, who knows; we didn't really have much interest in trying any others. Well, Scotty and I have to do some fishing or nobody's going to eat later. Let's go partner." He stood and joined his departing friend.

Excited squealing and laughter entered from the hallway in advance of Skye and Kesha's physical arrival. Ronni offered breakfast but they declined, and instead offered to join Juan outside to play some games with Davy. Nathan volunteered to help, and Davy, unsure of what to do looked to his mother for direction.

"It's up to you Davy. If you want to play with them, it's okay."

"Okay!" he yelped and started to follow the girls before stopping and addressing Jake. "Is it all right with you, sir? I said I was going with you."

Jake smiled, "It's fine little man; it would probably be too boring for a man of action like you. Run along and have fun." Davy grinned broadly and ran out of the room. Only Ronni and Jake remained; he spoke first, "Well, I guess we're on our own. You still up for a walk?"

"Wouldn't miss it," she said with a smile. "Now get off your butt and help me with these dishes."

"Aye, aye, captain," he said, half saluting, which elicited a chuckle from Ronni. They placed the dishes on a shelf that extended from the wall just below the lighted panels, and watched it retract. A low hum emanated from where the dishes entered the wall, lasting about thirty seconds. Five seconds after the sound ceased, the shelf reappeared with clean and dry dishes.

"Hmmm," Jake said, admiring the clean dishes. "I wonder how that works."

"I don't have a clue, but it does."

"It might have something to do with ultrasound ... but it doesn't matter now. Let's finish cleaning up so we can get going."

After clean-up, Ronni sent Jake from the room with a suitcase of her husband's clothes, saying she needed some time to get ready. After about ten minutes he went outside and found the air stuffy and hot, even though the sun's intensity was filtered through a lingering haze. Since being stranded here, Jake hadn't actually seen the sun; consequently there were no sharply defined shadows, although there was certainly shade. He wondered if some of the debris expelled into the atmosphere by the catastrophes from two centuries ago was still having an effect. About ten minutes later she joined him, wearing a sleeveless blue blouse with khaki shorts, sandals, and a canvas bag slung over one shoulder. The shorts were outdated, riding higher on her waist than the ones Jake was used to seeing, but they looked good, accentuating her slim waist.

"You look great! What's in the bag?"

"Why, thank you kind sir for the compliment," she replied demurely while executing a formal curtsy. "And the bag contains a little food in case this jaunt takes longer than a few hours." She smiled.

Heading south along the street, Jake took notice of the things Mack had observed and commented on some of them. He was searching for any indication of street names when he felt Ronni take his hand, interlacing her fingers with his. He looked at her and she smiled while asking, "Do you mind?" He smiled back and shook his head, his emotions on a wild roller coaster ride; on one hand he felt as breathless and excited as a school boy on a first date with the girl of his dreams, but he also felt as if he was cheating on Lisa. They walked that way for a few more blocks. He wondered if she was genuinely attracted to him, or had she just been lonely too long. Regardless of her motivation, he was glad to be with her.

Eventually Ronni moved closer and encircled her left arm through Jake's right and asked, "What was Lisa like?" The question took Jake by surprise and he was silent for a few steps until she continued, "If you don't want to answer, you don't have to; I was just wondering because I know you loved her deeply. If it's too painful, you don't have to ..."

He interrupted her gently, "No. I just wasn't expecting ... I mean the question took me by surprise." Feeling uneasy in an awkward situation and looking straight ahead he said, "She was beautiful, a pharmacist, and had a great sense of humor. It was, to quote a cliché, 'love at first sight.' We met in college and I thought she was totally out of my league until she showed interest in me. To this day, I can't understand what she saw in me."

"*I* can," she said quietly. "Go on."

"Well, she deserved better. After Nathan came along, she cut back her working and I had to work longer hours. We drifted apart … actually I was an ass. We divorced, and Nathan didn't like me very much for a couple years."

"You said last night that you were reconciling. What happened?"

"After the divorce was final, bitterness kept me away for about two years, but I slowly realized that I missed them both very much. With that came the realization that I was more responsible for what happened than she.

One night as I was living in Galveston, while supervising the construction of a new petroleum plant, I was drawn to the phone with an uncontrollable urge to call her. Figuring she would probably hang up on me, I had to try anyhow. As it turned out she was receptive to my call and we talked for quite a while. During the conversation I admitted my role in undermining our relationship, which encouraged her to open up more to me. We called each other several times, becoming close once again. I was happy at the possibility of reuniting. One weekend, I flew to Baltimore just to take her to dinner. She had moved out of our house in favor of a smaller, more affordable one. Nathan had to change schools, but it seemed to me that she had things moving in the right direction."

"Yes, it does. How did things go … the weekend, I mean?"

"During that weekend Nathan seemed distant but

cautiously friendly, probably owing to my long absence and how close he and his mother had become in those couple years. He had been eleven when we separated and nearly thirteen when we divorced; that was a lot for a kid his age to experience, much less accept."

"I'm sure it was hard on him."

"By the time I caught my return flight Nathan seemed to be coming around, even admitting he would like to see me again. Lisa gave me a long goodbye kiss before I left them at the curb, standing under the Departing Flights sign. On the plane my mind was at ease, and for the first time in years I actually felt hope for us.

As the project wound down, Lisa and I talked more often by cell phone because it was cheaper than landline, and we could communicate whenever we wanted."

"I'm still trying to get a grip on these cell phones; I heard about them when we first met. Keep going with your story but I want to find out about those types of things later."

"Okay. I'll try to remember. Anyhow, we spoke of feelings, love, and reconciliation, along with everyday problems, thoughts, and happenings. Things were looking great and with the project finally finished, I went to the airport for a second chance at my interrupted life."

He paused, a little too long, prompting Ronni to gently ask, "Is that when it happened ... I mean ... you know?"

Tears formed in his eyes as he remembered the call he received on his cell phone just before boarding Delta flight 1417. Why did he still remember the flight number he wondered. "Yes. I was waiting to board when I got the call from Lisa's father. Some distracted delivery truck driver had run a red light and hit Lisa's car broadside. He said stuff that I guess was to provide comfort; something about her never knowing what hit her and that she felt no pain."

"I'm so sorry for you," she said while taking his hand. "How did Nathan take it?"

"The next few days were a blur with funeral arrangements, the closed casket viewing, and the burial. I tried to console Nathan, tried to be strong for him, but I felt as if I was dying inside. You know, looking back, I didn't see Nathan cry during that time, or since. He seemed to withdraw into himself. I hoped this trip might help us both begin to heal."

"Don't be too hard on yourself; stuff happens that we can't control and we just have to make the best of it. That's what you did, right? Look at our present situation; we don't have a choice but to try to make the best of it. What else could you have done?"

"It's just that when I realized the mess I made, we started to get back together ... and then the accident. Nathan blames me for deserting both of them. In a way, that's what I did."

"No he doesn't; at least not anymore. I can see it in his eyes."

"I can't say I believe that; I wish I could. Hey," he said, changing the subject and looking up. "This looks like the tallest building we've seen so far. I'd like to get a panoramic view of the city; you game?"

"Sure! Let's go!" They entered the skyscraper and found it empty, reminiscent of the other buildings Jake had encountered. They located an elevator in the main lobby and entered. Once inside, they were confronted with holographic numbers from "1" to "58." Jake touched "58" and felt almost nothing instead of the expected upward acceleration. They exchanged quizzical glances and then looked at the wall where holographic numbers, seemingly in mid-air were progressing at an alarming rate. The rate of increasing numbers then slowed until "58" remained. The door opened silently and they stepped out into a vast room surrounded by windows.

"How did we get here? I didn't feel much movement," queried Ronni.

"I guess there have been some advancements in elevator technology over the years. I think it gradually accelerated to a high speed and then gradually decelerated to rest. Anyway, I didn't sense much movement either." They walked to the windows.

"Now that's what I call a view!" exclaimed Jake gazing over the gleaming city that stretched nearly to the horizon. Only a few buildings appeared to be taller than the one they now occupied; some of the lower ones had unique shapes, such as a domed building about two blocks away that seemed to be made of glass and chrome. Unfortunately, its beauty was marred by several massive holes and cracks in its surface. Jake stared eastward to where the ocean was visible beyond the buildings, appearing tranquil with few swells. He couldn't help thinking about the absurdity of their situation, and stopped short of blaming it.

"It certainly is a beautiful view!" said Ronni. "I'm glad we came up here; it gives a new perspective on the struggles we've been going through."

Jake turned and asked, "What about your husband, Tom?"

She was quiet for a few moments, seeming to reflect and then smiled, "He was my rock with clear blue eyes and dark wavy hair. He owned a chain of clothing stores along the east coast and was a fantastic employer, always treated his employees with respect. They thought the world of him, as did I. We were coming back from a combined business trip and vacation to Venezuela when we crashed. In addition to the clothing business, Tom was also a gun collector and dealer. He met with another collector down there and bought some antique guns the day before we flew back. He was so excited. He said some of them dated back to the Civil War and were worth much more than he paid for them. We were happy on that trip, never thinking our lives were about to change drastically. After he died I thought my world was over, and if it wasn't for Davy, it could have been." She looked into his eyes and smiled sheepishly, "Now I'm glad I survived." She moved closer and wrapped her arms around his waist. He hugged her back, and they remained that way for a few minutes before moving apart and refocusing on the view. They resumed discussing their former spouses, which naturally led to sharing information about their families and lives before meeting Lisa and Tom. Jake felt the former awkwardness dissolve and finally felt comfortable; it was as if they had known each other forever.

Finally he suggested they continue their exploration, to which she agreed. They re-entered the elevator and after examining the choices, Jake touched "1". Again, there was little sensation of movement as they watched the numbers decline until the rate slowed and stopped on "1". The doors opened and they found themselves facing a large open area surrounded by several closed doors instead of the lobby they anticipated. "Hold the door," he instructed, "while I check this out." He walked from door to door and found them all locked with instructions to *Stay Out and Authorized Personnel Only*.

He walked back to the elevator, entered while describing what he had seen, and touched "2". The doors closed for a few moments and then opened when the holographic display remained on "2". Peering through the open door, they saw a large open area, much like a subway station, including a sunken section that should have housed subway tracks, but was devoid of any. They walked to the sunken section for a closer look and found the vertical sides lined with, what appeared to be metallic badges. Anxious to find an exit, they re-entered the elevator and touched "3."

This time as the doors opened, they gazed at a series of hallways leading in seemingly all directions. They stepped out and found the walls decorated with signs and arrows. The signs appeared to be street names or building names. "This is interesting, but let's see if we can find our way out of here," urged Ronni, with growing alarm. They stepped back in and touched "4."

When the doors opened, they saw an extremely large open area with several elongated bubbles extending from the floor. They walked to one of the bubbles. Jake estimated it to be approximately nine feet long by five wide, and noticed it was sitting in a trough about a foot deep; the trough being only slightly wider than the bubble. Upon closer inspection Jake saw the same metallic badges lining the sides of the trough that they had seen on the previous floor, and the bubble was sitting on wheels. He looked up and said, "This is a car!"

Chapter 35

The car intrigued Jake but Ronni grabbed his arm. "How about we find our way out of here before looking at the cars? I'm getting concerned."

"Yeah, you're right. Let's try the next floor." They walked back into the elevator and touched "5". This time the doors opened on the lobby. They stepped out, breathing a collective sigh of relief and then turned to look at the elevator they had just emerged from. "Boy, are we dumb," stated Jake with a nervous chuckle as he pointed to a plaque beside the doors that read "LEVEL 5."

"Yeah," she smiled sheepishly. "Neither of us saw it. It would have saved me a lot of worry."

"Well, at least we have a better idea of how this city operated."

"What do you mean?"

"Level one must be the operational center housing the computerized mechanical brains that kept it running smoothly; level two looked to be the mass transit level; level three seems to be the walking level to the different buildings without going out in the weather or having to cross streets and interact with traffic; and level four must be for personal transportation. Ingenious! Hey, let's check out the cars downstairs."

"Let's do it!"

They returned to level four and stood together, surveying the area. There were about twenty-five to thirty vehicles parked at various places, all very much alike in design, resembling elongated bubbles on wheels and varying only slightly in color. They walked to one but couldn't see inside because the viewing area appeared to be mirrored. Circling the vehicle, they found no door handles or anything that looked to be a way in. Moving on they found the next vehicle was just like the first, and the next, and the next. While examining the fifth one Jake brushed against the left side and a door opened, not as a normal car door opens outward, but appeared to slide silently down within the side panel while a portion of the bubble slid upward to afford room to enter comfortably.

"Check this out," he urged while peering inside. "This is something!" She moved by his side and examined the interior, which included four-bucket seats.

Jake walked to the right side and brushed his hand on the door area. It opened the same way as the left one had. "Get in." She sat on the front right bucket seat and ran her hand over the seat.

"What's this material?" she asked as Jake lowered into the other front bucket seat. "It feels wonderful, soft yet firm."

"I agree but I don't have any idea." He continued to examine the interior. In front of him where a dashboard should be was a black panel stretching the entire width of the vehicle. A console extended from the bottom of the center of this panel downward to the floor. Overall, there was much more room inside than it seemed from outside. On the front of the console was the outline of a hand, so Jake placed his right hand inside the figure. Immediately the black panel lit up, and a message appeared that caused the two to glance at each other in disbelief.

WELCOME JAKOB RICHARD MEYERS
WHERE DO YOU WISH TO GO?
TYPE DESTINATION NAME OR NUMBER

"How did it know your name?"

"I don't know, unless ..." he paused to mull over possibilities. "Unless all the computerized systems are linked together to share information."

"I don't follow."

"Do you remember me mentioning that before we started looking for Nathan we were taking shelter in a house, or rather a group of pods connected to form a house-like structure? There were lighted panels inside that we found linked us to the computer system of the structure, much like the panels you used to operate your kitchen. The previous owner had not accessed the computer for over a hundred thirty years so it had to be reprogrammed. I had to place

C.P. STEWART

my hand inside a square and claim to be the new owner in order to reprogram it. That's the only thing I can think of because of the spelling. It asked me to pronounce my name and then asked if it was correct. I didn't bother to correct it, figured it wouldn't make any difference. Huh, imagine that; my fingerprints, ... er, handprint seems to be, quote, in the system, end quote." Smirking as he made the comment.

"That's incredible. But I don't know if I should be alone with someone who's in the system." She feigned disgust but was smiling. "Hey, let's go for a ride!"

"Where should we go?" Jake asked while searching the walls for some indication of where they were presently located. In case they *did* leave, he wanted to make sure they could get back. High on one wall he found a sign with a large *7445 New Surfway, Station 56, Parking Area 4B*. He pointed to the sign and asked, "Can you remember that?"

"You remember the first part, I'll handle the last two."

"Deal. Now where *to* my dear?" Jake exaggerated the question in jest, imitating someone he pictured as being very stuffy and quite rich.

Ronni playfully mimicked the attitude, "Why dahling, I think we should travel to Miami. Do you agree?"

"Certainly." He found a touch pad keyboard displayed in what had been the black panel and touched M I A M I. The panel responded.

YOU HAVE CHOSEN MIAMI
STATE CLEARLY YES NO

∞ 296 ∞

"Yes." The doors silently closed and all four seats slowly swung around 180° so the passengers were now sitting in the two rear seats. The vehicle proceeded forward in the trough toward a tunnel. Jake looked over at Ronni, shrugged, and then crossed his arms because the car was driving itself. Looking forward, Jake noticed a panel and console that appeared identical to the one he had faced before the seats rotated; a few quick alternating glances verified that the same information was being displayed on both. The roof was transparent, giving the illusion of riding in a convertible with no top or windshield frame.

The tunnel was well lit and the walls appeared smooth, not like the tunnels Jake remembered with concrete or concrete block walls. The ride was fairly smooth with only occasional minor bumping. After about three minutes in the tunnel, they were suddenly surrounded with daylight and landscape as the vehicle accelerated to 200 kilometers per hour, according to one of the displays in the panel. The ride became perfectly smooth, as if riding on air. "How fast are we going?" Ronni asked as she watched the scenery flash past.

"Two hundred kilometers per hour."

"No, I mean how fast in miles per hour. I don't understand that metric stuff."

"Let's see," Jake made a mental calculation and said, "A hundred twenty miles per hour, faster than I've ever gone in a car since I was eighteen. You like?"

"This is fantastic!" exclaimed Ronni, head swiveling as she looked at the passing landscape. "Are we outside?"

"No. If you look ahead you can see the landscape and skyscape narrow into a circle. We're actually in a tunnel, but seeing what's above ground."

"How? It looks so real."

"I remember seeing this at the library two days ago. It said all major highways and roadways were moved underground for safety and convenience."

"How is this safer?"

"Well, for one thing you don't have to worry about animals or other people coming out of nowhere in front of you. You also don't have to be concerned about weather problems: wind, rain, ice, and snow. In addition, if you notice how smooth and quiet this ride is, we're not polluting the atmosphere with any exhaust because there's no gas burning engine."

"No engine? How's it run?"

"Electromagnetism, like the monorail at Disney World."

"What's Disney World?"

"You know, Dis ... oh, that's right, Disney World wasn't opened until 1971, I think; you came here in 1965. Do you remember Disneyland in California?"

"I heard about it and always wanted to go there; it looked like such a fun place."

"Walt Disney built one here in Florida and called it Disney World. It turned out to be much bigger and better than Disneyland. Anyway, they moved people between parts of Disney World on a monorail, a train magnetically levitated and propelled by electromagnetism. This car runs the same way, except we are traveling inside a trough lined with magnets. The article also said sensors on the front and rear kept cars from running into each other."

"Oh," she said quietly, not sure if she totally understood the concept, but knowing enough about it to accept what he was saying. "What about the convenience part?"

"You don't have to drive; just sit back and let it go. Besides, if it's raining or snowing, you don't have to drive through it or step out into it. Just imagine, this state is prone to hurricanes, and you could jump in your car to drive wherever you wanted with no trouble, even if a hurricane was raging above." She pursed her lips and nodded as if to show she was catching on to the idea.

Jake continued, "What we're seeing is projected from a fiber optic cable that is suspended a little over a yard above the surface. We are seeing exactly what is going on aboveground."

"That's amazing!"

They traveled in silence for a few minutes, watching the scenery until their attention was demanded by a tone from the panel and a printed message.

OBSTRUCTION AHEAD
INITIATING DETOUR

They had seen alternate passages branching off at various locations along the way, but this time they turned onto one, smoothly and with no lean. Five minutes later a new message appeared.

DESTINATION MIAMI ATTAINED
PARKING AREAS INACCESIBLE OR FULL
PARKING IN NEAREST PROXIMITY TO CITY

The exterior scenery disappeared and they were again looking at the inside of a tunnel. The ride became a little rougher and Jake guessed wheels had been deployed. The vehicle pulled into a totally deserted parking area and stopped. The doors slid open and the system shut down.

After exiting, they took an elevator to ground level, stepping out into the lobby of what appeared to have been some type of commercial building. The room was devoid of furniture and had two hallways leading in diagonally opposite directions toward the rear of the structure; the right one was filled with debris, as if there had been a cave-in. Jake walked to the left hallway and peered down its length; more debris closed the other end.

"I'm not sure where we are, but this isn't how I imagined Miami," said Ronni. "Let's look outside."

Once outside they found the street deserted, just like the city they had left earlier. The neighboring buildings were low, none higher than three stories and appearing more residential than commercial, leading Jake to surmise they were probably in a suburb instead of Miami proper. Since Miami sits on the ocean, Jake checked the sun's position, and pointing east said, "This way."

Walking hand in hand they ascended a slight grade to its summit, expecting to see the magnificent city of Miami with its beautiful waterways and buildings. They stopped, astonished. Miami now lay in destruction, with building ruins poking through thick sand dunes and water, a few at odd angles. What showed of the partially submerged structures was layered with stains, various shades of brown and green stripes at irregular heights.

They regarded the scene and then each other. Jake spoke first, "Doesn't look like there's anything to see here. If what the car said about full parking lots is true, this must have taken everybody by surprise, and few had a chance to leave. I don't remember Miami being on the list of cities that were bombed ... I wonder what happened, maybe a tsunami or something. I also wonder if additional cities were destroyed." They stood awhile, unable to avert their eyes from the scene.

Without breaking her stare, Ronni quietly said, "What do you say we eat and then start back?" He solemnly nodded, and she opened the canvas bag after locating a shady level place along the street to position a small blanket. While they ate, their conversation was somber at first as they occasionally glanced toward what remained of Miami. Jake then took the opportunity to explain what life was like in 2005, which garnered Ronni's interest. She listened with rapt attention to descriptions of advances in automobiles, satellite dishes, cell phones, GPS, computerized checkout, etc. She also learned that men walked on the moon a mere four years after her disappearance.

After eating, they stretched out on the blanket facing each other, heads propped on a hand each. Ronni spoke first, "You know, this is the first time in three years I had the opportunity to get away from the apartment. It sure feels nice. Ending up here the way we did, with the plane crash I mean, just seems so unreal. Something like that shouldn't happen, and yet here we are."

"I know. I sometimes feel like we were part of a huge lake when somebody threw something in the water and we were the drops that splashed out, never to be a part of that lake again."

She leaned in and they kissed. After separating, she said, "Well, if you and I were supposed to splash out, I am certainly glad you and I splashed out to the same place." They kissed again, the kiss becoming more passionate.

Jake pulled back and said, "It's getting late. We probably should start back."

"I guess you're right. I'll gather the stuff, but before I do, I was wondering about something."

"What's that?"

"Well, it's been bothering me about what you said with reference to the Azujos being ... you know ... eating people.

"Yes, I'm sorry I had to tell you about that."

"I was thinking, why do they do that if they can get food from the computerized systems that seem to be everywhere? I mean they can at least eat baked goods like we do."

"I don't know the answer to that for sure, but I think

they have evolved into being driven to eating meat, which I don't think you can get from these computerized systems. I'm a little surprised that they appear to be cooking the meat, judging from the adaptations we saw on the dead one we examined, specifically the teeth and claws. Those are characteristics you would expect to see on wild animals. Maybe they are still evolving. I think we better go now."

While replacing the picnic materials into the canvas bag, they both couldn't help glancing at what remained of Miami. Jake then happened to look down and focused on something beside a nearby building that appeared to have been a residential structure, not too different from houses they were familiar with in the twentieth century. He walked over for a closer look.

"Come look at this," he said, pointing at the ground. Ronni moved beside him and saw a partial footprint in a small section of sand.

"Where'd that come from?" Ronni asked. "It looks fresh, and whoever made it wasn't wearing shoes."

"It has to be fairly fresh; otherwise the wind would have obliterated it," Jake said, looking around for signs of anyone's presence. He walked to the rear of the building while searching. "Well, it looks like there may be some others alive and living down here. Look at these."

"Do you think they might be Azujos?"

"I don't know, but it's a possibility. Look at the indentations just beyond each toe print; we didn't check the feet of our dead Azujos, but if his feet developed much like his hands, his footprints would have looked like these. Anyway, I'd say it's too bright for any of them to be out, but maybe we should go anyhow. If someone watched us and is hiding, it's either because he's afraid ... or setting a trap."

Ronni nodded agreement and picked up the bag. As they turned toward the street, three black-clad figures stepped out to block their way, faces obscured by dark hoods. Ronni screamed as Jake grabbed her hand and started to run behind the building.

The dark figures gave chase between the buildings as Jake and Ronni raced past the rear of two houses and then ran toward the street along the side of the second house. As they made the turn Jake glanced at the three pursuers. They didn't seem to be armed, and they ran, or rather loped, hunched over with heads mostly aimed downward. They weren't wearing shoes and what clothing showed intermittently under the robes appeared tattered and stained.

"Hurry," urged Jake as they reached the street where they had finished their picnic just minutes before, and turned west in the direction of where the car was parked. They stopped in their tracks; two additional figures blocked their way.

"Now what?" Ronni voiced panic.

"This way!" Jake barked, pulling her toward buildings across the street and headed between them with the two pursuers closing in and the original three hurrying across the street to continue the chase. They turned right, and as they ran behind the structure Jake noticed movement beyond the next building – two more headed toward them! He saw an open door to the right and pulled Ronni in. He closed the door and searched frantically for something to bar it with, not knowing if he made the right decision, but it seemed like the only option left open to them at the time. Suddenly they both were grabbed tightly from behind, hands covering their mouths.

Chapter 36

Jake struggled to free himself but was held so tightly he could hardly breathe. Ronni was squealing as she tried to cry out. They were dragged into the middle of another room where a third person, a thin fiftyish woman stood beside a hole in the floor, which they were forced through to strong, waiting hands below. Jake and Ronni were released with the exhortation to keep quiet. It was then that Jake took notice of the captors as they climbed down after the woman; his was a blond man who appeared to be in his twenties, and Ronni's had dark hair and seemed slightly older. The woman pushed a lighted panel on a wall and the hole over them immediately closed. Soon, footfalls were heard on the floor above.

"This way," the blond whispered and led the band into a wide tunnel. Jake recognized the tunnel as a vehicle passageway, probably something that connected each dwelling with the main highway system. Once inside the tunnel, a door closed behind them. They moved quickly for about five minutes until their progress was blocked by a section that had caved in. A hole in the debris existed to one side, obviously having been used often, as evidenced by how worn the edges were. Once through the hole, they continued for a couple of hundred yards before stopping. The blond man pushed a lighted panel and led everyone through a suddenly opened door, which shut behind them. Ronni looked at Jake, bewildered at what had taken place.

"Who are you and where are we?" Jake asked.

"In due time," responded the blond man, "Follow me." They moved through a labyrinth of tunnels, finally emerging in a large furnished room.

"Thy time hath come; sittest thou and let us speak," said one of the six. Jake and Ronni sat together on a lounger, not knowing what to expect. Were they prisoners? Had they been rescued? ... Or both?

They were joined by an older man, possibly early sixties, along with two women, both perhaps in their twenties, a pre-teen boy, and a girl around four or so. Eleven people sat or stood within the confines of the area, silently waiting for something, or someone to begin. The blond man took the initiative.

"I am Solomon. Who might thee be, and from whence hast thou come?"

Jake spoke, "My name's Jake Myers, and this is Veronica Langham. We came here on a day trip from a city to the north, don't really know its name, and were preparing to return when we were chased by, what I assume were Azujos."

"So, ye expect us to believeth thou didst come from a city ye don't even knoweth the name thereof? Why shouldest we accept that as God's truth?"

"Because it is," answered Jake.

"And what wast the reason for thy pilgrimage?"

Jake was becoming annoyed at the interrogation thus far and shot back, "Look, we didn't come here to cause trouble, and we certainly didn't come here with any intention of causing any of you harm ... matter of fact, we had absolutely no idea there was anyone still living down here. We appreciate your help in saving us from the Azujos, but if you would kindly direct us to our car, we will get out of your way."

The older woman interrupted, "Solomon, be thou at peace." She then turned toward Jake and Ronni, "I am sorry for the questioning ... please grant us thy forgiveness. I am known as Sarah and I begat Solomon and Jeremiah there." She indicated Ronni's original captor as the latter. "I am sure thou didst not wish harm on us and we wilt try to get thee back home as quickly as we art able ... but we all must remain in safety. Thou shouldest not depart from this safe place until we art sure thou canst."

Ronni said, "Thank you Sarah. I ... we appreciate all you've done for us, but I have a small son that I need to get back to as soon as possible. He saw his father killed by the Azujos a couple years ago, and I don't want him to worry about me."

"I doth understand thy feelings; an offspring shouldest

always cometh first. Solomon and Jeremiah, arise and go forth; bring news of when they may depart." The two men left without further utterance. Turning to Ronni she said, "While we bide our time, I will introduce my family. This is my husband, Malacai," she indicated the older man who had recently entered. Pointing to the two women, she said, "These are wives of our sons. The fair haired one, Ruth, belongeth to Jeremiah, and the other, Rebekah, belongeth to Solomon. The children art Jeremiah's. That is Rebekah's brother, Luke." This last introduction was of the man who had helped them in their passage through the hole in the floor earlier, a stocky man probably in his late teens. All of these people were dressed in cloth and skins of some type, much like men and women of the frontier.

"While we're waiting," Jake ventured, "how long have you lived here? I thought Florida was pretty much deserted."

The older man, Malachai, spoke up, "We hath lived our lives entire here, as did our ancestors who didst live before, and those before them. We art a peaceful family, as art the other families who livest here."

"Are you saying there are other people living here?"

"Yes. Dost thou findeth that troubling?"

"Troubling, no; surprising, yes. How many other families continue to live around here?"

Malachai paused to think, and then said, "I am not of certainty. We haveth meetings and worship with mostly six other families. We also shareth stores and whatever we need.

We art particularly close with the family Donarte, who liveth in quadrant three of the city."

Following this disclosure, Jake had many questions but didn't know what to ask first. He felt he should just go for it. "What is your family name and in what quadrant are we right now?

"We art the Hoolden family, part of the tribe Benjamin, and we art now within quadrant one."

"Do you know what happened to the city of Miami?"

"The story hast been told from generation to generation, the story of Noah's flood. Our ancestors who survived the great flood read to us of it in the book. We learned to read from them reading to us as we grew. Generations hath done thus. Our forefathers had not many possessions following the great flood, a few animals, a book, and God-given knowledge of survival. Out of those possessions we hath persevered and prospered. Our animals provideth us with nourishment, both from milk and meat, and clothing. Our crops provideth us with fruits and other food."

"How can you have those things with the Azujos around? In the city we came from, the Azujos only come out at night, and they seem very military-like, with light-shooting weapons. We also found evidence they eat meat, probably people. And yet, the ones we saw earlier seemed more like wild animals, with little disciplined structure, and hunting in packs. They also chased us in daylight. Why?"

"The blue-eyed creatures art known well to us. The creatures abideth in the underground passages of quadrant one and art forever prowling, searching for meat, as thou sayest. Through time, the creatures hath not discovered our stores, nor our stock. As to being about in daylight, I knowest not how, but I hath seen many creatures wearing face-coverings."

Jake pondered this, and then asked, "If the Azujos haven't found your animals and crops, where do you hide them?"

Malachai seemed uncomfortable at the question, but replied, "We hath them underground a distance from here. They are where only we knoweth and doth not say to anyone for fear the creatures might findeth them."

"But they have access to the lower levels just like you do. What keeps them from finding what you hid? Also you said you had animals. I researched the past and found that there was a shortage of meat; how did you get meat-producing animals?"

"We hath created cave-ins to block progress, and only we knoweth the way. Cattle, sheep and goats are kept in underground caves our fathers hollowed over many years. Our crops art grown in a multitude of caves using water. There art many passages with hidden doorways; we hath labored endlessly to keepeth the creatures out. The prophets foretold of the flood, so our ancestors gathered at least two of each living being they couldst capture, as taught in the book, and herded them away until the waters lowered. Through generations, the animals -- goats, cattle, sheep, and fowl, hath multiplied. We art a humble, but proud people living in the land of Oosa."

"I haven't seen any of you carrying weapons, so what happens when you run into …" Jake's question was interrupted by the return of Jeremiah and Solomon.

They stood wordlessly as Malachai addressed them, "Is the pathway now safe to returneth these good people to thy destination?"

Jeremiah turned to Jake and said, "We must first knoweth of thy destination before we art able to leadeth thee."

Jake looked at Ronni as if expecting her to supply some information, and then refocused on Jeremiah. "I don't really know where the car is parked. We used an elevator that led from the parking area to ground level in a building not very far from where you rescued us. I might recognize the building if I saw it again."

Jeremiah responded, "Thou shalt not walk on the ground because of the cursed creatures. It is best to travel below ground. What canst thou tell us of the building of which thou speakest?"

Jake thought. "All I know is it had two hallways leading diagonally toward the back when looking from the elevator. Both hallways were caved in."

Jeremiah and Solomon exchanged quizzical looks and then both looked to their father for direction. Malachai asked, "What is this 'diagonally' of which thou speakest?"

Jake squatted and traced the floor plan with his finger, which elicited a smile of recognition from Solomon. "I knoweth the place of which thou speakest. Father, do we haveth thy permission to lead these people to the Farston structure?"

"Yes, my sons." He then turned to Jake and Ronni and said, "Depart now, and God be with thee whithersoever thou goest."

Jake and Ronni both thanked their hosts and left to follow Jeremiah and Solomon through the tunnels. After a shorter time than Jake expected they entered the parking area and saw the lone car parked there. They thanked the two brothers, entered the vehicle, and following the destination prompt pressed in "7445". The seats again rotated and the vehicle moved forward through the tunnel into daylight scenery, once more reaching 200 kilometers per hour with an air smooth ride. The passengers sat back, rotated their individual seats until they were looking at each other, and tried to relax.

"What an experience," Ronni said. "Who'd have thought people would be living underground there? I'm so glad they were friendly."

"Me too, and I was certainly surprised too. I'm still confused about the Azujos though. I wonder why they behaved so much differently back there than they do where we live. It just doesn't make sense, and it sounded as if they roam around up here a lot. Well, as Malachai said, they wear some type of face-coverings; what that actually meant still leaves me baffled."

"Well, I just hope we don't meet up with those Miami types again; they were scary. Don't get me wrong, I'm scared of the ones we know, but they are more predictable, at least about only coming out after dark. By the way, Malachai said something about the land of Oosa; what was that about?"

"I'm not sure, but I wonder if he meant the USA. If nobody has said it as an acronym for generations, maybe they say it as a word – UUSSA."

"You may be right. What about the way they talked … it was kind of strange."

"I guess that's what you might expect if the only book you were taught from, and incidentally learned to read from, was the Bible. It must have been a King James Version. It was different. I'm confused about the part regarding how they prepared for the flood. Malachai said his ancestors, being warned about an imminent flood, gathered two of every animal, but where would they have found high enough ground to permit their survival; Florida is pretty flat. I also wonder about their crops; it sounded like they use hydroponics to raise vegetables and fruits. If so, how did they learn about it? Maybe knowledge was passed down through the generations because hydroponics was discovered way back in history and was in use in our time."

"What's hydroponics? I don't think I've ever heard of it."

"I think it's a way of growing plants without soil, just using nutrient-rich water. They could use it underground, like Malachai said, and use artificial light without actually planting anything in soil."

"Oh. I guess it makes sense."

"We've got to share this experience with the rest of our group as soon as we get back; I know they'll be interested in hearing about it."

A short silence followed after which Ronni teased, "Well, it looks like Miami might not be the best place to take a honeymoon."

Jake thought back to the Miami they had just experienced and didn't feel much like joking, but forced a reply, "You're right of course, and incidentally, don't you think I might be too old for you? I wouldn't want to be accused of robbing the cradle."

"When were you born?"

"1964, why?"

"Well, considering I was born in 1934 and you were one year old when I came here three years ago, I'm the one who needs to worry about being called a cradle robber." They both smiled, realizing that age norms just didn't apply to their situation.

"You've got a point there. I guess I must have a thing for older women."

It was early evening by the time they parked in the parking area. They took the elevator to the fifth level, and walked hand in hand into the street. As they approached the apartment and saw Davy still playing outside with the four teenagers, Ronni stopped and turned to face Jake. "I had a wonderful time today, even with all that happened. Thank you."

He smiled and traced the back of his hand down her cheek, "It was my pleasure."

Chapter 37

F our days passed quickly with everyone settling into new routines and finding his or her place within the new society. Mack and Scotty were regarded as the unofficial leaders of the colony, while Callahan and Mason seemed to hold jurisdiction over their respective passengers. Ronni stepped in whenever needed, to help or to offer advice in addition to her role as overseer of the kitchen. Skye and Kesha watched Davy as often as they were able; both had planned to major in Early Childhood Education at their respective colleges. Nathan could often be found helping with Davy, since it put him into close proximity to Kesha. Darryl, always looking for something to do, spent a good amount of time on *Blue Heron*, tinkering with the engines and cleaning the vessel from fore to aft. Veni helped when he wasn't keeping in shape by running on the beach or working with homemade weights, both activities could usually find Audryan involved. Juan kept his eye on Skye and found excuses to talk to her whenever possible. Carl Fontaine and Amy Kaufman seemed to pair up by default; neither put forth any effort to join in other circles, the mere act of which seemingly caused them to gravitate to each other. The Atwoods, in their mid-seventies, were hardly ever seen, spending nearly all the time in their second floor room. Mason and Callahan compared many stories of passengers and occurrences at sea. Through it all, Ronni and Jake mostly kept their distance but communicated with their eyes; eyes that expressed a close friendship that clearly was blossoming into much more. Occasionally, they found opportunity to sit and talk or take short walks while holding hands.

The sun was low on the horizon as Ronni walked outside to get Davy, who was playing with Skye. "Time to come in you two. We don't want to press our luck by being out here too long."

Skye looked up and sent Davy inside. She rose and asked a question that had been on her mind since her first visit to this apartment. "Don't the Azujos know you're here? If so, why don't they get in after dark and take people?"

"They know we are somewhere, but we don't think they know we're here. We know they're smart but we've tried to make sure we don't leave any evidence of our presence outside the building. For instance, I am going to use that branch over there to erase footprints any of you left in the sand. We can also watch through windows from a lighted room at night without anyone outside seeing us."

"What? How can that be?"

"We found the process by accident, and now we can turn

any or all windows into something like what we used to call *one way mirrors*, except it's more like *one way walls*. You see, one day shortly after we started living here, Davy was playing around one of the windows while my husband Tom was outside watching us. Suddenly, the window disappeared and all he saw was a continuation of the wall. It scared him and he came running in to see us doing the same things he had been watching from outside. Mack and Bobby found out how to do it and now we don't have to worry about Azujos seeing any sign of life in the building."

"But what about *our* rooms?"

"Don't worry, Mack and Scotty changed all the windows before you arrived. Look up at the building and see if you can find any windows." Skye scanned the building and found the only evidence of her window was a faint outline, the same for all of the windows.

"That's great! I feel a lot safer now, I was doing everything in the dark; guess I didn't need to worry."

"Besides, we close the main door before dusk and only a few know how to open it. We're pretty safe here. Wait a few seconds while I use the branch and then we'll go in together." Skye watched Ronni sweep the sand while backing up; after she threw down the branch, they walked through the main door into the building.

Once inside, they moved to their respective rooms; Ronni joining Davy in their room. Davy edged up to his mother and asked, "Do you like Mr. Myers, Mommy?"

"Why yes, Davy; he's a very nice man, don't you think?"

"Yes. I like him too. I feel safe around him. I'm glad he saved you from that bad man."

"I am too, now wash your hands, dinner's almost ready." He ran to the corner and pressed the little triangle just as people started to arrive.

After dinner, some residents departed for their rooms while others remained and engaged in conversation. Callahan was talking with Darryl about the maintenance being performed on *Blue Heron*, Mack and Scotty were discussing how things had changed with the new arrivals, and Juan and Nathan were comparing notes on the college girls. Jake was playing with Davy while Skye helped Ronni clean up.

By the time the dishes were clean and Skye departed, only Jake and Davy remained. Jake rose to leave. "It's time to turn in. Good night." As he walked past her, Ronni gave his hand a quick squeeze and watched him go.

"Good night stranger," she said after him.

"Good night. See you in the morning."

In the faint moonlight, a lone figure emerged from the shadows, furtively moved to the main entrance, and opened it. Others filed in noiselessly.

Jake was suddenly wakened from a sound sleep by something slapped onto his mouth and being forcibly turned face down, burying his face in the pillow while his hands were pulled behind and shackled. In the dim light of the room he saw Nathan receiving the same treatment at the hands of dark figures. A voice ordered them to put on their shoes, which they did without the use of their hands and then they were herded into the hallway. There they saw the rest of the first floor occupants standing along the wall, all with their hands tied behind and what looked to be duct tape over their mouths. Several Azujos were standing guard in the barely lighted area. All the prisoners were standing in their underwear, except Ronni in a nightgown and Davy in pajamas.

Ronni's eyes pleaded with Jake, but he was powerless to do anything except wait like the others. Soon they heard footsteps descending the ramp from the second floor followed by the appearance of more prisoners. Juan, Carl, Darryl, the three college girls, Amy, and the Atwoods were ushered into the hallway and forced to stand along the wall with the other prisoners. Juan's eyes blazed with determination, Darryl's with unbelief, Audryan's with fierce anger, and most of the rest expressed terror, some through their tears. Jake counted nineteen Azujos, each wearing their characteristic black hooded robes and carrying their light-shooting weapons. Through tears, Skye regarded Ronni with questioning eyes, and received in return a helpless shrug while surveying their situation. Other than the order to put on their shoes, none of the Azujos spoke, but just appeared to be standing guard.

Footsteps again descended the ramp and a cloaked figure entered the hallway. When he was close enough, he pushed back his hood to reveal the person known to most of them as Cranston. He walked past each prisoner until reaching the last one and then retraced his steps, repeating the process. After arriving back where he started, he turned and addressed his captive audience.

"Hello friends, my name is Manny Contraldo and it's so nice to see you again ... especially you," he cooed, tracing his finger along Ronni's jaw line, causing her to close her eyes and recoil from his touch. He stared coldly at her for a few moments and then returned his attention to the rest. "I bet you're surprised to see me; actually you came very close to never seeing me again, because I was almost dinner for my hooded friends here," he paused for effect and then continued, "But I did a little bargaining. After all, it only made sense for them to release one day's meal in return for, let's see ... " he paused while counting the prisoners, " ... eighteen meals; well, seventeen if *you're* nice to me." He had returned his gaze to Ronni.

Manny walked slowly until he faced Callahan. "So Mr. policeman from Pittsburgh, I didn't know if you'd recognize me sometime, but it doesn't matter now. When my friends get to you, I guess they'll be havin' pork. Oink, oink," he mocked, and then moved on to face Jake, where he thrust his face very close.

"So, you think you know all about me; well you don't know *shit!*" he hissed. "I suppose since you found out about me, you also know about the real Allen G. Cranston. Too bad for him ... I needed a car ... and when I looked through the car, guess what I found. No guess? I found a reservation for a boat ride, a perfect way to skip the country. The only trouble was ... any guesses? You and your kid!" His volume had risen to a crescendo with the last part. He calmed somewhat before continuing in an even voice, "I could have easily done away with the dear captain and his flunky and sailed on to safety, but I only had one knife ... bad odds with four men to dispose of, wouldn't you say, *Mister* Myers? When we jumped so far ahead in time, I thought I had it made, and things were going well until the *Pittsburgh Pig* showed up!" His voice had risen again. He turned to address everyone in a Shakespearian tone, "But now, alas, it is time to break up this little party. You will go in groups of four along with four of my hooded friends to discourage any mass heroics from so large a group." As an afterthought, he paused in his exit and turned around, "Oh and many thanks to Captain Bankowski for the very versatile duct tape; it was nice of you to park so close ... made it really handy."

Manny walked to the Azujos on the end closest the exit, whispered something into his ear and then left. While the guards were conducting the grouping process, three Azujos escorted Ronni and Davy into the night bringing terror to Jake's throat.

Chapter 38

The Azujos waited about fifteen minutes after Ronni and Davy's departure before herding the first group of four prisoners into the night. The first group included Kesha, Audryan, and the two Atwoods. Jake was beside himself; he wanted to get loose and kill these creatures, and then he would take the greatest pleasure in dismantling Contraldo one body part at a time. Contraldo, what had he done with Ronni? His guess was that they would all ultimately end up at the stadium and he figured she would be there in about another half hour. What worried him most was what would happen to her between the time she arrived until the rest of the group showed up. He wanted to be in the next group so he could get there sooner, but they weren't permitted to move around. His wrists hurt; looking at others' shackles he saw they had used wire ties, narrow locking strips of plastic, and he knew how strong they were. Contraldo must have gotten them from Mason's boat along with the duct tape. He felt helpless. Making matters worse was the thought of what the drugs could do to Davy; a child that young might not survive.

He was lost in thoughts of how to get free when the next group was taken; this included Darryl, Carl, Amy, and Skye. Each time a group left, four Azujos accompanied them; now only eight remained. His mind raced but he still didn't see any way out of this predicament. He struggled to free his wrists but to no avail; he knew his restraints were too hard to stretch and they cut into his flesh when he tried. The only thing the remaining prisoners could do was look at each other, and await their turn.

As Nathan, Veni, Scotty, and Mack were leaving with four other Azujos, the remaining four prisoners' eyes darted between each other and the guards. Jake tried to wriggle his hands through the ties once more. Again, nothing. He glanced at Nathan who looked back with an expression of resignation as he was herded from sight. A slight movement caught his eye and he looked at Juan who was alternately moving his eyes between Jake's eyes and hands, obviously trying to send a message, but what message? Jake narrowed his eyes and furrowed his brow. Juan repeated the same movements, to which Jake gave a slight shrug. Juan turned slightly, permitting Jake to see that his hands were working out of the bindings; they weren't out yet and it appeared he needed a little help. Jake met his eyes and nodded once.

Finally it was the last group's turn to leave, and the guards prodded them to move with the ends of their weapons. They exited the building and began walking westward, seemingly toward the stadium. As they walked behind Mason and Callahan, Juan continued to take a path that brought him ever closer to Jake until they were walking side by side. Since they *gradually* moved into close proximity, the guards didn't seem to notice and continued walking while looking straight ahead. Two guards led the way while the other two flanked the prisoners.

Juan held his bound hands to the side closest to Jake, who grabbed the tie with a couple of fingers and pulled, but it didn't budge. He looked at Juan, the hazy moonlight casting muted shadows on his features as he nodded his head three times. Understanding the gesture, Jake grabbed the tie again as they walked and watched Juan nod once, twice, and on the third nod he pulled hard as Juan pulled the other way; Jake felt the empty tie in his hand and glanced over to see him nod.

The guard walking to the right looked back at Jake and Juan, who had quickly returned his hands behind his back as if still bound, and then slowed to walk behind them. Now, two guards walked in front, one to the left, and one behind the prisoners as they continued their trek. Jake felt safer when the guard was walking beside rather than behind. Now anything Juan and he did could jeopardize the other two prisoners in front of them, because there was no way to communicate or warn of any escape plans.

Another block passed when Jake glanced at Juan and saw him nodding slightly toward the two prisoners walking in front of them. He shook his head no, but not enough to alert the rear guard. Juan patiently nodded toward the rear guard, then toward the side guard, then toward Jake and finally toward the two prisoners. Not understanding, Jake gave a slight shrug. Juan tried again, this time taking more time to try to get his message across. He nodded toward the rear guard and then toward the side guard, a pause, and then he nodded toward Jake and then quickly toward Mason and Callahan. Jake thought he understood and nodded agreement, hoping he grasped the true meaning of what Juan intended; if he didn't do what was expected at just the right time all four could end up dead.

Jake watched Juan out of the corner of his eye as he slowed his pace and fell behind. The guard moved to him and attempted to push him forward with his weapon. As soon as he felt the guard close behind, Juan rammed his left elbow into the guard's face and grabbed the weapon with his right while Jake threw a body block on the back of the other prisoners' legs, forcing them to fall. Juan felled the side guard with a single burst and a sweeping prolonged shot dropped the front guards as they wheeled around. The rear guard started to rise but Juan's fist connected hard and he went limp.

Juan ripped the tape off his mouth first and then the others. Callahan had a laceration on his forehead and Mason was bleeding from a gash on his shoulder but they were glad to be free.

"Get our hands free," Mason ordered as soon as his tape was pulled off. Juan tried all three but the wire ties were too strong to break. He had a thought.

"I'll blast them off with the light-shooter, bend over so I can see better."

"Whoa!" exclaimed Mason. "I wanta keep my fingers!"

"Don't worry; I'll put the business end against the material and give a short burst.

Ready?" Mason bent over, closed his eyes and extended his hands as far behind as he could. He heard a *puht* and his hands were free.

Callahan motioned for Jake to go next, and then assumed the position while Jake rubbed his freed wrists.

"We hafta go after those sonsabitches!" Mason said, "We gotta save th' others."

Jake stated the obvious, "We can't just go in there and expect to come out alive, much less get anyone else out; we need a plan and I might have one. First though, I want to thank Juan for his quick thinking and superb reflexes; without either of which we would still be prisoners." Mason patted him on the back while Callahan nodded approval.

"I never regretted hirin' this young man." After a reflective pause he prodded, "Okay, what's yar plan?"

"I think we should wear these guards' robes and try to pass ourselves off as them until we get inside and see what's going on."

"Sounds good to me," responded Callahan. "But we need weapons and I don't think we have time to go back to the apartment."

"Use these," suggested Juan, picking up the rear guard's light-shooter he had used to free their hands. "I'll show you how to use it."

They each grabbed a light-shooter weapon and Juan

gave them a quick lesson in its operation. Each made a few practice shots and then began their preparations. After removing the hooded robe, Jake used Juan's zip tie on the unconscious guard's wrists, pulling it tighter, and used the best piece of duct tape on his mouth. Juan removed the robe from the left guard's body, but the other two robes were unusable because they were both cut about in half.

"It looks like we need to change the plan," Jake stated. "Instead of all four of us using the disguise, I think two are going to have to act as prisoners."

"You and Juan take the robes," recommended Callahan. "Captain Bankowski and I will be the prisoners; Lord only knows we've had plenty of practice over the last hour or so. One thing though, I prefer to have a weapon with me in case something goes down."

"These weapons are fairly small; I think you could carry it behind your back if the top part is hidden under your shirt. Fair enough?"

"Sounds good, let's go."

Juan gazed down at the unconscious guard and asked, "What should we do with him?"

Jake stepped forward and said, "Maybe we can use him if he cooperates." Handing his weapon to Callahan, he instructed, "Hold this on him to let him know we mean business."

He squatted beside the guard, lifted his head and gently slapped his face a few times. The guard moaned and opened his eyes to find he was staring at the barrel of one of their weapons. His eyes grew wide in the faint moonlight and he tried to speak, "Umm ... ummmm ... "

Jake said quietly, "If I remove the tape will you be quiet?" The guard peered up at him, seemingly not comprehending. Jake tried again, but this time it was more of a demand than a request, "I am going to take off the tape, don't make a sound." The last part he emphasized by pointing at the weapon. The guard looked terrified and glanced back and forth between Jake and the weapon aimed at his face.

Jake removed the tape slowly until he was sure the guard would remain silent. He asked, "Where did they take our people?" The guard stared quizzically at him, still appearing terrified but saying nothing. Once more Jake tried but increasing his tone into an order, "Where did they take our people?"

The guard's panic intensified as he stammered, "N..no ha...hablo Ingles." Jake looked at Juan questioningly.

"He says he doesn't speak English," explained Juan. He then knelt beside the guard and spoke in Spanish; the guard's fear seemed to diminish as he answered. Juan listened and then translated, "He says they are at the stadium like we figured."

"Ask him what they plan to do with them," instructed Jake.

Juan again spoke to the guard and waited for the reply. The guard's eyes moved from Juan to Jake to the weapon still aimed at him before speaking haltingly, with fear perceptibly growing. After speaking slowly, his pace quickened and his words came very quickly while his eyes darted be-tween his captors. When he finished, Juan interpreted, "He is afraid of us, but he said they are to be used in something called the *Festival of Sustenance*, a type of ritual, involving sacrifice for the nourishment of his civilization. He says he doesn't like it, but it is needed for their survival because of the lack of food."

Jake thought a moment and then said, "Ask him when the Festival is scheduled."

Juan exchanged words with the guard, then looked up and said, "He used a couple words I'm not familiar with, but I'm pretty sure he said today at dusk."

Callahan cursed, and then said, "That doesn't give us much time since they're probably drugged by now. We need to get there as soon as possible."

Jake rose and strode off toward a building speaking over his shoulder, "Juan, find out why he speaks Spanish and the other ones we met speak English, and see if you can get him to help us." He disappeared into the building while Juan returned his attention to the guard, and a lengthy exchange took place.

Inside the building, Jake found a vacant wall in the semi-darkness and stood studying it for a moment. He aimed his light weapon at a point on the wall, and using a continuous light burst, traced out a rectangle roughly six feet by four feet. He dug his fingers along its edge and pulled, causing the sec-tion to fall on the floor. The section was constructed in three layers, the second of which consisted of a type of insulation. He pried off the back layer to expose the insulation and then pried the insulation off in one piece. It was very light and was probably blue in color, just like the insulation he had seen in the demolished ruins at the apartment inhabited by Callahan and his passengers. At the time it didn't hold any significance, but he had suddenly remembered it, and a hypothesis needed to be tested. Carrying the insulation, he approached the others from behind the guard. As he came within range, Juan related, "He says some speak Spanish, some English, and some are bilingual; it depends on the family one is brought up in. He said his family doesn't socialize with the English speaking ones because they are generally, what he called them is roughly translated as *too vicious*. He is willing to help to a point, but he fears for his life if anyone finds out."

Keeping the slab of insulation between him and the guard, Jake walked into the guard's visual area and spoke, "Find out how old he is."

Juan asked, "Cuantos anos tiene usted?"

The guard appeared agitated and glanced quickly in different directions while answering, "Dies y seis."

Juan responded, "He says he's sixteen, my age, but he's acting funny. What did you do?"

"I'm testing a theory." The guard's eyes were darting everywhere and he was getting more frantic. "Ask him what's wrong."

Juan exchanged words with the guard and then related, "He says he hears you talking but you're not here."

"Does he mean he can't see me?"

Juan asked the question to which the guard quickly replied, "Si' ... si'!"

"He says he can't see you." Jake lowered the insulation and the guard focused on him questioningly.

"It's just as I thought," explained Jake. "At night they don't actually see us, they see heat, so when I put this layer of insulation in front of me, it acts as a barrier to heat. I think we now know something they don't even realize, and it just may give us the edge we need."

Chapter 39

Callahan and Juan, dressed in the hooded robes escorted Mason, acting as a prisoner through the streets toward the stadium while Jake moved with them a short distance behind, peering over his insulation shield. The guard had been too frightened to help, so Juan explained they would pick him up on the way back if things went well. They re-taped his mouth and used Callahan's undershirt to bind his ankles, rendering him immobile and carried him into the building where Jake had acquired the insulation.

Jake estimated the time to be about an hour before the earliest signs of dawn, and for the insulation to be useful they had to confront any Azujos they met in the darkest conditions they could find.

They were approximately a quarter mile from the stadium when two Azujos met them. After a quick inspection, one of them spoke, "Why are you so late, and where are the other prisoners?" Jake kept the shield in front as he continued forward.

"They tried to escape and we had to kill them," Juan lied

and then added, "The other two are watching the bodies until we deliver this one."

"You know the orders! Zebular will have your head!"

"Not this time!" The voice seemed to come out of nowhere, and as the two frantically searched for its origin, Jake reached around his shield and fired two quick bursts dropping both guards. "Two more robes for the taking," he said while removing one; Mason grabbed the other before dragging the bodies behind a building.

Now all four were wearing black robes with hoods covering their heads. They figured that if they walked with their heads bowed, none of the Azujos would be able to detect their different eyes. Even with the hooded robe, Jake continued to carry the shield in front while following the other three. As they approached the stadium they noted that only one of the massive doors was open, flanked by two guards. Callahan whispered to keep moving.

Upon walking past, one of the guards commented, "Nice day."

Callahan replied, "Yes it is."

The two guards shouted, "Stop!" Callahan, leading the way stopped abruptly and the other two followed his example, all nervously readying their weapons. One guard moved behind while the other walked to face them, advanced to Callahan and jerked back his hood. At this, Callahan's point blank shot caused the guard to spin around and fall unmoving on the ground while Jake clubbed the rear one with his weapon.

Mason turned around and asked, "Why didn't ya kill 'im?"

"He was between us and I didn't want to take a chance on the beam going through him and hitting either of you. This thing is like a powerful laser and I think it could easily take out more than one person at a time."

"Well, he isn't in front of anyone now," Callahan observed as he put a beam through him. "Let's go!"

Jake, shocked by this act of violence on an unconscious individual, had to force it from his mind as they dragged the bodies into a secluded area outside the stadium. "We found you prisoners in a room this way." Jake pointed to the right and started in that direction.

They hurried through the hallway. As they passed the first offset room Jake shuddered, thinking of the sights he encountered there. Getting close to the second offset room where the prisoners were found last time, they broke into a jog, causing Mason to start puffing almost as soon as they quickened the pace. The hallway was considerably darker than the last time, but a dim glow illuminated their way. Suddenly the offset room was upon them, and they almost passed it in their haste. Mason was panting and wheezing as they readied their weapons and started into the hallway leading to the room.

Peering into the room, they saw the prisoners tied to exposed girders, all slumped and supported by their shackles. As they entered, a movement to the left caught Jake's eye causing him to drop instinctively and turn to fire, stopping at the last instant as he identified the mover as Nathan, who was fighting sluggishly against his restraints.

Juan ran to Skye who was also showing some movement, while Jake quickly moved to Nathan. "Nathan," he said pulling the tape off his son's mouth. "Are you all right?"

"Umm, I ammmokaaay," he slurred. "I tried to not taaake theedruggg." The last sound was exaggerated as he attempted to answer his father. "I remememberedd las'tiiime theygaave usss sommmthin' todrinkk an' I spittt itoutt wennn they lefttt thissstiime."

"Okay Nathan, you did the right thing," Jake said as he untied his son while surveying the room. He saw Mason and Callahan freeing prisoners and setting the unconscious forms gently on the floor; Juan had left a semiconscious Skye to free Audryan when Jake felt as if a sledgehammer had hit him in the gut. Ronni and Davy weren't here! He released his grip on Nathan, who slid down the girder until he was sitting. He made a slow sweep with his eyes to make sure he hadn't missed them and then panic set in. *Where could they be? Was there another room similar to this one?* He vowed to check out every inch of this place and pray he could find them, because if they weren't in the stadium ... retaining his sanity kept him from pursuing that prospect further. He had to get going. *Now!*

"I'm going to look for Ronni and Davy!"

"Hold it!" The command came from Mason. "There

ain't no way ya're goin' out there alone. Let's sort this out an' we'll get ya some help."

"I guess you're right but we can't waste time," he shot back while freeing Veni, and then he had to focus totally on his task when the unconscious young man went dead weight upon release; it was all Jake could do to keep him from falling on his face.

When all prisoners were free, Jake spent a few minutes trying to bring Nathan back to full functionality, but the process was slower than he hoped. He analyzed their situation with mounting despair; there were twelve newly released prisoners, ten of whom were unconscious from some type of drug, and the remaining two were still in a fog. How were they going to transport all these people out of the stadium, much less get them back to the apartment. He was so desperate to find Ronni and Davy he was having trouble concentrating, but he knew he had to focus on the immediate problem first.

Callahan stepped forward and said, "Meeting ... now!" Jake, Juan, and Mason looked up and when he saw he had their attention, he said, "I don't know if you've noticed but there's no way in hell we'll be able to get these people outta here for at least four or five hours, and that's helping to carry them; it'll be more like eight hours until they might be able to walk on their own. Remember I've been there, that stuff they make you drink is very powerful."

"Nathan and Skye aren't totally out," interjected Jake. "Nathan told me he waited until they left and spit out his dose; maybe Skye did the same."

"Okay, that means two will be ready earlier and can work with the others; that'll help. It's going to be daylight soon so it's probably best if they all stay here until they can walk out on their own. How about I go with Jake to search and you two stand guard here until we get back?"

Juan glanced at Mason and then back to Callahan and agreed, "Sounds like a plan; go ahead, we've got things covered here." Jake was on his feet and Callahan had to hurry to catch up.

Reaching the main hallway, they pulled up their hoods and started to the right. They peered into every space that was large enough to be a possible holding area, and after about twenty minutes found themselves back where they started. They rejoined the others and reported that Davy and Ronni were not in the stadium.

"Well where can they be?" asked Mason. "We saw 'em taken by th' guards so they should be here someplace."

Jake's emotions were exploding from within; he remembered feeling the same disbelief coupled with a sense of loss and hopelessness when he heard about Lisa. He had forced the obvious from his mind, but he now had to face it head-on. Contraldo had her and he had absolutely no idea how he could find out where.

"The guard!" he suddenly cried with urgency. "I've got to get back to our prisoner!"

Callahan voiced the question Mason and Juan were wondering, judging by their expressions, "Why?"

"Ronni and Davy aren't here because Contraldo has

them somewhere else. I would guess it might be where these people live, or at least somewhere the guard might know about. If he hasn't escaped by now, I need to find out what he knows or doesn't know."

"It's worth a try. I'll stay here on guard; take Captain Bankowski with you and you'll need Juan to translate."

Mason spoke up, "You're the cop and I'm too slow; you go an' I'll stay. No arguments, get goin'!" Seeing the wisdom in his suggestion, Callahan nodded agreement and left with Juan and Jake.

The three men headed east from the stadium, noticing streaks of deep red along the horizon. A few minutes later the building where they had left the guard bound and gagged came into view. Arriving at the structure, they entered and found the guard where they had left him.

Juan removed the tape while Jake instructed him on what to say, "Ask him where they took the woman and child."

A dialogue took place before Juan looked up, "He said he doesn't know; he thought they were taken to the same place as everyone else."

"Did he ever meet Contraldo?"

Another exchange and then Juan translated, "He says he never saw him before the apartment. He said he was just following orders."

"Who gave him the orders?"

After a brief exchange, "His superior is someone named Jorenzo."

"Who gives orders to Jorenzo, and where can we find him?"

This time a lengthy dialogue took place in which the guard became animated at times. Juan translated, "Jorenzo takes orders, as does everybody, from someone named Zebular, but he says this guy is very scary, someone we need to avoid at all costs. They all live underground in the transportation tunnels, something like subway tunnels. Every family lives in a *nest area*, or that's the best I could translate what he said, and this Zebular lives in a larger area with several helpers, probably what we would call bodyguards. He says Zebular is very dangerous because he is powerful, called him something like the *judicial supervisor* of the entire colony. He also said the sun is coming up soon and he needs to return to his daytime land."

"Ask him if he will take us to Zebular's nest."

As Juan was speaking the guard was emphatically shaking his head no, and then he responded, after which Juan replied, "He says it would mean certain death for him and his family if he was caught. He would rather have us kill him now, at least that way his family would be safe."

"Okay, I understand. Thank him for his help and tell him we'll let him go free if he does two things for us, first give us directions to Zebular's nest and second, show us the best route to get underground and close to Zebular."

Jake and Callahan watched as another animated conversation took place in which the guard interspersed rapid speech with shaking his head, but by the end of the dialogue he nodded affirmatively. "He agrees but is anxious to return home." The guard then resumed talking and a lengthy dissertation followed with Juan interjecting at times. Standing, Juan related, "He gave me directions to Zebular's place, and I think I understood enough to find it."

"Let him go, and again tell him thanks." Juan rolled the guard onto his stomach and used a short burst from the light-shooter to free his hands while Callahan removed his shirt from the guard's ankles. The guard rolled to a sitting position and took Jake's offered hand to stand. He said something to Jake, who looked to Juan quizzically.

Juan smiled and translated, "He said his name is Darmak, and you seem to be honorable; he wishes you good luck." Jake smiled and extended his hand only to have Darmak stare at it, and then look at Juan. After Juan explained in Spanish that shaking hands is a sign of friendship and trust, he placed his hand in Jake's and smiled. Jake nodded to him while handing back his hooded robe; Darmak quickly donned it, and hurried out into the early morning light, cringing and trying to shield his face.

The three men followed Darmak to a commercial building situated on a corner and entered. They watched as he went into an elevator, pointing to the floor choices and held up two fingers before the door closed and he was gone.

"Let's give him some time before we follow." Jake suggested.

Callahan countered, "While we're waiting I think we should go back to the apartment and get guns that I'm more familiar with." Then as an afterthought, "I also would feel better with more clothes on."

"You're probably right, but let's hurry," urged Jake turning to go. Ten minutes passed before they reached the apartment. "Get the guns and we'll meet at the main door."

Jake jogged to his room and dressed quickly; he was first to the door and waited impatiently for the other two. When they finally arrived, he could tell something was bothering them. "What's wrong?"

Callahan answered dejectedly, "They took all our guns; there's nothing left."

Chapter 40

D o you like your new quarters?" Manny asked sweetly. "I think we'll have a nice life here, don't you think?"

Ronni, bound to a chair, looked at him incredulously. "Never!"

"Ah now, I know you'll grow to love it."

"I'll tell you what I would love; let us go and get out of my sight!" she hissed, struggling to free her hands.

He walked to her, lowered so his face was about three inches from hers and whispered while sliding his hands down her arms, "Too bad, you're mine now, whether you like it or not; we're going to have a good time together." She spit on his face causing him to recoil, wiping his face with his shirttail. He regarded her with rage, "You'll pay for that! You'll damn well regret that!" He calmed slightly and then said evenly, "I'll let you think about it, and while you're at it, think about your little boy. Keep in mind that I can do anything I want with him and you can't do a thing."

"Don't you dare touch a hair on him, you scum! If you hurt him in any way I'll kill you!"

"I don't see how you're in any position to give me orders. Now think about your lack of options and I'll be back soon. If you're not more cooperative, I guess I'll just have to give our hosts another offering, a smaller portion perhaps." He wheeled and left the room, exchanging a few words in passing with the two guards outside, and then he was gone.

She strained against her bindings until she couldn't stand the pain any longer, thinking about Davy the whole time; she didn't have any idea where they had taken him, and she was concerned about how he was dealing with everything. He had seen his father killed, and Ronni remembered his silence that lasted three months, an eerie silence accompanied by an almost total absence of emotion. *What is his mental state now,* she worried; is he going through the same thing, thinking he was going to lose his mother too. She winced against the pain and tried to free her hands again. Contraldo was an animal … no, worse than an animal! Why had he singled *her* out instead of one of the college girls? The only reason she could come up with was he saw her before any of the others and had become fixated. He seemed to be someone used to getting his way, not caring about anyone but himself.

Manny was savoring his victory and congratulating himself on outsmarting everyone as he left the apartment for the second time in two hours. He had the woman he wanted, and even though she was resisting him at the moment, she would come around; he had the proverbial *ace-in-the-hole,* her son. He knew the bitch would do anything, and even pretend to enjoy it if her son's life was at stake. He couldn't wait to play *that* card! Just thinking about her pretending to enjoy the things he had planned excited him immensely. In addition, he had eliminated everyone who knew about him, and even a few others thrown in to sweeten the deal with Zebular; but just in case any of them escaped their intended fate, as improbable as it seemed, he had swiped all their weapons from the apartment. Life was good!

Having difficulty with the stolen weapons forced him to stop. He stuffed four handguns into his waistband and filled his pockets to overflowing with shells, which freed up his hands to carry the shotgun and the extra shells that wouldn't fit in his shirt pockets.

He walked into the Holloway Building, which had housed some type of business offices at one time, crossed to the elevator and entered. He touched the holographic number "2" and watched the surface world disappear as the doors closed. He patiently watched the LED numbers change from "5" to "4" to "3" to "2" and felt the elevator stop softly. The doors opened to reveal the large vacant area that reminded him of a standard subway station without the tracks; this was more like the Squirrel Hill Tunnel, a traffic tunnel he was familiar with in Pittsburgh. The lighting was dim throughout these tunnels, but bright enough to see where you were going. He chose the tunnel that headed west and began walking.

Chapter 41

Jake, Juan, and Callahan, armed with the light-shooting weapons, headed back to the commercial building where they had last seen Darmak. After entering the elevator, Jake touched "6" which resulted in Juan's concern, "Wait a minute. We're supposed to go down to two, not up to six."

"Don't worry, just a little detour," assured Jake and then as the doors opened, "Let's go." He led them through the building, checking each room until he found what he was looking for. "In here!" He led them into a room that was devoid of furniture and wall coverings. He used his weapon to cut out a section of wall approximately five feet by four feet, and pulled it until it fell out. He then cut out two more of similar size while the other two watched, intrigued. "There's one for each of us; get the insulation out like this." Jake started peeling the back layer off and the others followed his example.

Once they had freed the insulation, Callahan asked, "What are we going to use these for? It's daylight now."

"Look at the color."

After examining the pieces, he stated the obvious, "Blue, why?"

"Actually it's dark blue, and if my theory is right, I think the shields will still work but we're going to have to be a little more careful."

"I don't get it," Juan said, confusion showing on his face.

Jake replied patiently, "Remember how they couldn't see me behind the shield in the dark because it blocked the heat?" They nodded and he continued, "Well, it seems their eyes *are* shifted toward the red end of the spectrum and that means it is a definite possibility that they can't see violet and quite possibly blue. If that's the case, they will probably see gray, like much of the background. Regardless, I think we stand a better chance hiding behind these so they won't see heat, and if we remain fairly still, we should appear to blend into the surroundings."

"Okay, it's worth a try," conceded Callahan as he turned to leave. They reached the elevator and touched "2". As the elevator door opened to the second floor, they were squatting behind the shields, ready to fire at anyone that might be awaiting their arrival. The area was clear.

"Which way, Juan?" Jake asked.

Juan thought a minute, trying to remember Darmak's directions and then said, "Straight ahead four stations and then right for two stations."

They started forward then turned right after reaching the fourth station and were approaching the second station when they heard shouting ahead and flattened against one wall, pulling up their insulation shields. A minute later they were forced to remain motionless as eight Azujos approached from the direction of the shouting. The Azujos passed by without noticing, and continued until the sound of their footsteps disappeared after them.

"That was close!" Callahan observed. "Did you notice anything about those guys?"

"Do you mean the dark goggles?" asked Juan.

Jake said, "I saw them too, and that means they must be headed outside, but where?" After a thoughtful moment he speculated, "What if they're headed to the stadium … Captain Bankowski has the only weapon! What should we do?"

"You're right, there's no way he'd be able to hold them off," agreed Juan. "We need to help him."

"But we don't know for sure that's where they're going," argued Callahan. "What if they're going somewhere else?"

"I'm pretty sure that's where they're headed," countered Jake. "I bet they got a report about the ones we killed and are going to try to secure the area before their prisoners get away. Nathan's back there and Ronni and Davy are probably here somewhere. We need to split up."

"I'll go to the stadium," volunteered Juan, standing. "It would be suicide for only one to keep going down here so two need to stay, and besides, I've had the most experience with these light-shooting weapons. Since the troops already left, I'll be behind them, something they won't be expecting." Looking Jake straight on, "Don't worry, Nathan'll be okay." Without another word he picked up his insulation shield, shook hands with both of them, and then he was gone.

"Are you sure that kid's only sixteen?" Callahan queried while looking in the direction where he had just seen Juan disappear.

"I've wondered the same thing many times over the past week. I pray he'll be all right ... and everyone else too. Let's get going and maybe we can help him if we get Ronni and Davy out soon."

They resumed their trek toward Zebular's place. Becoming suddenly aware of approaching footsteps, they flattened against the wall, hiding behind their shields. Five Azujos marched by, one in the middle flanked by two in front and two behind, all wearing dark goggles and headed in the same direction as the previous group ... and Juan.

Callahan watched them retreat from sight then turned to Jake, "We better step up the timeline; looks like Juan's going to need some help." A minute later they were standing in front of a large door that they surmised must lead to Zebular's place. While weighing their options, they were interrupted by a high-pitched voice from behind.

"Hola, are you looking for something?" They quickly turned to see a young boy with long thin hair and large light blue eyes standing in childish innocence. The boy appeared to be approximately eight to ten years old and was dressed in a yellow jumpsuit that seemed to be made of the same material the adult Azujos wore under their hooded robes. Seeing the strangers' faces, he took a cautious step backward saying, "You are surface dwellers and don't belong here."

Not wanting to spook the child into alarming anyone of their presence, Jake thought fast and said soothingly, "Hello there young man, my name is Jake, what's yours?"

The boy appeared confused as if not knowing what to do, but after a lengthy silence replied hesitantly, "My name's Apheris."

Trying to make gentle conversation, he continued, "Do you live close by?"

Apheris stepped backward again and seemed ready to run, but inexplicably, possibly out of curiosity, remained in place and pointed across the tunnel to a small door that was open. "Over there."

Wanting to assuage the child's uncertainty, Jake sat against the wall, setting his weapon and shield at arms length and motioned for Callahan to do the same. This seemed to help Apheris relax a little, and he came closer by two steps.

"Tell me about your family. Do you have brothers or sisters?"

The child reacted to the non-threatening posture of the two strangers by taking another two steps toward them and answered without trepidation, "I have two brothers, Samale and Hectar; they're younger than me. Our mother lives with us."

"What about your father?"

Apheris examined the floor while answering, "The man who lives there killed him." He pointed to Zebular's door.

"Where is that man now?"

"He just left. He's a bad man; we are afraid of him because he does bad things."

Jake looked at Callahan and said dejectedly, "We're too late; we'll never find them now."

"Find who?" queried Apheris, curious, "Are you looking for somebody?"

Jake tried to capitalize on the child's dislike of Zebular by offering, "We think the man who lives here took a friend of ours and her son who is about your age and we can't find them."

"I didn't see Zebular with the people you're looking for," stated Apheris, causing Jake's heart to sink; then he added, "They were with a surface dweller like you."

Buoyed by this information, Jake asked, "Did you see where they went?"

"They went that way," he said pointing southward in the tunnel, "Five doors on the right, I think."

Jake and Callahan stood so quickly it caused Apheris to jump back, but he relaxed when Jake responded, "Thank you very much Apheris, your help is greatly appreciated. We have to try to rescue them now, so go back home and take care of your mother and brothers, you're the man of the family." Apheris didn't reply, but the huge smile exposing neatly pointed teeth spoke for him. Callahan and Jake hurried in the direction indicated.

Chapter 42

Manny entered the room and stashed the stolen weapons and ammunition in a corner before approaching Ronni, still bound on the chair.

"Hello my love," he said in what Ronni thought of as a sickeningly sweet tone. "Are you ready to consummate our relationship?" He said bending to kiss her lips. She didn't move until his lips touched hers and then she bit him ... as hard as she could.

He jerked back and instinctively swung from the right, his fist catching the side of her face, causing her head to jerk to the right with enough force to topple her and the chair. "You bitch!" he screamed while wiping blood from his rapidly swelling lower lip. "You'll pay for that!" he promised as he jerked her back to an upright position and then hurried from the room. She didn't understand what he said through the fog that deadened her senses, but she had the sensation that she was sitting again ... and then there was darkness.

Jake stopped in the tunnel, glanced down and then

stooped to pick something up, which he held out for Callahan to see.

"Shotgun shell. We're on the right track." Jake nodded agreement and continued forward until he spied the door Apheris had indicated, and the two Azujos standing guard.

"That has to be the place. Now how do we eliminate the guards without announcing our presence?" Jake wondered aloud.

"We need a diversion," Callahan said. "And I think I can provide it. Stay behind your shield and follow me." Before Jake could answer, Callahan hoisted his shield in place and was moving toward the guards. Jake did likewise.

Callahan walked past the guards, careful to make sure to keep his insulation shield between him and the guards. The guards didn't seem to notice and continued to stare straight ahead. When Jake was close enough, Callahan, who was now on the other side of the guards spoke, "Hey you slime balls, I'm over here." The guards turned in the direction of the sound and frantically searched for the source, until felled by two quick bursts from Jake's weapon.

Jake prepared to open the door, but Callahan stepped over the bodies and pushed him aside saying, "Let me go first."

Bowing to Callahan's police training, Jake agreed and readied his weapon to follow his partner. The former policeman kicked the door open, stepped in, and checked the corners and behind the open door. "Clear!"

While he was occupied with securing the room, Jake

stepped in and saw Ronni near the far wall, approximately twenty feet away. He ran to her and felt her neck; finding a strong pulse, he informed Callahan that she was alive. As he raised her head he saw a large bruise on her left cheek and a left eye that was swollen and darkening.

He laid his weapon at her feet and moved behind to untie her hands. He almost had her right hand free when a movement caused him to look up to see Contraldo with a bound and gagged Davy in the open doorway. Callahan, facing away from the door, saw the alarmed expression on Jake's face and spun around just as Contraldo fired, the bullet slammed him backward. He groaned and gagged, then lay motionless on his back, blood spreading across the front of his shirt while a narrow dark line trickled from the corner of his mouth.

Chapter 43

Juan hurried to the stadium and arrived in time to see the last of the Azujos pass through the large entrance. Fearing they would leave one or two to guard the door, he brought the shield up and walked behind it. Reaching the doorway and finding it unguarded made him feel more secure, thinking that if they had been expecting an attack from the rear they *would* have left guards. He kept the shield in place and stepped off with renewed confidence.

Nathan and Skye had fully recovered from the drug, but the remaining prisoners were still affected to varying degrees. Most of them could stand and walk, though shakily, while Amy Kaufman was little more than semi-conscious, Carl Fontaine's condition was somewhere in between. The drug had been too strong for the frail Peggy Atwood, and her husband, George, was grieving quietly over her body. Mason stood guard while conversing with many of the prisoners, figuring the act would help to bring them back to full consciousness quicker. Nathan was helping Kesha regain her balance by helping her walk around the room. It was then they heard voices, and Mason hurried to peer into the hallway. What he saw made his blood run cold; several Azujos were approaching and he realized he had the only weapon to protect the prisoners. He ducked into the offset hallway and darted back to the room.

"They're comin', an' a lot of 'em! I got th' only weapon an' there's no way I can fight 'em off." After quickly considering the options, he ordered, "Everybody stand where ya were tied and pretend to be out cold; maybe that'll buy me enough time to take 'em by surprise." All but the Atwoods and Amy Kaufman, who was too groggy to understand, did as instructed. Mason hoped the three crumpled figures might be enough of a distraction to allow him to kill as many as possible with a continuous burst. He pulled his hood up and stood with the light-shooting weapon in his arms, trusting he looked like a guard on duty. He heard their rapidly approaching footsteps and managed to keep his head down as they entered the room and stopped, removing their goggles while keeping their weapons at the ready.

One of the Azujos walked to Mason and said, "Nice day." The greeting sounded familiar, but he couldn't remember if it had any significance. Then as he was about to respond, he recalled where he had heard it - when he, Jake, Juan, and Callahan had entered the stadium a few hours ago, one of the on-duty guards had said it, and whatever Callahan had replied must have set off a red flag because the guard knew they weren't Azujos. This had to be a password or something.

He couldn't remember what the wrong response was and he had to say something, so he said, "You're right." The troops pulled up their weapons, aiming at everyone … and one was aimed point-blank at Mason. While ripping the light-shooter from his hands, Mason's hood was violently jerked back to expose his face.

He watched with dismay as the one aiming at him ordered his troops to re-bind the prisoners, and then looked him in the eye and said, "Too bad, you should have answered *bad day*." The other Azujos moved to the prisoners, and as they were starting to reattach their bindings, a voice sounded from just inside the room.

"Drop your weapons! Now!" The Azujos searched for the source of the voice, not about to release their weapons until they knew an actual threat was present. A light burst felled one and then another; when the third one dropped, the rest began firing in various directions. It was then that Juan's weapon sputtered and stopped firing. The Azujos were still firing in all directions, the prisoners ducking to keep from getting hit and wondering why the guards couldn't see Juan hiding behind a piece of blue foam. George Atwood charged and was shot point-blank as he dove into one of the Azujos, his momentum bowling him over onto the floor.

Juan chose the closest Azujos, who was within four feet of him, and attacked. He cast the shield aside, lowered his head and stepped into the guard, grabbing his right arm while ducking under that arm and rolled onto his left hip throwing his right arm up through the crotch. As the guard hit the floor, Juan swept up his light-shooter. As another Azujos shifted his gaze to the scuffle, Veni charged forward and tackled him, knocking his weapon from his hands and then landed a hard blow with his fist. The other three Azujos seemed to be in a state of confusion and indecisiveness; sensing this, Mack, Scotty, and Mason charged into them. Two of them were disarmed, but Scotty's adversary, taking advantage of his missing arm and slowness, rolled him off and stood, weapon still in hand and aimed it at Scotty's head. Audryan sprung into action and tackled the guard, throwing him to the floor so hard they slid across the floor a short distance until the guard's head rammed the wall rendering him unconscious. She picked up his weapon and joined the other conquerors in standing over the five defeated Azujos.

Nathan approached Juan and said, "We are *so* glad to see you! How did you do that, hide in plain sight I mean?" Skye ran forward to hug Juan.

"I'll tell you later, we need to get out of here now; there might be more coming. Carry those that can't walk."

"Where's my dad? Did they find Ronni and Davy?"

"We were closing in when these guys marched past us and I left them to help out here. Don't worry, he'll be okay." Juan hoped he wasn't making an empty promise to Nathan, but for now, worry would only slow them down.

Mason had the five remaining Azujos tied to the girders and then directed everyone to leave. Before anyone could react, a stern voice boomed just inside the room. "Stop and drop everything … or die now!" All heads turned to see five Azujos, light-shooters aimed at them. Weapons dropped as all eyes remained fixed on the hooded figures blocking the escape route. The individual that seemed to be in charge impatiently motioned toward the left and barked, "Everyone move over there."

Juan whispered to Mason, "Distract them." Mason moved with the others as Juan held back, moving slower and putting him in close proximity to one of the four subservient Azujos.

Mason looked over his shoulder at the main Azujos and then pretended to trip, falling into Mack and both tumbled to the floor. All eyes were attracted to the commotion as if they were metal attracted to a magnet. Juan did the same *Fireman's Carry* takedown on the near guard, just as he had done earlier on the other guard, and again came up with the guard's weapon. The other four Azujos' awareness shifted to the struggle.

While their attention was diverted from the prisoners, Veni again led the attack, charging into the one that was giving orders and tackled him. The remaining prisoners were on the other three guards. With every Azujos involved in a fight, Juan stood back and watched the fun. Veni swung and connected with the main Azujos' face, eliciting a curse. As he swung again, his target moved his head to one side, causing him to miss. Veni, being off balance, was open for a quick move from below and was thrown off. The Azujos rapidly collected his light-shooter and shot Veni, the pulse striking him in the left shoulder. He quickly turned his weapon and aimed it at Juan ordering him to drop his weapon. Suddenly, the situation had reversed, and Juan did as instructed. He ordered the prisoners back into one corner and then strode to the center of the room.

"My name is Zebular and I was going to keep you alive until tonight for our festival ... but you are all going to die now. First, my inept guards, who are too weak and ineffective to serve me anymore. I will recruit new guards upon my return." He then shot each of the Azujos in the room, including the five that were tied to the girders. "And now for the surface dwellers, starting with *you*." He aimed at Juan.

Juan heard the characteristic *puht* that had permeated the room during the past minute as each guard was dispatched. Strangely, he didn't feel the expected pain and watched in total surprise as Zebular fell on his face, dark goggles smashing on the floor. Confused, he looked around and saw one Azujos emerge from behind a shield made of insulation.

The guard crossed the floor until he was close to Juan, lowered his weapon while removing his goggles, and said, "Hola amigo." Then he held out his right hand.

Taking the hand, Juan spoke in Spanish, "Darmak! Muchas gracias me amigo, pero por que' corer el riesgo ..."

Cutting him off, Darmak spoke and Juan listened, nodding his head occasionally and interjecting words in Spanish. Not sure what was transpiring, the prisoners watched the exchange with curiosity while attempting to decipher what was actually going on. They appeared to be safe for now, but how safe … and for how long?

Juan, sensing the tension among his comrades, turned toward them and said, "I would like you to meet Darmak. Apparently, the Spanish speaking Azujos are not as vicious as most of the English speaking ones. He took a great risk by killing Zebular, who was a powerful leader of their people, but he says the world is better off without him. I started to ask why he would risk danger for him and his family and he told me Zebular was a butcher, a tyrant and a killer. His entire race is richer without him, but just in case any of his followers might want retaliation, he will tell them he is the only survivor of a great battle. He doesn't believe any others will attempt to kill us, but just in case, we should be very careful and stay indoors at night." Everyone filed forward and shook Darmak's hand as a gesture of gratitude, and then watched him leave.

Mason and Mack gathered the body of Peggy Atwood and her critically wounded husband. Carl supported Amy, Audryan and Scotty helped Veni, and the rest were able to walk out of the stadium. Most of them were cautiously thankful to be alive so far.

Once outside, Juan announced that he was heading back to where he left Jake and Callahan earlier. Nathan said, "I'm going too. I need to find my dad."

"You might need this," Juan said, handing over a light-shooter. "I'll teach you how to work it on the way." Gathering the insulation shield, he commanded, "Let's go!"

Chapter 44

Jake's gaze alternated in horror between Callahan's body and the swollen lip curled into a sneering smile on Contraldo's face.

"Aw, too bad, *Jakey's* lost a friend," Manny taunted. "Maybe there's no future in being Jakey's friend. Actually, there's no future in being Jakey; what do *you* think?" Jake's eyes searched out Davy who was cowering in a corner, cheeks wet with tears and visibly shaking. "What's the matter Jakey? You look like the little boy who got caught with his hands in the cookie jar. Do you have something going with my woman?" While talking, Manny was moving closer, circling Jake and Ronni, whose head still hung limply.

Jake instinctively circled, keeping Ronni as a barrier between him and Manny. "Aw, Jakey," Manny continued to taunt, defiance in his eyes. "Are you hiding behind a woman's skirt? I would have thought better of you." Jake realized he had been doing exactly what Manny accused him of, but rationalized that he was Ronni and Davy's only hope at this point, and if he died … he cringed to consider what would happen to them.

Manny held the gun more directly at Jake and instructed him to stop moving. He stopped about two feet in front of Ronni's left knee, and after a furtive glance downward, calculated there was no chance of reaching the light-shooter in time. Manny stepped around and leveled the revolver at Jake's head while kicking it away.

With a mocking pout, he said, "Bye bye, Jakey Boy." Suddenly a streaking figure came out of nowhere, spearing Manny in the back and driving him into Jake, who knocked the gun free. Jake glanced to see Davy rolling on the floor, still bound and gagged, and then leveled a punch that landed solidly on Manny's jaw, knocking him down. He got up and swung, connecting a punch that made Jake think he'd been hit with a rock. His lower lip was cut on the inside by his own teeth and he could taste blood that was collecting in his mouth. He swung again but Manny ducked and connected a smashing blow across the side of Jake's face, causing him to stagger backward.

Trying to clear his head, Jake backed away for a moment; Manny attacked and connected with two solid left jabs but Jake ducked under his right cross and hit him with an uppercut to the stomach, doubling him over and then connected with a right cross to the head which spun Manny around, but he remained standing. From that point, Jake, who had never been in a fistfight, much less a life-or-death struggle, was no match for Manny's street fighting experience. For every solid punch he landed, Manny hit him three or four times. Both eyes were swelling, he felt like a couple front teeth were loose, blood gushed from his cut and swollen lips and he was bleeding from gashes on his forehead and left cheek.

After a vicious flurry of punches, Jake went down at Ronni's feet and had only enough strength to lift his head and watch as Manny kicked him in the ribs so hard he heard loud cracking accompanied by extreme pain that felt like his side had exploded. Manny retrieved his revolver and swaggered until he stood over him.

"I got to hand it to you, Jakey Boy," Manny glared down with several minor cuts, some bruising on his chin and a swollen eyebrow. "You had more fight in you than I figured you would, but it's no matter. Let's finish this now, for good." Jake resigned himself that this was the end; he didn't have any energy left, and watched with strange detachment, as if seeing the scene on television as the gun was aimed at his face. No fear. No energy. Just pain and resignation.

Chapter 45

Juan and Nathan started off running, but after a couple of blocks Nathan was wheezing and had trouble catching his breath. Juan waited while Nathan stood gasping, hands on knees, sweat and saliva dripping on the street. "I'm sorry," he said between gasps. "I'm not used to running."

"That's okay, I'll wait until you're ready. In the meantime, look at your weapon. Aim it across the street and push the top button." Nathan did as instructed and heard a *puht* as a quick burst of light blasted a small hole in the building. "Now push the bottom button." A longer *puuuht* ensued and a long gap opened in the building as Nathan moved the weapon slightly.

"Wow! Okay … gasp … I'm about ready."

"What if we keep the pace down to a little faster than a walk? You know, like jogging."

"Go ahead. I'll try to keep up." Juan was already beginning to jog and Nathan fell in behind. This time, Nathan felt better because he could match Juan nearly stride for stride, and after his initial exhaustion had past, he felt something resembling renewed energy.

Juan paused at the building he, Jake, and Callahan had entered earlier. "What's wrong?" asked Nathan. "Where's my dad?"

"This is where we went underground, but I came out another building that was much closer to where I left them. We can make better time up here. Let's see ... it should be ... that way." He pointed and started jogging at the same time, Nathan followed.

Ronni's right arm wind-milled upward into Manny's outstretched arm causing the gun to fly into the air. Just then Davy kicked one of the stolen revolvers across the floor, coming to rest against Jake's hip. Realizing he had been granted one last chance, Jake felt for the gun, wrapped his battered hand around the grip, and fired at the shadowy figure running through the slits of his swollen eyes. The figure stooped to pick up something and then fired back. The bullet whizzed past Jake's head so close he heard it, and then he painfully rolled onto his knees and fired again at the retreating figure as it disappeared through the door.

Holding his side, Jake rose to see Ronni smiling up at him. "You look like hell," she observed.

"You don't look too bad yourself," he managed, and then looked around to see Davy standing by the door and staggered to him. "Thanks for saving my life," he said as he knelt, ripping the tape off his mouth and untying him. "Take care of your mother." And then he was out the door.

"Jake! Jake, don't go! Please don't go!" He heard Ronni screaming after him, but he knew he had to finish this with Contraldo or he would be back. At the very least, he knew he had bought Ronni and Davy some time.

Davy moved quickly to his mother and finished untying her. She stood and then sat back on the chair to keep from passing out. She slowly shook her head to clear the cobwebs that seemed to have all her thoughts tied together in a cloudy mess.

"Mommy… are you okay? Mommy?" Davy implored, sobbing.

Regaining her composure, Ronni put her arms around him and assured, "I'll be okay; just stood up too fast. I feel better now. Let's go help Mr. Myers." She took Davy's hand and walked as quickly as possible with the child in tow.

After about five minutes, Juan and Nathan entered a door, beside which was fastened a bronze-looking plaque engraved with the words "HOLLOWAY BUILDING." After entering the elevator, Juan touched "2" and readied his weapon. The door opened to an unoccupied area of level two. Nathan followed as Juan cautiously advanced through the tunnel, shield held in front. A few minutes later, he stopped and motioned for Nathan to move against the wall.

"What is it?" Nathan whispered.

"Bodies ahead ... look like Azujos. Let me go first." He raised the shield and moved carefully to the bodies. Finding them dead, he turned his attention to the room, standing open beside the dead Azujos. He entered and quickly surveyed the surroundings: an empty chair with ropes and a strip of duct tape lying on the floor, the cache of guns and ammunition stolen from the apartment, and Callahan. Nathan was suddenly behind and peering over his shoulder.

"Oh, no!" Nathan exclaimed upon seeing Callahan's body. "Where's my dad?" he urgently pleaded while looking around the room.

"Look here," said Juan, squatting and pointing at something on the floor.

"What is it?"

"Looks like a blood smear. There's another one. I don't think they're from Callahan. Must've been a fight."

"Where'd he go? We need to find him; he might be hurt!"

"Don't worry, we'll find him." Juan said, leading the way out the door. Once outside, he motioned in the direction opposite the way they came. "We didn't see any sign coming in, so let's go this way." They jogged southward until Juan suddenly stopped and urged, "Shhhh ... listen."

Chapter 46

Jake ran as best he could on weak legs while holding his side and wiping blood from his eyes and face. He stopped for a moment and listened; running footsteps farther down the tunnel spurred him as fast as he could run in that direction.

Entering an open station area, he was spun around by something slamming into his left shoulder. At first he thought Contraldo had punched him, but when he glanced down he realized he had been shot. Looking up, he saw Contraldo and fired at him, the bullet hitting the wall about an inch above its intended target. Manny turned and fled up some stairs. Jake, holding his shoulder with his gun hand raced after him.

Climbing the stairs weakened Jake even more, but he reached the fifth level in time to see Contraldo running outside, headed obliquely across the street. He exited into the street and heard a ricochet to his right causing him to duck behind a corner of the building for cover. Peering around the corner, he saw Contraldo hiding behind a corner of the building diagonally across the street.

Jake was becoming light-headed and realized his shoulder wound was bleeding more due to his exertion on the stairs. No matter, he had to get Contraldo. He stood on wobbly legs and limped across the street as fast as he could, firing at the face peering around the corner. He suddenly felt like he was living the movie "High Noon", in a running gun battle with a bad guy. As his shot ricocheted off the building a few inches above Contraldo, he saw him back into the alley while returning fire.

Suddenly he heard a scream, so horrifying it seemed to be born in the depths of hell, resonating and gathering terror until being unleashed on the world. He staggered across the street toward more screams mixed with unintelligible sounds, and then silence.

Jake reached the corner where he had last seen Contraldo, and cautiously peered into the alley; what he saw sickened him. Contraldo had backed into an immense spider web and was staring past Jake through terror-filled unseeing eyes, while a spider, with what had to be a four-foot leg span, was beginning to wrap his unfeeling body in a cocoon-like web. Overcome with nausea, Jake turned away and vomited in the street.

Trying to distance himself from the ghastly sight, he managed to stagger to the other side of the street, before the world spun and disappeared.

Nathan tried to hold his breath but was having great difficulty; then he heard it … faint footsteps, running.

"This way ... hurry, but be quiet as you can," Juan directed and resumed jogging. As they progressed, the footsteps
sounded louder, like someone was climbing stairs. Entering
the next station, they saw a stairway. As they began to climb,
Juan noticed drops of blood on approximately every second
step. He kept this observation to himself, not wanting to
increase Nathan's concern.

As they reached the fourth level, a scream from outside stopped them, "Jake ... noooooo!" Juan and Nathan
exchanged glances and then continued to ascend the stairs,
running. Exiting the building, they immediately saw Davy,
approximately a hundred yards away, standing by Ronni,
who was sobbing and cradling Jake's limp form.

"Dad!"

Chapter 47

O minous dark clouds with occasional lightning domi-
nated the late-afternoon sky as mourners gathered on
a windy dune around three fresh graves located next to that
of Bobby Blackhorn. Mack and Mason had begun digging
shortly after dawn; everyone else had waited until they had
finished and cleaned up.

"Is everyone here?" asked Mason. Thunder rumbled in
the distance causing some to cast a wary eye skyward.

"Nathan chose to remain in the apartment," answered
Ronni. "This has all been so hard on him."

Mack stepped forward and bowed his head, the others did
likewise. "Lord, it wasn't but a few days since we met here last
on the occasion of turning one of us, Bobby Blackhorn over to
you. Now we're here again to give you these people. None of
us knew them but such a short time, although in that time they
touched all of us with caring, bravery, and love of fellow man.
They gave the ultimate sacrifice by laying down their lives that
others might live. Please accept their souls and give comfort to
those of us left behind. We ask it in Jesus' name. Amen.

Ronni approached one of the graves as rain started to fall, cheeks already moist. "Thank you dear friend for doing all you could to save my son and me. We will all miss you." She placed a bouquet of wild flowers on the grave and Davy added a flower of his own. They lingered by the grave while everyone else filed by, and then turned toward the apartment. Ronni knew she would come back before dusk and remove the flowers so the Azujos wouldn't know bodies were buried there. She put her arm around Davy's shoulders and started back as rain intensified.

Instead of entering her apartment, she stood in the hall until Davy was in, then she walked down the hall to where Nathan sat against the wall, crying. "How ... how was the funeral?" he asked between sobs. "I should have ... should've been there ... but I just couldn't." He stood, the sobs somewhat less frequent and continued, "You know ... I, I never cried for my m ... mom an' now I'm cr ... cryin' for b ... both of 'em ... and I can't ... can't stop. I fee ... feel like such a ba ... baby." The sobs increased and Ronni took him in her arms, holding him until he finally relaxed a little.

"Don't let that worry you; everyone understands why you couldn't be at the funeral. They all know how it feels to lose someone, especially someone as close as what you have experienced. Just remember that I will always be there for you ... no matter what.

"Th ... thanks." Nathan wiped his eyes with his shirttail. "You're a special person and I can see why my dad liked you so much. I'm sorry you got beat up."

"Oh, it's not much comparatively," she said, touching her hand to her swollen cheekbone. If it wasn't for your father, things would have been a lot worse."

Yeah, I guess so. I was sorry about Mr. Callahan."

"I was too. I was also sorry to lose Mr. Atwood last night, but he wouldn't have had much of a life here without his wife. Let's go in."

Nathan opened the door and they entered. "Any change yet?" she asked, moving past him into the room and then she stopped, staring at the battered figure on the bed.

"Not yet," answered Nathan, wiping his eyes. "It's been over twenty-four hours; I hoped he would show *some* improvement by now."

"I wish there was too, but some things take time, and we've done all we can. From what Davy told me, he took quite a beating but he wouldn't quit; you would have been very proud of him. He did this for us ... me, all of us; I'll never forgive myself if he ..." She stopped and wiped her eyes.

"I *am* proud of him, but I just want to tell him. I blamed him for my mother's problems and I blamed him for my problems. He didn't deserve that. I just want him back so I can tell him I love him." Ronni pulled him close, tears spilling from his eyes as he buried his face in her shoulder.

As she comforted him, she glanced down at the bloodied, swollen, and bandaged individual, then closed her tearing eyes and added, "I want to tell him that too."

A sound gave start to both of them, and turning they

saw an eye peering through a swollen slit, and a weak voice said, "Okay ... you both said it ... now let a guy ... get some rest ... you both ... talk too much." Ronni knelt beside the bed and gently hugged him as he protested weakly, "Ow ... hurts."

Epilogue

Snow swirled inside with the bundled man as he came through the front door, which he quickly closed against the cold. He fingered a remote in his pocket and his boots opened to allow him to step out. After storing his boots, he walked through the hallway while removing his coat. As he was hanging it in the closet, warm arms encircled his waist from behind.

"Welcome home stranger." It was an appreciated greeting and he took comfort in hearing the endearing name she had used since shortly after they met, three years ago. He turned and wrapped his arms around her.

"It's nice to be home; it's really cold out there. I'm looking forward to staying in tonight. How are the kids?"

"They're fine, Nathan's on *School-Link* submitting his senior term paper and Davy's doing his Algebra homework in his room. Oh, and the little one's been keeping me on the run all day; I don't know where she gets her energy. She's like a battery-operated toy ... oh excuse me, a chip cell-operated toy; I still have trouble talking in today-speak."

"She's probably just like her mother was at that age. You know, what goes around comes around."

"Yeah, blame it on the mother," she said with a smirk. "Dinner will be ready in about ten minutes." They kissed and separated, she to the kitchen and he to the living room where he picked up the remote and accessed the communications system.

"Hey, did you check messages today?"

"Nope, been too busy chasing my clone. Why?"

"Mason left a message to call back. Do you want to do it now or wait until after dinner?"

She joined him in front of the wall screen, "No, do it now. We haven't heard from him since right after we came north. I wonder what he wants." Jake concentrated on the remote while he pressed REPLY and watched the twelve-digit number that belonged to Mason's videocom appear quickly on the wall; almost immediately he was on the screen.

"Hey southerner, how's the weather down there?" Jake initiated.

Glad ya called back. Weather's good now, 'bout in the mid-seventies; sure beats th' hot spell we been havin'. How're things with th' Myers family in P-A? Bet ya're wishin' ya was back down south."

"The weather sounds a lot better than what we're having, high twenties and a snow storm just beginning. Other than that, I'm glad to be away from there; some good memories, but some awful ones too. We're happy here, living in a neighborhood with actual neighbors that have regular teeth and eyes." Ronni whispered in his ear and then he added, "Except for Halloween; we see some pretty dreadful looking creatures then." He chuckled. "How is everyone?"

"Well, most parts of Florida's still pretty much deserted, so Juan had to move to Atlanta for college. His parents started a bank account for 'im when he was born an' by now, interest an' all, he's got close to three million; he can afford any college he wants. Lucky it was in one o' the few banks still 'round. I'm his actin' guardian."

"That's nice to hear. I don't think many of us would have survived if it weren't for him. He's a quick thinker and isn't afraid to do what needs to be done. What's his major?"

"Some type o' engineerin', mechanical or electrical, not sure; that stuff gets me confused."

Well, the company I work for could use an engineer with his abilities. We're running the TUR and have started work on the Transatlantic Railway. It's a monumental project that will take decades to complete."

"What's TUR stand for?"

"Transcontinental Underground Railway. Have you heard of it?"

Naw, I been fishin' nearly every day since I found a place 'round what's left o' Jacksonville that has both diesel and regular gas. Only a couple refineries make it now 'cause there's not much market for it anymore. Darryl's a wizard with engines an' with his help *Oblique View* and *Blue Heron* are both available for charter. Actually, we all moved up here a year ago and are livin' pretty good. I got quite a few people comin' for trips, now that we live in a well populated area. We call our company *Antique Charters*, an' our motto is *Out to Sea; Back in Time*; catchy, huh? Ya know, nobody makes parts for somethin' as old as our boats, but there's a place here that'll make any part we need if somethin' breaks. We jus' take th' broken part in, they put it in a glass chamber an' th' computer scans it an' makes a new one. They do it while we wait. By th' way, why would anyone build an underground railway?"

"Well, as many as five hundred passengers at a time can get on in Newport News, Virginia and travel to San Francisco in less than an hour. Not too many people want to teleport, and this is a safe, quick alternative."

"How can a train go that fast? That sounds impossible."

It uses different technologies than we were used to. First of all, it uses a tunnel, suspended on all sides to the surface of a larger tunnel. All the air is pumped out until it's a vacuum before the train starts. It travels so fast because of no air resistance."

"But doesn't goin' that fast hurt people?"

"Not on these trains, because the speed is increased and decreased slowly. I'll tell you more about it when there's more time. What about the rest of the apartment crew?"

"Mack an' Scotty send their regards to all o' ya, 'specially Ronni and Davy. They really miss 'em. They live jus' down the road; help Darryl an' me an' we split th' profits. Th' muscular one, what was his name?"

"Veni Fassenetti."

"Yeah, him. He and that Audrey Hepburn ..."

Jake interrupted, "Audryan Hepbrun. Remember, it was close but not quite the same."

"Oh yeah, well they moved somewhere near Charlotte, another place with a lot o' people, an' opened a gym or somethin' like that ... a fitness center, yeah, that's it, a fitness center. They're partners an' as I understand it, he got married to someone from that area. I guess there aren't many fitness centers anymore, so they have a lot o' customers."

Ronni had left the room during the conversation and returned with a toddler in her arms.

Mason continued, "Those two, Amy an' Carl got married an' moved somewhere up north, not sure where; guess they figured they'd been through so much together they may as well make it permanent. They reminded me o' a coupla lost souls an' I'm glad they found each other."

"Hi Mason," Ronni broke in. "Look at our new addition." She held up the wiggling toddler for him to see.

"Beautiful! Ya'll have to call Mack an' Scotty; they'd love to see that. What's 'er name?"

"Lisa."

"I shoulda guessed."

"It was great talking to you, Mason, but I need to get back to the kitchen so this guy can have dinner. See you, and tell everyone we send our love." She sat Lisa on the floor and then hurried to the kitchen.

"What happened with the Azujos? Are they nearby and still keeping their distance?"

"Not very many o' 'em 'round' here, jus' a few outside th' city. It actually got to the point that it wasn't too bad where we used to live. Once in a while one of 'em got to feelin' his oats an' came 'round lookin' for somethin', but all in all it was a lot better'n it was when we first showed up. Mack, Scotty an' I went explorin' the city 'bout two years ago an' ya know what we found?"

"Not really, what did you find?"

"Well, we went in a bank, ya know like a savins' an' loan. Inside, there wasn't jus' money; there was a huge vault loaded with frozen meat. Do ya believe it? A vault of frozen meat. Guess that stuff ya told us 'bout meat bein' valuable was pretty much on. Anyways, we met with that Darmak guy an' showed 'im how to get in. Last I heard he's a big wig with his people, they elected him to some kinda office. He was good to us, keepin' th' loonies away an' all. Funny how things work out."

"Yes it is." His reverie interrupted by Ronni's voice from the kitchen.

"Ask him about Skye; she was so nice to Davy."

"Ronni wants ..."

"I heard," interrupted Mason. "Tell 'er that Skye an' that other one, her friend ... Kesha, well they headed north like ya'll did; I think they used th' tele-whatever that thing is insteada drivin' like ya did when ya'll went north. I'm not sure jus' where, but I think it's somewhere 'round Philly. That's

pretty close to ya, isn't it? Well they was goin' to some college up there, should be 'bout ready to graduate I suppose.
I think Juan has kept in pretty close touch with Skye all the
time they been in college. Who knows… might be another
weddin' in the works one o' these days."

"Well, Nathan might get a thrill out of hearing Kesha's
not too far away, he had a thing for her, remember? Actually
they should have about another year to go so he may have
the opportunity to get together with them before they
graduate."

"By th' way, ya got any Azujos up there?"

"From what I can determine they were everywhere, and
I guess there are still some pockets here and there given that
many were killed off. They're called by different names depending on where you live. If you mention Azujos up here,
people don't know what you're talking about. The ones
around here're known as *Night Beasts*. The ones up north
generally live in caves in the mountains and live off wild
game. Since there are less people, and therefore less hunt-
ers, some wild animals like deer have made a big comeback.
I don't know much about them, the ones up here I mean,
but I've heard they're somewhat like the ones Ronni and I
encountered in Miami. Remember them?"

"Yeah, I remember what ya told us. They seemed to be
even more wild than th' ones we dealt with. I wonder how
those people that helped ya are doin'. It's a good thing they
was 'round when ya needed 'em. By th' way, do ya have any
regrets, Jake, 'bout movin' north or anythin'?"

"No, I'm good … we're good. I'm negotiating for a position in the chemical treatment section of the colony at L5 but you know you've got loonies no matter where you go. My present job is supervisor of TS-1, that's Tunnel Section one from Newport News to Indianapolis; I monitor the conditions, movement, vacuum, and so forth. Well, two days ago we got a message that some group plans to destroy part of it if the government doesn't come up with some serious money. Things have been a little tense but we're on top of it for now. I hope and pray it stays that way."

"Ya can't seem to get away from th' crazies, can ya? Well, I hope it all works out an' ya can catch 'em b'fore they do any damage."

"Yeah, me too. I never thought I could be happy again, but here I am, happier than I've ever been, and I don't want some idiot or idiots ruining that."

"No, me neither. Well, I jus' wanted to touch base with ya'll an' see how things're goin'. I'll let Scotty an' Mack know what's happenin' an' I'm sure ya'll be hearin' from 'em b'fore long. Don't be a stranger, call sometime, ya hear."

"Will do, and thanks for the updates. Stay healthy and God bless." The screen went blank as Jake mulled over the last thing Mason had said. "No Mason," he whispered. "I'm *happy* being someone's stranger."

THE END